# SHADOWS OVER LONDON

# CHRISTIAN KLAVER

# SHADOWS OVER LONDON

CamCat
Books

CamCat Publishing, LLC
Brentwood, Tennessee 37027
camcatpublishing.com

This is a work of fiction. Names, characters, places, and incidents are either products of the author's imagination or are used fictitiously.

Hardcover ISBN 9780744303766
Paperback ISBN 9780744303438
Large-Print Paperback ISBN 9780744303490
eBook ISBN 9780744303377
Audiobook ISBN 9780744303223

Library of Congress Control Number: 2021931132

Book and cover design by Maryann Appel

5 3 1 2 4

*To Katie . . .*

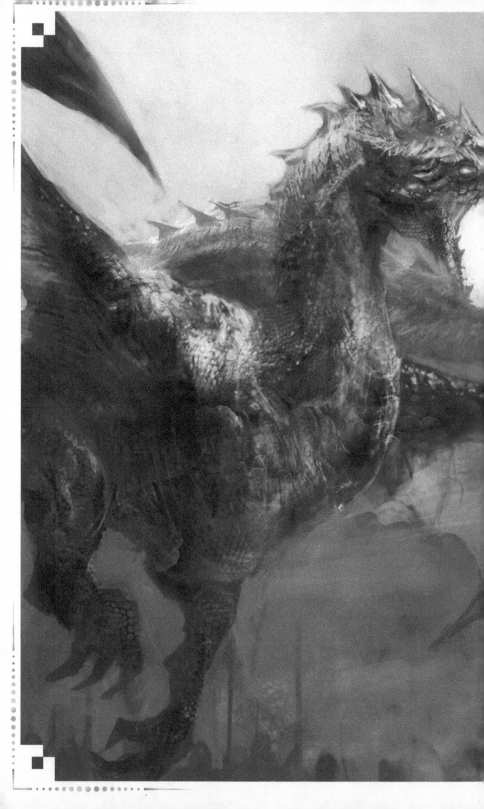

*Myths are public dreams, dreams are private myths.*

– Joseph Campbell

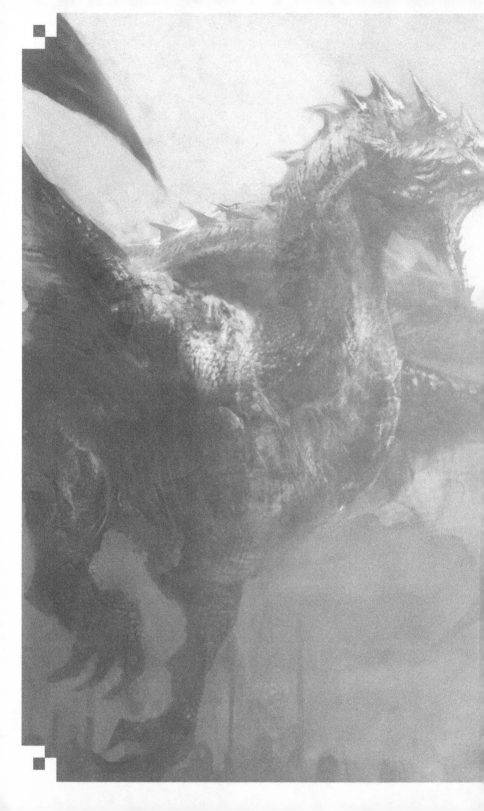

# PROLOGUE

## The Faerie King

Some dreams are so true that it doesn't matter if they actually happened that way or not. They're so true that they've happened more than once. My dreams about the Faerie were like that. Most of the rest of England got their first glimpse of the Faerie on the night London fell. But not me. I saw my first Faerie ten years before that, on my sixth birthday.

My name is Justice Kasric and my family was all tangled up with the Faerie even before the invasion.

Because I'd been born on Boxing Day, the day after Christmas, Father always made a grand affair of my birthday so that it wasn't all swallowed up by the other holidays. That's why, long after Christmas supper had come and gone, I stood at the frosted window of my room looking out into the darkness trying to guess what kind of surprise Father had in store for my sixth birthday. I was sure that something wonderful was coming. Maybe a pony . . . or even *ponies*.

I crept quietly out of my room. I didn't want to wake Faith, my older sister. I didn't see or hear anyone on the top floors, but then I heard movement from down in the front hall. Father. He clicked his pocket watch closed, tucked it back into his dark waistcoat and pulled the heavy black naval coat off the hook by the door. I was sure he'd turn around and see me crouched on the stairs, but he only stood a moment in the shrouded half-moonlight before opening the front door. A cool mist rolled noiselessly past his ankles as he went out.

I was in luck! Where else would Father be going except to feed the ponies? I pulled on my rubber boots and threw my heavy blue woolen coat over my nightgown, determined to follow.

When I opened the door and looked out into the front garden, the mist hung everywhere in soft carpets of moonlit fleece. Father was nowhere in sight, but I could hear him crunching ahead of me.

I paused, sensing even then that some steps took you further than others. The enormity of my actions lay heavily on me. The comforting, warm interior of the house called for me to come back inside. It was not too late to go back. I could return to the rest of my family, content with a life filled with tea settings, mantelpiece clocks, antimacassars and other normal, sensible notions. The proper thing would have been to go back inside, to bed. I remember shaking my head, sending my braids dancing.

I followed Father outside into the still and misty night.

We went across the front garden, past shrubs and frozen pools, and descended the hill into the snow-laden pines. His crunching footsteps carried back to me in the still air. I followed by stepping in the holes he'd left in the snow to make less noise, jumping to match his long stride. The stables lay behind the house, but clearly, we weren't heading there. We lived in the country then, amidst a great deal of farmland with clumps of forest around.

The silence grew heavier, deeper, as we descended into the trees, and a curious lassitude swept over me as I followed Father through the tangled woods. The air was sharp and filled with the clean smell of ice and pine. On the other side of a dip in the land, we *should* have emerged into a large and open field. Only we didn't. The field wasn't there. Instead, we kept going down through more and more snow-laden trees.

The treetops formed a nearly solid canopy sixty or seventy feet above us, but with a vast and open space underneath. The thick shafts of moonlight slanted down through silvered air into emerald shadows, each tree a stately pillar in that wide-open space.

I worried about Father catching me following him, but he never even turned around. Always, he went down. Down, down into the forest, into what felt like another world entirely. Even I knew we couldn't still be in the English countryside. You could just feel it. I also knew that following him wasn't about ponies anymore and I might have given up and gone home, only I had no idea how to find my way back.

After a short time, we came to an open green hollow where I crouched at the edge of a ring of trees and blinked my eyes at the sudden brightness. The canopy opened up to the nighttime sky and moonlight filled the empty hollow like cream poured into a cup. This place had a planned feel, the circle of trees shaped just so, the long black trunk lying neatly in the exact center of a field of green grass like a long table, and all of it inexplicably free of snow.

Two pale boulders sat on either side like chairs. The silence felt deeper here, older, expectant. The place was waiting.

Father lit a cigarette and stood smoking. The thin wisp of smoke curled up and into the night sky.

Then, the Faerie King arrived.

First, there was emptiness, and then, without any sign of motion, a hulking, towering figure stood on the other side of the log, standing as if he'd always been there waiting. I'd read enough of the right kinds of books to recognize him as a Faerie King right off and I shivered.

The Faerie King looked like a shambling beast on its back legs, with huge tined antlers that rose from his massive skull. He wore a wooden crown nearly buried by a black mane thick as lamb's fleece that flowed into a forked beard. His long face was a gaunt wooden mask, with blackened slits for eyes and a harsh, narrow opening for a mouth.

Except it wasn't a mask, because it moved. The mouth twitched and the jaw muscles clenched as he regarded the man in front of him. Finally, he inclined his head in a graceless welcome. He wore a cloak like a swath of forest laid across his back, made entirely of thick wild grass, weeds, and brambles, with a rich black undercoat of loam where a silk lining would show. Underneath the cloak, he wore armor that might once have been bright copper, now with rampant verdigris. He leaned on the pommel of a wide-bladed, granite sword.

The Faerie King and Father regarded each other for a long time before they each sat down. A chessboard with pieces of carved wood and bone sat suddenly between them. Again, there was no sense of movement, only a sudden understanding that the board must have always been there, waiting.

They began to play.

The Faerie King hesitated, reached to advance his white king's pawn, then stopped. His leathery right hand was massive, nearly the size of the board, far too large for this task. He shifted awkwardly and used his more normal-sized left hand. Father advanced a pawn immediately in response. The Faerie King sat and viewed the board with greater deliberation. He finally reached out with his left hand to make his move, and then stopped. He shifted in his seat, uncertain, then finally advanced his knight.

I could feel others watching with me. Invisible ghosts hidden in the trees. The weight of their interest hung palpably in the air. Whatever the outcome of this game, it was important in a way you couldn't help but feel. However long it took, this timeless shuffling of pieces, the watchers would wait and I waited with them. With only a nightgown on under my coat, crouching in the snow, I should have been freezing. But I didn't feel the cold. I only felt the waiting, and the waiting consumed me.

Father and the Faerie King had each moved their forces into the center of the board, aligning and realigning in constant readiness for the inevitable clash. Now Father sliced into the black pawns with surgical precision, starting an escalating series of exchanges. Around us, it began to snow.

As the game went on, Father and the Faerie King lined their captures neatly on the side of the board. Father looked to be considerably better off. The Faerie King grew more and more angry, and he squeezed and kneaded the log with his massive right hand so that the wood cracked and popped. Occasional bursts of wood fragments flew to either side.

Father's only reaction to this violent display was a long, slow smile. He took another Turkish cigarette calmly from a cigarette case and lit it. I was suddenly very chilled. That kind of calm wasn't natural.

The smoke from Father's cigarette drifted placidly upwards. His moves were immediate, decisive, while the Faerie King's became more and more hesitant as the game went on. The smile on Father's face grew. I watched, and the forest watched with me.

Then the Faerie King snarled, jumped up, and brought his massive fist down on the board like a mallet. Bits of the board, chess pieces, and wood splinters flew out into the snow. Twice more he mauled the log, gouging out huge hunks of wood in his fury. Then he spun with a swiftness shocking in so large a person and yanked his huge sword out of the snow. He brought it down in a deadly arc that splintered the log like a lightning strike. Debris and splinters had flown around Father like a ship's deck hit by a full broadside of cannonballs, but Father didn't even flinch. Two broken halves of smoldering log lay in the clearing.

"Perhaps next time," Father said, standing up, the first words either of them had spoken. He brushed a few splinters from his coat.

The Faerie King stared, quivering, his wooden face twisted suddenly with grief. Then his legs gave out and he collapsed in the snow, all his impotent rage spent. He sat, slumped with his mismatched hands on his knees, the perfect picture of abject defeat. He didn't so much as stir when Father turned his back and left.

I couldn't tear my gaze away from the rough and powerful shape slouched heavily and immobile in the snow. White clumps were already starting to gather on his arms, shoulders, head and antlers, as if he might never move again.

Father climbed directly to my hiding place and stood, looking down at me with amusement in his glacial-blue eyes. I'd forgotten all about hiding.

He warned me to keep silent with a gloved finger to his lips, then put a hand on my shoulder and steered me away from the hollow. Father fished his watch out of the waistcoat pocket and checked the time as we climbed back up the slope. We walked for a bit, surrounded only by the sound of crunching snow and the spiced scent of Father's smoke.

"Well," he said finally. "I've always encouraged you to be curious, little Justice, but *this* is a surprise. Did you follow me all the way from home?" He didn't sound cross at all, only curious. So it was a family trait.

"Yes." I looked back the way we'd come. It was hard to imagine that *I* was the biggest surprise of this night.

"You must be cold," he said, "yes?"

I *was* cold, suddenly. Father draped his coat around me, then picked me up and carried me like a princess. The soft wool of his coat was warm and comforting, as were the familiar scents that clung to it. The Turkish tobacco with cloves and ginger. Ordinary, familiar smells that sluiced away the strangeness of the night.

"Father, what was that horrible thing?" I asked

"Oh, not so horrible, Justice. Not really. Though I suppose the church might not agree. But then, you'll learn to think for yourself and not take *their* word, eh?"

"Yes, Father," I said. I knew exactly what the church would have to say about a creature like that, but maybe that wasn't so important.

"Well," he said after a time, "now I have a problem. This needs to be a secret, you see? But I know how little girls talk. Perhaps a bribe? What would it take to keep this our secret?"

He didn't need the bribe and we both knew it. I would have done anything for him.

But he'd asked, so I said, "A pony?"

He laughed. "Well, I don't have a pony on me, but . . . here, hang on tight." He shifted my weight a little so that he could fish around in his coat pocket.

He handed me a chess piece from the game, one of his knights. At least it *looked* like one of the wooden pieces from the game back in the hollow, but how could it be? The Faerie King had bashed them all to bits and I hadn't seen Father pick anything up when he left. Still, there it was.

"Would this horsie do?" he said.

I looked closer. The piece wasn't just a horse's head, but an entire stallion carved in loving detail. It reared up, riderless, wild and beautiful. More than beautiful. The dark wood gleamed, reminding me of the glossy flank of a living horse.

"It's wonderful," I said, taking it in both hands. It was warm to the touch. "I couldn't feed a regular horse, anyway."

"You are very wise for such a small child," Father said.

"Does it have a name, Father?"

"Why, of course it does. All important things have names. Remember your promise here not to tell a soul about what you saw, and I'm sure we'll discover her name together."

A sudden sleepiness overcame me. It felt impossibly late, near morning. He must have carried me all the way home because my next memory was Father climbing the steps inside our house and then lowering me into bed. He moved carefully so as to not wake Faith, my older sister.

Moments or hours later—I could never be sure—I sat up.

Father was gone. I was in my nightdress only, with no sign of my coat. In the bed across the room, Faith was in the deepest kind of sleep, immobile, as if it would take a prince to wake her.

But the sweet smell of Father's Turkish cigarette still lingered in the air.

I looked for the chess piece, but to my disappointment there was nothing in the bed, nothing on the dresser. There was no sign of the chess piece anywhere.

So, for many years I discounted the memory of that night in the forest, believing it only a lovely and somewhat frightening dream. I didn't find out how wrong that idea was until much later.

# CHAPTER 1

## Father Comes Home

It wasn't until I was fifteen, that I thought seriously of the Faerie King again.

We were in London now. Had been for six months now, so that Mother could be closer to her doctors. This meant trading the sun-dappled glades, small brooks, and ageless mystery of the woods in the countryside for the raucous, vibrant, smoky, fog-drenched, teeming bustle of London.

The dim street lanterns shone dully in the darkened, rain-slick streets, illuminating little. Vague shapes of people, horses, carriages, and other things moved like shadows out there. I pressed my face against the leaded glass, trying to see more but not having much luck.

There was activity in the street beneath me, our groom helping Faith into another carriage that would whisk her to some fashionable part of town for yet another ball. Same as last night. And the night before.

With Henry sent off to Harrow's Boarding School, and Faith gone so often, it would be another night of having the house to myself. Faith's laugh drifted up from the street and I saw her stop and say something to the groom, her hand briefly on his arm. He nodded eagerly, completely besotted with her. Everyone was.

Before London, Faith and I had been inseparable. But her presentation to court and moving to London had changed all that. Now, I hardly ever saw her. She was a debutante and part of London *Society*.

Now the house would be empty, with no one to talk to. Mother would be here, of course, but that wasn't much help. Neither was the loathsome Mrs. Westerly, Mother's maid. None of the servants inside were that interesting and I wasn't often allowed outside.

Father, of course, was away at sea.

I heard Mother's slow footsteps pass in the hall outside my room and thought briefly of dashing out and trying to talk to her. Engage her in something, *anything*. But the idea faded as quickly as it had come, smothered by the remembrance of a hundred other failed attempts. Since Faith's introduction to Court, Mother had focused all of her declining faculties on Faith's progress in *Society*.

I was only a year behind Faith, and should soon be introduced to the Court and to *Society* myself. (You could always hear the capital 'S' and italics when Mother said *Society*.) The problem was: I didn't have a knack for Society and we all knew it. Superficially, I didn't look so very different from Faith. Both of us were slender, and we both had the same pale-gold hair.

But while Faith simply *reeked* of coquettish elegance, I was too curious about everything, Mother said, and it made my face all thin and ferrety. Also, I asked too many questions. Boys don't like questions. Men even less so.

With my ear to the door, I waited for several minutes after I heard the footsteps pass, then stole out into the darkened hall.

I had two places of refuge. The first was Father's study. The lock was an ornate brass monstrosity shaped like a widespread elm that was harder to pick than any other lock in the house, but I'd had lots of practice. Once inside, I locked the door again and tugged one of the carpets to cover the bottom of the door so I could light a candle. Then I pulled out Father's collection of maps and nautical charts. The room always smelled of leather books and Father's cigarettes. I knew I'd be safe in here.

Father had been an officer in the Crimean War before leaving the service and becoming a merchant captain for the East India Trading Company. Being a sea captain meant he spent more time sailing to India and back than he did in London, but whenever I was here in his study, he didn't seem so far away. I walked to the great map on the wall and traced Father's course with my fingers. Coming back from India would be faster now with steam power and the Suez Canal, but that didn't seem to change the fact that Father was almost never home. He simply commanded more voyages than he had before.

I left the wall and pulled out some of the books of maps that offered more detail. Flipping through the pages, I found England first and noticed a few with pencil marks outlining a number of the railroads, which was curious. But England and her coastline weren't as interesting to me as more foreign places. I'd already memorized most of the English coast. Now, the maps showing

India, China, the Americas. *These* were the magical places to me. Oh, to sail to *those* places!

I imagined standing on the deck of a ship someday, with the rocking horizon stretched out before me. With a hold full of cotton, silk, indigo dye, tea, or opium to sell, I could make all the money I might need to stay free. Forget Society and their chaste and interminable little dinners. I would eat salted pork, ship's biscuit, fruit from the islands, or fish pulled up from the surrounding seas. I would love and marry who I wished, perhaps no one at all if that was what *I* wanted. I could go anywhere, meet anybody, *be* anybody, instead of living amidst the inescapable, awkward and stifling life in London Society with nothing to live for but my husband's dreary successes or even drearier failures and nothing whatsoever of my own.

A bit of stray streetlamp glow leaked in from the street. I took Father's navy coat and an old battered hat from the coat rack and slid open the study window. Another marvelous feature of Father's study. No one came in here when Father wasn't home, so there was little risk of discovery.

I went out to my second refuge: the roof. With Father's coat and hat protecting me from the cold, wet and soot, I could sit and watch the will-o-wisps of the gas streetlights down below. Carriage lanterns moved in the fog and the call of cabbies' cries and the clatter of horse's hooves echoed all around. The entire city seemed alive and spread out beneath me. I sat above it all, wrapped in the anonymity of London's yellowed and ageless fog.

After a while, I climbed back into Father's study and pulled the leather-clad Mariner's Diary off the shelf. I looked a little at the merchant ships like Father captained now, but turned quickly to the navy vessels, which Father had worked on and commanded years ago. There were a great many pictures in this edition and I entertained myself for a short time identifying how each was rigged, where the wind must be coming from, and what the sea must have been like based on the position and disposition of the sail. I lost myself in the drawings of sail and rigging and the minutiae of life at sea and finally fell asleep in Father's big leather chair.

At first, I dreamed of running close-hauled on a fair wind. Next, I dreamed of the Faerie King sitting in a strange forest, immobile and covered in snow.

◆◇◆◇◆◇◆

I woke slowly and sat a moment drowsily staring at shadows on the ceiling. Morning! It was bloody morning already. I jumped to my feet and the Mariner's Diary crashed to the floor. Scooping it up, I smoothed the pages and went to put it back on the shelf, but stopped, staring.

There, in a corner of the room, sat a chess set that hadn't been there before. At least, I hadn't seen it. The room had been dark. Seeing it sent a shiver through me, bringing back both last night's dream and following Father in the woods, so long ago.

It wasn't just any chess set, either. It was *the* chess set. The same set of carved wood and bone I'd seen in my dream in the forest. Only, suddenly, I was sure it hadn't been a dream at all.

Someone was in the middle of a game, with a bunch of captured pieces lined up off to the side. I reached out with a shaking hand and picked up one of these, the knight. The warm and polished surface tugged at something deep, deep inside of me until my legs felt weak. The details of the horse were perfect, just as I remembered from that night in the woods. Father had given it to me then, hadn't he? And then I'd lost it. I clutched it tightly. Now that I'd found it again, I didn't want to ever give it up. I tucked the chess piece into a pocket of my dressing gown.

Dazed as I was, my gaze swept the room to see what else I'd missed in the darkness last night. A smoking stand sat in easy reach, filled with recent ash. That's why the room always smelled so strongly of Father's cigarettes. There were a number of new items on the bookshelves. Some of the older books on the top shelf were gone, replaced by collection after collection of children's storybooks: Faerie tales and ghost stories. The shelf at the very bottom held curios.

Father had been home recently—within the last month—and hadn't told anyone. It had been months since I'd seen the room during daylight and gotten a good look around, hadn't it? None of this was here then.

So someone had come into this room recently, smoked, muddled with the books and added things to Father's collection. It had to be Father. I imagined him sitting at his desk, smoking, pondering one of his maps while the rest of us slept. I was hurt beyond belief that he'd been home and hadn't told me.

I knelt down to look at the new things on the bottom shelf. The closest object was a jar sealed with wax, which I picked up. Inside, suspended in amber fluid, a tiny, lifeless girl washed slowly back and forth. Both horrified and irresistibly drawn to get a better look, I held it up to the light.

She was smaller than my hand, with delicate wings like a dragonfly. Her face was beautiful, but feral, even in death. The long red hair on her head fell down past her shoulders, but she also had tufts that ran down her spine and along the backs of her arms and legs. Fine hairs that floated like seaweed in the preserving fluid.

Her hands were grotesque, barbed and curved talons that dangled down to her knees like oversized butcher's hooks. But the worst was her mouth, which gaped open to show rings of teeth like a river lamprey. A freakish combination of beautiful and repulsive that made me shiver. A small card next to the jar labeled it simply: "Faerie—Pix".

There were other objects there: a collar, elephant figurines, a bowl of broken stained glass in green and red, and a sextant. These things also reminded me of the time in the woods, convincing me even more that my memory of the Faerie King hadn't been just a dream.

I jumped as something heavy thumped downstairs. I wasn't expecting any of the family up and it didn't sound like the servants. I needed to get out of here before someone caught me.

Closing the door of the study behind me, I went back out into the darkly-paneled hallway, half expecting the Faerie King to be there waiting for me. Next to an umbrella stand, perhaps. A high window at the far end of the hall let in more wan light. It couldn't be too many minutes past dawn. The family portraits in the hall glared at me accusingly: Father, Mother, Joshua, Benedict, Faith, myself, and lastly, Henry, the youngest. I glared back.

Another loud noise from downstairs, a door slamming, I thought. Loud voices down there, too. Lots of voices.

I glanced at the stairs that led down to the front hall. It wouldn't do to get caught out here by Mother or Mrs. Westerly, but curiosity drew me to the stairway like a mouse to the trap. I looked down into the front hallway to see dozens of men in white breeches and rough jackets, clearly sailors, passing back and forth in raucous industry. The door to the street was propped open, letting in noise from the street and a cold draft I could feel all the way up here.

There was a knot of men standing in the foyer, one of them giving orders. "...warm clothes," he said. "It's a long trip and they'll need them before the day is out."

Father! The man giving orders was Father! I clutched the railing, looking down at him, and felt my legs about to give way. Despite my discovery that he'd been in the study, actually seeing him in the flesh when his ship was supposed to be halfway across the ocean was still a shock.

My nightgown was rumpled and my hair a fright. I still had Father's coat on too, but I didn't care. I tore down the stairs. Another sailor made to grab me, but I was already past him and barreled right into Father with a happy little shriek.

"You're home!" I shouted. "Why didn't you tell anyone?"

"There's my little Justice," he said warmly. "Of course you'd be the first to greet me. Good god, girl, you're getting taller."

"You were already home!" I said. "Days ago! Maybe weeks!"

He looked at me a minute and nodded. "That's quite true."

I stamped my foot. "Why didn't you tell anyone?"

His only answer was a secretive smile. He turned to a man in an old-style, indigo officer's uniform. "Have them down here in two minutes. Two minutes, Mr. Caine, not a second more!"

"Aye aye, sir!" The officer rushed up the stairs, a line of sailors in tow. A few more sailors strong-armed our sleepy-eyed servants back into the kitchen while yet another pair wrestled a clanking barrel past us. They dropped it with a metallic crash in the hallway and pried it open. Then, each of them pulled two handfuls of iron spikes out and flung them down the hall with an enormous racket. They dragged the keg further into the house and disappeared. I gawked at that a second, then turned back to glare at Father, who still hadn't answered me.

Father always looked more like a gentleman than a sea captain: dark suit, black satin cravat, and a gold watch chain dangling from his vest. His face was tightly set: a man engaged in an unsavory task. "I know I've always raised you to think for yourself," he said to me, "but we're going to do some things that won't make a lot of sense today. Can you follow orders, even when they don't make any sense to you? *Can you trust me?*"

I didn't even blink. "Yes, Father. Of course."

"There's a good girl. I'll hold you to that. I brought coats for the others, but I see you've got one. Good. We have to get everyone out of London. It's not safe."

"Where are we going?" I said, but Father just gave me a look. *No questions,* was what that look said.

"Rachek?" Mother called out from the top of the stairs. Two men had her by either elbow and were ushering her firmly down. Her skin was pale, and her dark eyes were unfocused, glazed with the effects of her medicine. She was deeply confused, but still regal, somehow. Coppery hair drifted around her in glorious disarray, a guttering candleflame. Father's face lifted, and then his mouth hardened. A flurry of emotions passed across his face and then his expression was guarded and stern again.

"Rachek?" Mother said again. "You're home? What in the world is going on? Are these men under your orders?" Her head lolled as the sailors half-carried her down the stairs.

Father met them at the bottom. He looked her over quickly. "Martine, dear," Father said softly. "You look pale. Another few weeks, and they would have had my wife out from under my very nose."

Mother looked at me standing next to Father and her eyes focused briefly on me with sudden anger. "Justice! I should have known you'd be involved. Two peas in a pod. The lies, the secrets. No wonder you were always his favorite!"

Father's eyebrows shot up in surprise, looking at both Mother and me in turn.

"I didn't do anything!" I said.

I looked at Father in appeal, trying to keep my bottom lip from quivering while my heart fell. Mother's anger with me had been going on for forever, it seemed, and try as I would, I couldn't get her to forgive me.

"I've kept things from you," Father said to Mother, "but I'm not doing that now. We're in terrible danger and I'm trying to save us. I hope you all see that someday."

Mother gave Father one last look of disgust. "I can't bear it. I just can't," she said. She shook her head, refusing now to meet his gaze.

Father nodded at the two men holding her and they dragged her towards the front door. Another man waited with a coat. Yet another man scurried by with Mother's medicine bag. Father's face, watching them go, was hard.

Immediately, two more men brought Faith down. "What's going on?" she whispered as they escorted her to the front door and wrapped her in a coat. "Are you part of this?" I shook my head, but she glared spitefully back at me. "I bet you are."

Just like Mother, assuming this was my fault. At least with Faith, I knew that she believed the worst of me because Mother did. I wished I knew why *Mother* felt that way.

They took Faith out into the street.

Because I was off to one side, I was the only one who could see down the kitchen hallway. The greasy brown hair, pockmarked face and hostile gaze of Mrs. Westerly appeared for a moment in the kitchen doorway, peering vulturously out. Father might have seen her, if he'd turned around. But he didn't. He was talking urgently to two more sailors. Westerly saw Father and her black eyes narrowed into a shocking expression of hatred. Her mouth opened in a drawn-out and silent stoat's hiss.

Father turned suddenly, and saw her.

"Her!" he snapped at his men. "Fetch her out here!"

Mrs. Westerly hissed again, this time loudly, and disappeared into the kitchen. Four of the burly men hustled after her, but they came out of the kitchen a thirty seconds later, shaking their heads.

"Bolted, sir," one of them reported. "Out the back door and into the street, maybe. We couldn't find 'er anywhere."

Father nodded, clearly unhappy but not sure what to do about it. Finally, he seemed to remember my presence and nodded at me.

"You go now, Justice," he said. "Like you promised."

"But . . ."

"Come, Miss Justice," a soft voice at my elbow said. "You *did* promise." A small, young, blonde man with a pointed yellow beard took my arm. He wore an ox-blood suit, with jacket and waistcoat, and yellow bits of disheveled hair peeked out from underneath an equally ox-blood derby.

"Who are you?" I said.

He gave me a sly grin and the yellow mustache and beard quivered. "You're quite right to insist on introductions," he said. He had a voice of rough honey and a Parisian lilt. "My name is Sebastian Sands, magician." There was an odd, aristocratic courtesy about him that made me revise my first estimate of his age upwards by ten or twenty years. Thirty? Forty? I couldn't tell, but I let him escort me out anyway.

Outside, yellow walls of fog pressed all around. The street smelled of garbage and standing water, like London always did.

Unseen hansoms and footsteps rattled by in the fog, heard once, then lost again. London was never still. A dimly seen crowd had gathered to watch the strange goings-on despite the early hour. More sailors were unloading clanking barrels from a cart, but Mr. Sands steered me around them before I could get a better look.

A man standing guard opened the door of a large, reinforced carriage. It looked like something to imprison the queen, with iron bands across the paneling, bars on the windows, but no glass. The guard had both cutlass and pistol.

"Even the Royal Navy doesn't hand out weapons unless action is coming," I said. "What enemy are you expecting in the middle of London?"

The sailor's face remained like stone. I looked back at Mr. Sands, who tugged at his little beard thoughtfully.

"Justice," he said. "That's a peculiar name for a girl, isn't it?"

"It was my Father's idea," I said. "I think he wanted all the virtues, only he didn't have enough girls for seven. We had an older sister, Prudence, only she died as a baby. I've only got the one sister now."

"Only one sister?" He said. Something about the idea seemed to amuse him.

"Yes," I said, trying to match his flip manner. "Maybe if I'd had a few sisters before me, someone else could have been Justice and I'd have been Temperance or Charity or maybe even Faith, only Faith's already Faith so . . ."

"No." Mr. Sands shook his head sadly. "You couldn't possibly be any of those, I'm afraid." With those astonishing words, he ushered me up into the carriage and closed the door.

The lock on the outside slid home.

# CHAPTER 2

## The Storm

I pushed at the locked door, which was stupid because I'd heard them lock it, but I did it anyway. Nothing.

"What's happening?" Faith said. "Did Father tell you what's going on?"

"I don't know." A hope sprang into my head prompted by all the sailors and casks and sailcloth and the smell of salt. "Maybe we're going to sea?"

"Pretend all you like," Faith said. "I'm sure whatever this is, you know more about it than you're telling. You like secrets more than anything, don't you? Isn't that right, Mother?"

For answer, Mother opened her bag, a foul thing of oil-stained leather, and took out one of the small vials that held her medicine.

The interior of the carriage smelled immediately of oranges and licorice somehow gone acrid and foul. She took a small sip and said to Faith, "Don't bother fighting it, dear. Men rule the world and the best that women can do is find one they can trust. I wish to hell that *I* had."

"Of course we can trust Father!" I protested.

"You don't know," Mother sneered. "You don't *know* what he's done. To me, to all of us." She another, longer swallow, and then seemed to lapse into a silent torpor, ignoring us and staring out the carriage window at the rolling, yellow fog.

Faith pressed her face against the bars, shouting out. "Father! Father! Where are you taking us?"

More shouts came from outside, drew closer.

"Mother!" Faith shrieked. "Make them stop!" But Mother didn't respond at all. She just sat there, staring vacantly out into the fog, even when the carriage door opened again.

Three of Father's men shoved my brother Henry inside with us. It needn't have taken three. Henry wasn't very large. He was also stunned and completely unresisting. They pushed him in and he fell down on the carriage floor.

I have three brothers, but my two older brothers went away to school when I was much younger, and I never got to know them very well. But Henry was a year younger than I, and always dear to my heart, as he, Faith and I had grown up together.

Henry sat up, his sandy hair tousled, his eyes wide with fear. He was still in his bedclothes, same as the rest of us. Well, most of us, anyway, if you didn't count Father's coat and hat that I was wearing.

"Lor!" Henry said. "Justice? Faith? Mother? What's going on? I was in my bed at Harrows when they pulled me out. Bundled into a carriage and then out into the street and now here, into another carriage? What is all this?"

"We don't know," I said.

Henry moved and there was the clink of heavy metal. I leaned forward. Henry was wearing manacles!

"Henry!" I gasped. "You're in irons! Why!"

"Because Father's lost his mind," Faith said. "That's why!"

"I resisted!" Henry said. "Fought like a pirate when they pulled me out of bed, I did!" Then, seeing our stunned expressions, he smiled sheepishly. "All right, then, I panicked when they pulled me out of bed. Screamed like a girl and bit one on accident. He's the one that called me a whole *mess* of foul names and then put these on me." He laughed ruefully. "I'm not even sure Father knows about it. I only saw a glimpse of him when they pulled me out of the other carriage and threw me in this one."

"Faith," I said. "Give me a hairpin." I didn't wear any. Never did, really. But Faith always had some in, even when she went to bed.

"Come on now," I said. "Give me a hairpin, won't you?"

Faith stared. I shook my open hand at her until she finally pulled one of the pins out of her hair and handed it over.

"Lor!" Henry said. "Really? You can get these off? They chafe something terrible!"

"Just hold still," I said. The pin wasn't very strong, and it was a heavy lock, but slow pressure got the lock open at last.

"How did you do that?" Henry asked.

I held the bent hairpin out to Faith, but she only looked at it and said stiffly, "Where is Father taking us? I know you know."

"I *don't* know," I said. It dawned on me that if I'd paid more attention to Father's maps of England, I might have some idea. But I hadn't.

"Yes, you do," Faith said, glaring at me. She ignored the hairpin.

Henry looked at me questioningly, but I shook my head and he nodded. The two lanterns hung on the outside of the carriage provided the only light, but his open, honest face practically shone with trust. It had been months since I'd seen Henry last and I was worried that he might have changed in school, grown apart from us, but he was just as I remembered him. He got up and brushed the sandy hair back from his face. His sleeping clothes were gray wool, worn, and two sizes too big for him, clearly assigned from Harrows.

"Maybe it's some kind of mistake," Henry said. "Maybe Father just made a mistake, is all."

"Father knows what he's doing," I said. "He says we have to get away."

"Get away from what, Justice?" Faith said. The past year's distance between us was all summed up in her cold and suspicious look. I could only lift my hands helplessly. I didn't know. Faith scoffed and turned away.

"Are you injured, Mother?" Faith said. She sat carefully next to her.

Mother didn't answer. She was still staring fixedly out the window. When Faith gently took Mother's hands in hers, Mother muttered something unintelligible and closed her eyes.

"Mother?" Faith said softly, "what do you know about this? Do you know what Father's up to?" Still no answer.

"Lor!" Henry said. "Is she always like this?"

"It's not her fault!" Faith snapped, angry tears in her eyes. "It's the medicine, sometimes it makes her like this."

"What kind of bloody medicine is *that*?" Henry said.

"A concoction of Mrs. Westerly's," I said distastefully.

"She always comes out of it in a few hours," Faith said. "When she does, she'll know what to do."

I didn't want to wait that long. I scrambled to the door, trying to get a better look at the hinges and the latch in the weak lantern light. Father clearly wanted us to stay here, so I would, but it didn't hurt to look. The latch was on the outside, but I might be able to finesse it open from this side with some kind of tool, if only I had one. I noticed two of Father's men watching me through the window bars. I watched them back. Two other men were switching out the carriage horses, so we probably had a long trip ahead of us.

I prayed that Father would explain himself soon. He had to, didn't he? He couldn't lock us all up without some kind of explanation, could he? I touched the bars over the window. They were black, rough, and very cold. Disturbingly hideous, rousing equally disturbing feelings since my family and I were the ones behind them. Whatever Father was doing, he wasn't taking things lightly.

Father materialized out of the fog and spoke to one of the men. I kept hoping that he'd come over and offer some kind of explanation to this mad scene, but he never did.

The officer, Caine, appeared behind him. Now that I got a closer look at the uniform, it didn't look at all familiar. Not like any uniform I'd seen before. A deep and vivid indigo, with wide, white lapels, heavy cuffs, and white frogging cord down the front. More cord ran down the back, white on blue, like a string of barbed thorns. Certainly not English. Not any of the other European sea powers, either. I was sure of that. Two epaulets marked him as a captain of at least three years seniority.

Mr. Sands joined them, and the three men conferred briefly, Mr. Sands looking tiny next to Father and the equally tall Caine.

Father was issuing orders to Sands, who nodded dutifully. I thought I caught the names of my other two brothers, Joshua and Benedict.

Then Father and Caine walked towards the carriage. Father met my eyes through the barred window, but didn't say anything. He looked like a haunted man. He put his hand briefly on the window frame of the carriage as he went by, but that was all. He joined Caine out of view in the driver's seat.

Mr. Sands stood alone in the fog a moment. Then he clapped his hands and a white shape clip-clopped itself out of the fog as if it had been waiting off stage for his signal.

"Oh!" I said. "Look at Mr. Sands' horse! It's magnificent!"

The stallion gleamed all over, an alabaster glory in defiance of the dirty streets. Proud and tall, with a matching white saddle chased with gold inlay. Sands mounted and leaned over and spoke a word into the horse's ear. It might have been a joke from the look on Sands' face, but the horse quivered with excitement. A light touch and word from Mr. Sands and the stallion bolted forward. The yellow fog swallowed them at once and they were gone.

"Mr. who?" Faith said. "How do *you* know his name?"

"Mr. Sands," I said. "He says he's a magician."

"You seem to know a great deal more about this than the rest of us," Faith said suspiciously.

"I *listened*," I shot back. "While the rest of you were fighting with him, I followed orders and listened."

"You . . ." Mother hissed, and I jumped. I hadn't even realized she was awake, but she had her eyes open now, glaring at me. Her head still lolled to the side as if too heavy for her to pick up. "You're *helping* him do this to us," she whispered. "I won't forget that." Her expression now was so hateful it sent a winter's chill right through me. Faith turned a heavily lidded gaze on me, too, as if Mother's condemnation was all she needed to condemn me, too.

I couldn't make my mouth work to deny her condemnation, either. I was just as trapped as the rest of them, wasn't I? Except that I told Father I'd obey. No one had forced me to do that and none of the others would have, I was sure.

"I won't forget," Mother repeated. She closed her eyes again, shutting us all out.

Mother hated me now. It had been bad before between us, but this burned our bridges entirely.

Father's shout to get the horses moving made us all jump. A sudden jerk and the carriage rattled into motion. We turned a corner at once and we nearly hit another cab, such was our rush. I saw the familiar face of the other cabbie, Mr. Divers, up on his hansom with the stalwart and friendly roan, Hercules, out front. Mr. Divers had to yank on the reins to prevent a collision between our two vehicles and man and horse watched us rattle by at an unsafe speed. Mr. Divers' whiskered face was full of surprise and then, we rattled on and I couldn't them anymore.

We were underway.

◄◊►◄◊►◄◊►

When I think about that carriage ride, a sort of mist descends. I remember the fright and uncertainty, but there was an undercurrent of *certainty*, too. Nothing too terrible could happen, I was sure, because Father was behind it. Often, the sweet and spicy scent of Father's cigarettes would drift back to us from driver's seat and that reassured me. Whatever reasons Father had for dragging us out of our London apartments, they would make perfect sense once we found out what they were.

We watched the counties slide away: the dark buildings and early morning foot traffic and trade of Southwark first, then nearly identical Lambeth, and finally into the rural areas of South London where the buildings and street lights melted into open fields and trees brilliant with fall colors.

None of us spoke. There didn't seem any point. I was rubbing my thumb against the chess piece in my pocket so much the tip of my thumb was getting sore.

We stopped once briefly at an isolated farm where Father and Caine drove the carriage past an abandoned farmhouse and into a large barn. The doors on the barn were swung shut so that we had only the lantern light to see by before we heard the bolt drawn back on the carriage door.

We emerged, half blind in the cold darkness, finding no sign of Father, only Caine waiting for us.

He had his pistol out, eyeing us as if we were serious hardened criminals rather than three children and an ill woman. He pointed the pistol at a dirty latrine in the corner. He didn't speak, and there was no sign of Father.

"Where are you…" Faith started, but Caine cocked the weapon and pointed it with such a stern gaze that her question trickled off.

"No questions," he said. "Or you all get back into the carriage *without* using the loo."

Not even Faith had anything to say to that, though if looks could kill, there wouldn't have been enough of Caine to sweep out of a barn. Faith's glare notwithstanding, Caine had us back in the detestable and somewhat ripe carriage in less than ten minutes. I got a glimpse of Father as he climbed back up into the driver's box, but the lengths to which he'd gone to avoid even talking to us gave me a gloomy chill.

Caine shouted at the horses and we were underway again down another nameless muddy road. Faith caught my eye and gave me a look that condemned Father and anyone foolish enough to follow his orders.

Our carriage thumped and thudded over dirt roads now, and other than the drizzle of rain and the splash of a lantern swinging from the top of the carriage, our prison wagon might have been the only thing moving on the whole countryside. The sky was so dark and gray that several times I woke and thought we'd ridden the entire day away.

Inside, we four prisoners were cramped, bruised, outrageously grubby and even more dismal than the landscape, which was saying a great deal.

Mother, insensate in the corner seat now for hours, moaned softy.

"What's wrong with her?" I said. "How come no one told me she'd gotten this bad?"

"Mother said not to," Faith said. She was rifling through Mother's medicine bag again with an expression of bitter helplessness. "She didn't want anyone to even talk about it. She was usually fine a few hours into the morning, after her medicine. She'd be herself all the way through evening, on a good day. I'm sure she needs something, only there are so many *different* bottles here I don't know which to give her! Mrs. Westerly always administers it at home. Oh, Mother, wake up!"

The carriage turned now, and the horses started laboring up a steep incline. The sky above us rumbled in warning, long and deep and low. Caine yelled and drove the horses harder, cracking the whip repeatedly. The road leveled off and we picked up speed. A great deal of speed.

I could see the same thought in Henry and Faith's eyes, the same fear. *Too fast, too fast.* The wheels hissed through puddles and banged in the road, each jarring impact rattling our spines all the way up to our teeth and still we picked up speed. We flew now, far faster than anyone should go. Our wheels were going to smash themselves to pieces any minute.

The rain overtook us.

We could see the storm through the rear window coming fast. Half a minute later it had caught us. Rain splashed through the bars of the window and the sky lit up like fireworks followed by a crack, like a rifle shot.

"Aren't we going to slow down?" Faith said tremulously.

"We ought to," I said. "They're hurting the horses driving them like this."

"Do you hear that?" Faith said. "Music?"

"I don't hear *anything* over this noise!" Henry said.

"Me either," I said.

The wheels hit something in the road, and we were all sickeningly airborne. We held our breath, hearts pounding, until the carriage hit dirt again and kept going. The rattle was deafening. The bars across the window broke loose in one large section and the entire hunk of metal went spinning away.

Odd noises played around the edges of my hearing, sailing past in gusts to compete with the racket of the bouncing carriage: the harsh cawing of birds, the baying of hounds, a great host of pounding hooves.

I stood up and leaned out the window to try and see out. Henry was behind me so I stuck my hand to him and he grabbed it without hesitation. He wasn't any larger than I was, but it still helped to have someone to hold onto. With one hand on the edge of the window and him bracing the other, I leaned out to get a better look around.

"Justice?" Faith said from inside the carriage. "What are you doing?"

It was a monsoon out here. Woods flashed by, glimmering darkly in the rain, while a white-hot bolt cut raggedly across the sky. The lantern had fallen off, too, leaving everything black around us. The wind wailed and mourned. There had to be a crash. No carriage could fly along a dirt road like this and *not* crash.

I could barely make out the shape leaning out of the driver's box.

"You've got to slow down!" I shouted.

Father turned and looked back in my direction, but not at me. At something behind us. His hat was gone, leaving his hair plastered to his skull and water running off in rivulets. His face was a fish-belly white mask of fear with eyes shot wide open. He didn't respond to my shout, only pointed the dripping barrel of a revolver at something in the sky behind us and fired until the gun clicked empty.

Seeing Father's terrified face, more than anything before, brought the terror home. I knew he'd fought fearlessly in the Crimea. A navy man's life was filled with stormy seas, artillery fire, engagements at sea. They wouldn't give so many medals to a coward, would they?

I looked back just in time to see a flashing arc of lightning strike the back of the carriage.

The carriage twisted and I fell back inside. Everyone was screaming. The world spun and twisted and banged and crashed as we fell end over end. It seemed like it went on forever, bashing into each other over and over. Maybe being packed in like sardines saved us, because there wasn't as much room to fall. Maybe.

One last crash, and we all fell into each other again, *hard*, as the carriage banged over one last time and then finally lay still.

The horses' hoof beats, still running, gradually faded into the distance. Rain poured down through the open door above us. We'd lost the door somewhere in the crash. Another flash filled the sky. The storm that had knocked us half to pieces wasn't done yet. Not by a long shot.

# CHAPTER 3

## The Wild Hunt

I couldn't move, couldn't breathe, and something pressed on my chest hard enough to crush the life right out of me. But I fought. I was still alive, at least. God knew how, but I was going to fight to keep it that way. I wormed myself out from beneath the crushing weight, which turned out to be Henry and part of a broken wheel. Henry wasn't moving.

A terrible image of my family lying broken and dead in the road burned itself into my mind's eye. What if they were all dead and I was the only one left?

I put a hand on Henry's chest and I could feel him breathing. Thank god! That was two of us. What about the rest? Another burst of lightning showed me the hole above us, a flashing square where the carriage door had been torn off. Then, it faded. Water from the rain splattered down next to me in the darkness.

My hand found the horse chess piece in the pocket of my dressing gown. I knew this was all connected, somehow, to that night in the woods.

"What happened?" Henry's voice sounded younger than ever.

"We crashed," I said. The interior of the carriage echoed and everything was very dark and I wasn't sure where he was.

"Justice?" Faith said.

"Faith?" I said. "Thank god! What about Mother? Can you see?"

"Mother's here," Faith said. "She's all right, I think. Just dazed."

The next flash of light showed the three of us, Faith, Henry and me, looking around. I picked out Mother's still shape.

"Hold still," I said to Henry and shifted to get my foot up on his shoulder.

"Ow, what are you doing? Ow!"

"I need to look around," I said.

I ignored his further protests and climbed up through the open hole above us and looked.

Falling water hissed on the trees, dripped on my face, and plunked down on the muddy road. My hair, nightgown and coat were soaked through in seconds and the wind slashed across my face. I knuckled the water from my eyes and looked around. Rain and darkness veiled everything, making distorted shapes of the trees. The road ahead ran up a short hill and then curved to the right into the trees.

"Father? Anyone?"

When I looked back the way we'd come, lightning drenched the sky. I didn't see Father or Caine.

But I got a good look, at long last, at what was coming for us. A horde of hunters riding on a great black storm cloud in the sky.

The cloud was fearsome on its own: a long black expanse hanging so low that it brushed the tops of the trees. The cloud moved forward with an inevitable, terrible slowness, uncoiling like squid ink on the ocean floor. The sharp tang of rain came with it and the underside of the cloud flashed with lightning that arced down into the forest. Some of the trees were burning now, even in the rain. Flocks of crows darted in and out of the edges, all of them screaming like madwomen.

Riding on top of the cloud, bearing down on us as if running down a slope, was a hunting party.

A pack of bone-white dogs led the hunt, charging down through the sloped confusion of smoke, barking and howling to set your teeth on edge. Their eyes were sockets of burning coal, filled with the bloodlust of the chase.

The riders thundered behind. Men and women, wild haired and pale-skinned, naked and wailing. They rode sooty mounts with black holes for eyes and the toothy grins of sand sharks. Black streamers flew behind them, like pennants.

In the center of the horde, an enormous rider paused on a smoky rise and blew a horn of bone. The long, clear note drifted across the barrage of noise that shot fear straight through my heart. The rider's head was shaggy, his face bearded and his mouth filled with fangs. Antlers rose up from his head in graceful, tined arcs. At first, I thought it was the Faerie King I'd seen in the woods so long ago, but it wasn't him at all. The Hunt leader looked similar though, as if they shared a kinship. Whatever he was, he wasn't human.

All I could think of was running, only there was nowhere to run to, no escape.

Another musical note cut across the din, answering the horn with honey and velvet. I spun around to look further up the road and saw a soft yellow light coming, and coming fast.

Mr. Sands rode out of the darkness on that magnificent white horse, brandishing the unlikeliest of weapons: a violin. Every time he dragged the bow across the strings, it threw out shards of light like an active forge and his green cat's eyes danced in the light. I could feel the waves of heat come off him as he rode past the overturned carriage and took up position between us and the hunt.

The leader of the hunt blew his horn again in challenge and the hunt surged forward.

Mr. Sands answered, his violin soaring.

His hair was a rage of lambent yellow as he sat on that wondrous horse and played with all the glorious abandon of a brush fire. The sparks from Mr. Sands' violin didn't fall to the ground, but drifted around him like attendant fireflies, hissing in the rain and casting off a powerful scent of burning metal. He turned back and forth, his horse answering commands without any need for reins, trying to hedge the Faerie hunting party out. Behind Mr. Sands, I could see another figure riding behind, slumped against Sands' back, unconscious. Who the figure was or how they stayed on while Sands' horse was prancing around that way, I'll never know.

I was crouching on the side of the overturned carriage, still stunned into immobility by the scene in front of me. I shrieked when something pulled on my coat.

"Justice!" Father said. It was his hand on my coat. He was standing in the muddy road below me, reaching up.

"Sands won't be able to hold them long," Father shouted. "What about the others?" He jerked his chin at the overturned carriage. "Can they climb out?"

"I . . . I don't know," I said. I yelled down into the carriage. "We need to move!"

"We can't possibly move!" Faith's voice said from below. Her white hands gripped the edge of the wet doorframe as she hauled herself partially up. Her head rose slowly out of the carriage while the rest of her was still inside. Probably she was standing on Henry's shoulders, like I had.

"We just crashed, for god's sake," Faith said, "and god knows what kind of injury . . ." Her voice trailed off as she turned and stared at the flickering, fantastically unbelievable scene of hunt and magician facing off before us. The leader's horn sounded again.

Faith swallowed and nodded. "We have to move," she said.

Faith and Henry boosted Mother up, and I got hold of her hands and pulled until a burning sensation tore through my shoulders, but somehow we got her up. Then Faith and Henry clambered up after. We repeated the routing to get Mother off the carriage and down into the muddy road, but she was too heavy and Mother and I toppled into the muddy road. Finally, Faith and Henry got down and helped me get her up. She was barely conscious and we had to keep her propped up between Henry and me. Somehow, even in that bedraggled state, Mother managed to cling to the medicine bag.

"Here," Faith said, taking Mother's arm from me. Even now, she didn't trust me.

"Justice," Father said, grabbing my arm. "I need you to be strong. Get your mother and the others up this road. At the top, there's a gate. Go through that, close the gate and you'll be safe. Can you do that for me?" His eyes were the same clear and determined blue I'd always known.

"Yes, sir," I said. "Up the road. Gate at the top."

"Don't forget to close the gate, understand? Don't stop for anything until you're all behind that gate."

"Yes," I said, then, "Aye aye."

God only knew how I'd get them up that hill, but I'd do it.

"Good," he said, turning away. His coat was gone, his waistcoat torn in shreds, his hair wind-tossed. He held a black revolver in his hand, fishing more cartridges out of his pants pocket as he spoke.

I rushed over to where Faith and Henry were holding Mother up, and then looked back.

The floating embers from Mr. Sands' violin rose up to meet the rolling black cloud of the hunt above the trees. The yellow dots opened up, unfurling serpentine bodies and angular bat wings. Their eyes were pinpoints of white-hot flame and each beat of their wings spilled a cascade of sparks and ripples of heat in defiance of the rain.

"Dragons," I breathed. "Tiny dragons."

The rushing line of hounds yelped and skidded to a halt, shrinking away from the rippling wall of heat in front of them. The hunters behind had to jerk to a stop to avoid trampling them and the front edge of the horde came to a slow, chaotic stop. The storm cloud stopped with them, slowly flattening out in either direction. Two of the hounds had skirted far enough out to the edge and jumped the thirty or forty feet down into the wet ground on the side of the road with a sharp growl.

Mr. Sands was still casting forth firefly dragons with every pull of the bow across the violin strings. The horse he was on danced, keeping a careful distance between itself and the advancing hounds. On the horse's back, behind Sands, the form slumped against Sand's back was alternately lit and covered in darkness. It was an older boy with black curly hair that I knew well, and a pale face. I hadn't seen him in nearly half a year, but I still recognized Benedict, our brother.

"Benedict!" Faith shouted at me. She'd seen him, too. Sands must have gone and collected him after leaving us, and then brought him to meet us back here in time for all of this. The light flashed again and I got another look. Benedict was clearly unconscious. It was a miracle that the magnificent white horse could dance back and forth the way it did without throwing either Sands or Benedict, but it did.

"We have to get Mother safe!" I shouted at Faith.

Father, aiming very carefully, squeezed off two shots and two of the spectral hounds went down. A massive shower of sparks flew up from Mr. Sands' firefly dragons, but the cloud and horde were spilling over the fireflies like a flood over a dam, dropping snarling hunters and hounds down into the road.

Faith and I rushed after the rest of my family, who'd gone a short way up the road, but now stopped and stared at the fantastic warfare unfolding in front of them.

"Go!" I shouted.

Mother suddenly raised her head. "No," she rasped, "I'm not going along with this madness anymore! Whatever he has waiting for us up the road, I don't want it. We'll go into the woods. Find shelter and hide until daylight. He'll never find us there."

I looked at the thick, dark woods, flickering with light. We *might* be able to hide in there, which would ruin Father's plans entirely. But Faith and Henry were nodding at Mother's words and I realized that I was going to fail Father right when he needed me most.

I didn't think I could stand toe-to-toe arguing with Mother, especially not if Faith and Henry agreed with her.

Instead, I hastily shoved aside Faith and grabbed Mother by the hand and elbow. It was the same hand that still clutched, amazingly, the medicine bag. I hauled on bag and arm together, hoping that Henry would go along with it.

"This way!" I shouted, pulling for all I was worth.

It worked better than I'd dared hope. Mother shrieked and came stumbling after me, so concerned at the possibility of losing her medicine bag that she, in her addled state, seemed to forget all about wanting to go into the woods. Henry gamely held her up on the other side. Faith cast one dark look back at the battle, clamped her jaw, and followed.

Father was back there facing some kind of horde out of legend, but I pushed that from my mind. Father had asked me to get them up the hill, and I'd bloody well see it done. We passed around a clump of trees and the incline of the road increased sharply. We couldn't see the battle behind us anymore, but we could see flashes of light against the night sky and hear shots and screams, barking and the call of a hunting horn, as well as fire sizzling in the rain. My legs felt numb and my breath was already coming in gasps, but I forced myself on through the dark and wet. The storm rumbled behind us angrily. My coat and nightdress were soaked and heavy with rain and freezing to the touch.

We slogged on through the mud, up, up, up, forever, it seemed. Our ragged breathing as we struggled and the rain and the thunder behind us were the only noises. The forest petered out gradually, leaving a wide expanse of wet fields on either side.

A craggy shape rose up ahead, a darker patch of black lines in the gray all around. A black, heavy, iron gate. It was tall, nearly nine or ten feet, and ugly and rough, with a huge arch and fence as far as we could see in both directions. The bars were as thick as my wrist and both the fence and the arch had barbs on top. Someone really didn't want visitors, putting up a fence like that. We stood facing the gate, hollowed and bled dry of all emotion. The gate had a lock on it large enough to keep Germany out.

"I don't like it," Mother muttered to herself. "Don't . . . don't go in."

"We have to," I said. I tried pushing at it, and we all gasped as it swung open.

"It's not locked," Henry said.

"Come on, then." Henry and I hauled Mother through, and Faith, still hesitating, finally followed.

"Hold her up," I said to Henry. "I have to close the gate."

The heavy bars felt cold and rough to the touch and made my fingers tingle. I ignored that and pushed it closed anyway. The ponderous metal gate clanged closed with an oddly musical sound. Suddenly, we could no longer hear the storm behind us. The night was tomb-silent and black.

We stood on a white gravel drive that ran up towards the blocky shadow of a large mansion. Smooth, wet lawns with evenly-spaced black trees lined the way. Impossibly, it wasn't raining inside the gate.

Night had fallen, hidden by the storm. Peering through the bars, we should have been able to see the lights down the slope, but all we could see were the dark velvety folds of a valley swathed in darkness. Benedict was back there, somewhere in that silent darkness, and Father.

Movement on the lawn caught my eye and I saw a pair of shining eyes. They watched us unflinchingly. Another pair appeared from behind one of the elms, and then another and another. Dozens of pairs of glowing eyes looked at us out of the gloom.

"Where," Faith said, "have you brought us? Justice? What kind of place is this?"

With a flicker of movement, the glowing eyes disappeared.

With a sudden thud of hooves, Mr. Sands crested the hill on the other side of the gate. He was only a dozen feet away, but he was caught in a torrential downpour as we stood in a dry, clear night. Not a drop of rain even touched us.

Mr. Sands had Benedict slung across the horse's neck.

"Oh, thank heaven!" Faith said. I pushed at the gate, but it wouldn't open. It had opened before, but this time, when I pushed, there was a sharp painful tingle and I snatched my hand back.

Father came stumbling out of the darkness on foot just behind them, the revolver dangling weakly in his hand. He sang, a short, complex trill of notes that echoed something of the melody Mr. Sands had played on the violin before. The heavy black lock snapped open and they came through.

Father caught my eye. "Good," he said with a nod. "You got them all here."

I felt a swelling of pride.

"The boy's leg needs attention," Mr. Sands said. "Hit by lightning." He and Father shared a significant look.

Father carefully lifted away the torn flap of Benedict's trousers to reveal blackened skin. "I'll take him. You'd better check the perimeter."

"Yes," Mr. Sands said. "What about Caine?"

"Caine knew the risks." Father slid Benedict off the back of Mr. Sands' horse and cradled him in his arms. "We need to get him up to the house."

"He'll be safe here," Mr. Sands said to us. "You'll all be safe here."

"This," Father said, "is Stormholt."

He started up the gravel drive.

We stared at each other: Faith, Henry, and me. Mother was sagging between Henry and me, out on her feet again. There didn't seem to be any other choice. It was either Stormholt . . . or the storm.

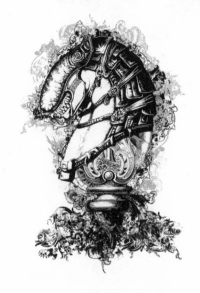

# CHAPTER 4

## Stormholt

We followed Father up the gravel drive, past poplar trees to the dark building above, all of us shivering from cold and fright. The sprawling mansion hulked over us, draped in shadow, with only a general impression of gables and peaks that shifted in the dark.

Father mounted the front steps and entered through a blazing square of light. We all followed.

I remember hands helping me up some stairs, and a warm blanket thrown over my shoulders. More hands thrust a crystal glass of hot wine into my hands, which I drank greedily, still standing. It was heavily spiced with a bitter flavor underneath and I remember very little after that.

I woke up with a hard gasp. No one else was there. I slid out of a strange bed and discovered I wore a number of bandages underneath a thin nightdress. I had two cloths wrapped awkwardly around my right arm and two more taped to my back. It all came back in a rush. Father's return and him dragging us out of the house, the wild carriage ride and subsequent crash, the Wild Hunt. Benedict getting injured.

I was banged and battered and covered with bruises, but fantastically, I was still alive. My hand found a lump in my pocket which turned out to be the wooden chess piece. At least that was safe. But was I?

I'd never been in this room before. The bed was clean and soft enough to sink my hand into. Bright purple curtains covered a stained-glass window that didn't open. A fire was going happily in the grate and I wondered wildly if I might need to escape badly enough to try and get up the chimney. Calm, calm. A painting hung over the mantelpiece depicting a British ship of the line with both gun decks blazing away at some unseen enemy. Automatically, I noted that the ship was 'reaching', with sails full and running perpendicular to the wind, probably running very fast to judge from the upflung spray off the bow. On a shelf underneath sat a model of a frigate, three masts and square-rigged in the English style. At another time, I might have wondered at the minute details like the staysails and the flying jib in front. But not now.

The model and picture convinced me that this room had been prepared especially for someone like me who loved ships, but the frills and colors on the bed were distinctly feminine. There weren't that many girls who would appreciate ships, so this room had been outfitted with *me* in mind. Even more convincing, the wardrobe was filled with frocks and dresses of my size. Lots of frocks and dresses. That all implied we'd be here a while—an unsettling thought that made my throat tight.

Father's coat, that I'd been wearing last night, was there too, brushed clean. Father might as well have stenciled 'Justice Kasric' across the ceiling of this room. What I didn't find was any kind of note telling me *why* we were here or where everyone else was or even if the others were still alive.

I dressed hurriedly and went out. The doors along one side of the hall all looked like bedrooms, most of them ajar. Henry's room was easy enough to identify by the swashbuckling paraphernalia, including a skull and crossbones flag on the wall, a miniature pewter cannon, and a real cutlass on display. A dream room for any fourteen-year-old boy, though *I* sure wouldn't give Henry a cutlass. The blankets were still rumpled. The bed had been slept in, which almost made me cry in relief.

The next had frilly lace on the walls, racks of delicate outfits and a dresser laden with copious amounts of cosmetics, undoubtedly for Faith. Looking at the things that Faith was concerned with, as demonstrated by the rooms, compared to what decorated my room, the gulf between us seemed wider than ever. Far more than the two years between us. I thought this bed had been slept in, too, but someone, probably Faith, had straightened the bedclothes so that it was hard to be sure.

Further along were two sparse rooms that were probably meant for Benedict and Joshua, but neither of these beds had been slept in. Father, or whoever had prepped the rooms, didn't seem to know anything about my two older brothers, because they weren't personalized the same way our rooms had been. That wasn't too surprising. Benedict had been studying at the seminary and Joshua was an adult now, and part of the Horse Guard. Neither had lived at home for years. I didn't know much about them myself. I knew Faith had corresponded often with Benedict, but that obviously wasn't much help to me.

At the end of the hall was a pair of doors of red mahogany and brass gilt, larger and grander than the rest. Maybe some kind of master bedroom. I tried them but they wouldn't budge. Perhaps Mother or Father's room? I pounded on the doors with my fist. No answer.

In the other direction I found a series of baths, many of them filled with steaming water but with no sign of the servants that had filled them. In fact, I didn't see anyone. I was starting to wonder if the place was actually empty and it was enough to make me feel as if I might wander through this endless house alone, forever. Before I got desperate enough to run screaming through the halls or set fire to the furniture, I went through another pair of mahogany and brass doors at the end of the hall and found Faith and Henry in a large parlor.

"Oh, thank god!" I said, running up to and flinging my arms around them. Henry gripped me tightly. Faith flinched when I hugged her, but I didn't care.

The room was done up in rich, red velvets and dark wood, and large enough to entertain all of Bristol. Thick dark carpets lay on the floor and dozens of couches, divans, and padded chairs were all around, and even the tassels had tassels. Two hearths blazed on either end.

The large table in the far end was laid out with the breakfast of all breakfasts. Sausages, fried eggs, salted fish, bacon, kippers, two puddings, toast, tea, and wine. Even a large bowl of fresh strawberries. It was all there on silver platters and china plates and crystal glasses lined up with military precision.

"Ha!" Henry said with his mouth full of kippers. "At leaſt we won't ſtarff."

Faith rolled her eyes at our younger brother. She was in a rose-colored house dress and a delicate ivory shawl and had clearly spent some time cleaning her long hair and getting it up into an elegant bun. I couldn't imagine taking a bath or finding the right dress at a time like this, but Faith had. She'd even found a pair of gloves somewhere. Henry was just as rumpled and disheveled as I was.

"Where's Father?" I asked. "How's Mother? Or Benedict?"

"No one knows!" Faith said. "We haven't seen anyone except each other and you. You were sleeping pretty hard, so we let you go on sleeping. No sign of Father or that little magician fellow. What did you call him? Sands? Not since last night. We think Benedict's here somewhere. We saw Father bring him in, remember?"

"Mother's here, too," Henry said, "but she's barricaded herself in her room. That big one at the end of the hall."

"I knocked on her door," Faith burst out. "I can hear someone moving around in there, but she won't let me in!"

Henry looked down into his cup. "I guess it's just the three of us for now." Right now, he looked even younger than ever and very scared. Probably that was how I looked, too.

"So," Faith said. "No answers from Father. Or Mother. We don't know what's going on and we don't know why we're here."

Henry threw his hands up "We don't know *anything*!"

"Here," Faith said. "Eat something, Justice." She was loading up a plate with bacon. She added a few slices of toast and strawberries and set it in front of me.

"Oh," I said. "Umm . . . thanks." I couldn't remember the last time my sister had done something nice for me, however simple. The toast was still fresh and warm from the oven.

"Why, Justice?" Faith said, and her voice was different, softer than before. "Why did Father bring us here? He must have told you why he's doing this."

Suddenly, her kindness seemed suspicious. "I don't know," I said. "I swear I don't."

Henry pushed his plate back onto the table, inadvertently knocking over one of the platters of toast. The muffled bang of the metal tray hitting the carpet was enough like thunder to make all of us jump.

Henry looked sheepish as he picked up the platter.

"I guess being followed by storms can make you jumpy about that sort of thing," he said.

"What *was* that in the road?" Faith said, ignoring Henry and leaning closer to me. "What kind of storm is filled with hunters on black horses? What kind of storm *follows* you?"

"I don't know," I said, "but I think we'd better find out."

"Does Father just expect us to sit here?"

"I can't believe that," I said, shaking my head. "He must know what he's doing, but he wouldn't want us to wait blindly. He's always taught us to know what we're getting into."

"You don't know what that storm was?" Faith persisted.

"No," I said.

"What about *this* place?"

I shook my head.

Faith narrowed her eyes, clearly not believing me. Her dark brown eyes and skeptical expression looked unsettlingly like Mother's. I stood up, partly just to be doing something, anything.

"If nobody's going to tell us anything," I said. "We'd better look around for ourselves then, hadn't we?"

"We?" Faith said.

"Yes," I said. "Why not 'we'?" I looked at another pair of double doors, also brass and mahogany, on the other side of the room.

Faith looked skeptical again, but she followed as I walked silently across the plush carpet and pulled on the gilt doorknob.

The door opened onto a long gallery stretching to our right and left, with another set of identical double doors twenty or so feet ahead of us. I went across to the new doors, but stopped when Henry said, "Lor! Will you look at that!"

"It's . . . us," Faith said.

And it was.

One side of the gallery had walls covered with pastoral scenery and sailing ships, like the one in my room. But on the other side, where Faith and Henry were looking, were large, ornately-framed portraits. Huge paintings taller than we were, like they have for royalty.

Henry, Faith, and I were all up there. We gawped at the regal and haughty representations of ourselves. Benedict and Joshua came right after, looking as equally unlike themselves as our own pictures did. Then, after a little bit of statuary, in an alcove, we saw similar noble representations of both Mother and Father.

"Does Father's face look smudged to you?" I asked. The entire display gave me an unsettling feeling, and I was anxious to get out of this part of the house.

Henry shrugged. "Not enough light, I guess."

We went back to the other doors. These opened onto a wide balcony overlooking the main hall below. The hallways and suites full of rooms behind us had seemed roomy, but now I saw that it was only the beginning. We peered down into the main hall directly below us.

It was huge. Mammoth. Everything—floors, pillars, walls, and high ceiling—were all done up in gray marble, veined and flecked like a beautiful and jeweled elephant skin. The railings were wrought iron, filled with French curves and topped with gleaming copper.

We faced a panorama of stained-glass windows, spanning the entire wall, showing an enormous tree. The frightening array of black branches and glittering leaves towered over us, many stories tall, so that shafts of emerald, gold and a few slivers of robin's egg blue slanted in, throwing color everywhere. The whole place, enormous and expansive, gleamed with it. We stood, the three of us, transfixed, drowning in light.

"Lor . . ." Henry said. "Look at that!" He let out a great whoop that echoed off the walls, then he tore over to the right-side staircase that led down into the hall. Faith and I went down the left side. The sunlight was warm on our faces and the light made us all look as if we were underwater.

"This is the way we came in last night, isn't it?" Faith said as we descended into the main hall.

"I think so," I said. I had only vague recollections of coming in last night, so I didn't remember it being this beautiful. Of course, it wouldn't have been lit like this last night.

Gilt chandeliers and pillars and wall sconces were everywhere. Sculpted satyrs, cherubs, and sphinxes sat in little alcoves and cavorted above the pillars and around the ceiling. There was no sign of our shambling entrance last night, so someone must have cleaned up the dirt and mud. In fact, everything was spotless, but I hadn't seen any sign of domestic help.

There were more rooms off to either side branching off the main hall, but none of these were lit. I looked down one of the dark, tunnel-like corridors and shivered.

"Unnatural," Henry said. "Don't fancy going down there without a candle, do you?"

"No," Faith said. I agreed. Better to stay in the light.

We went down more stairs into the foyer.

The stained-glass wall was so large and ornate that I almost missed the doors worked into the black trunk of the tree. Under the tree, there was a tiny depiction of a coastline. Buildings and ships were like child's toys in the monstrous tree's shadow. I felt like a small, grubby, blinking mole just looking at it. Still, mole or not, I needed out. I tried the doors. Locked.

We turned away, and then a snap like a rifle shot behind us made us all jump and look back as the locked doors suddenly flew open.

Sunlight poured in as Mr. Sands stepped through, leading his white horse. The horse was even more beautiful up close, pale and silky.

His hooves clicked unnaturally loudly on the marble. His hair and mane shone like porcelain in the spill of light, then emerald as Sands led the horse farther in.

I stood, frozen for a moment, then thought about getting to the door, which Mr. Sands had left open behind him. But before I'd taken so much as a step, Mr. Sands spun and closed it. I could hear the lock click emphatically shut.

"Good morning," Mr. Sands said with his hand still on the iron-and-glass door. He spoke casually, as if there was nothing unusual going on. He turned to the horse and pressed his forehead fondly to its cheek. It nickered softly in return. Sands was dressed as if going to a ball, with a black satin suit and a top hat to match, both accented with a canary yellow cravat and hat band. Despite the hat, his tufted yellow hair still managed to stick in all directions from underneath.

"Thank you, dear friend," Mr. Sands murmured to his horse. Mr. Sands still held the violin and I could see something that made me suck in a deep breath. I edged closer to get a better look. Yes. It was!

A white bone chess piece was worked into the lower part of the violin's body. It was cleverly done, in such a way to emphasize the white piece, rather than hide it. I thought of the chess set in Father's study and then the knight I still had in my pocket. It didn't escape my notice that Mr. Sands' piece and mine were from opposing sides. My knight was warm in my pocket.

"Acta Santorum," Mr. Sands said. The white knight glowed unmistakably. "Acta Santorum, Acta Santorum!" There was a brief shimmering, and soft soughing sound of air. The violin and chess piece flashed and then went dark, and the horse was gone. Gone as if it never was.

"Lor . . ." Henry said. "That's a neat trick! They'd love that at the race track."

"Acta Santorum," I said, struggled with my smattering of Latin. "Deeds of the Saints? Is that his name?"

Mr. Sands looked surprised. "Yes, that's right."

He tried to go up the foyer steps, but stopped with his foot raised, looking up. His confident and suave manner suddenly faltered.

"Mr. Sands?" Faith said. She hadn't moved from her place on the landing and the light shone down on her in glittering colored diamonds. Suddenly, her care with her clothes and hair didn't seem foolish or out-of-place, but the actions of a lady. Henry and I looked like disheveled children by comparison.

She held a glove in her hand, worrying the kidskin ever-so-slightly. She looked away briefly, as if searching for resolve, then back at him, her dark eyes pensive. Her hair shone like burnished gold, showered by the stained glass with a hundred shimmering emeralds.

"I wanted to thank you," Faith murmured. "What you did out on the road. That was the most magnificent thing I've ever seen."

"Oh," Mr. Sands said. "Um . . . it was . . . nothing really." He picked something off the steps. "Here, Miss. You've dropped your glove." He took another step up the short stairs so that he could extend the lost article to her, shifting and nearly dropping his magnificent violin in the process.

"Thank you," she said. "You are too kind." Her hand, taking the glove, brushed his slightly and the little man blushed.

"Is this your house?" Faith said. "You must be very rich. Father makes a little money, but not like *this*."

"Mine?" Mr. Sands squeaked. "No. It's, um . . . called Stormholt."

I shook my head. Un-bloody-believable. But I couldn't help myself from admiring her. This is what she'd been learning while she'd been away at Society, and she'd learned it well.

"And magic," Faith said. "How long did it take you?"

"I'm sorry?" Mr. Sands said.

"How long did it take to learn how to do that? To learn magic?" They weren't close, exactly. Nothing improper, but somehow the two of them, leaning slightly towards each other, looked like long-time intimates, while Henry and I were the outsiders.

"How long?" Mr. Sands said and he stopped suddenly. A tight smile twisted his yellow beard, and something of his confident manner came back to him. "I started learning magic, as you put it, much longer ago than you can possibly imagine, I'm afraid."

His head cocked suddenly, as if hearing something inaudible to us. His mustache and beard quivered in irritation.

"Forgive me," he said, speaking directly to Faith. He'd nearly forgotten about Henry and I. "I must go." He spun turned and went down the stairs without waiting for an answer. Whatever errand he'd intended inside the house was forgotten now. He got to the front door and put his hand on the black iron door knob.

"I do hope, Miss Faith," he said, "to talk again soon. Justice, Henry."

He sang a short phrase, similar to the musical phrase he'd used to open the gate last night. A musical key. The door clicked softly open. He passed through and it slammed heavily closed behind him, all the glass pieces trembling slightly in the iron framework.

Faith watched him go, tapping her finger against her lips. Then her face broke out into a broad smile.

"That," she said, "didn't go so poorly."

This time I said it out loud. "Un-bloody-believable." I walked up the steps and regarded her. "We've got flying horses and dogs and a magician that shoots *fire* out of a violin . . . a storm that's hunting us, somehow, Father and Mother both acting like . . ." I was at a loss for words. "I don't know what they're acting like, but your response is to . . . what was that?"

Faith spun on me. "We're locked in here, right?" she said. "It's not really a door or a gate, either, is it? It's *magic*. We're suddenly in a world *ruled* by magic, and *you* wonder why I'm interested in magicians? He's the one that can let us out, or hadn't you figured that out yet?"

"Of course I had," I said, "I just don't see what . . ."

"Of course you can't," she said. She smirked at me. "You'll understand better when you're older." She cast a sly glance down towards the locked front door. "He'll be back. These things take time, done properly."

I tried pounding on Mother's door myself, but didn't get any answer. I looked at the lock and thought about trying to pick it, but wasn't sure I wanted to burst in on Mother if she was in one of her moods. I was about to leave when I thought I heard voices from the other side of the door. Mother's and someone else's. A lower, deeper, one. I pressed my ear to the door. I still couldn't make out the words, but definitely two voices? Mother and Father? I wasn't sure, but thought it didn't quite sound like Father. After listening for another minute without being able to place the voice or make out any of the words, I finally left.

I went back down to the front hall and stared at the long expanses of marble. No one else was in sight. The front doors were still closed. The locks and doorknobs were made of the same black iron as the gate outside. On impulse, I walked down into the sunken foyer and tugged on the black metal doorknobs. Nothing.

I gave up on the door, turned, and nearly jumped out of my skin.

Joshua, my eldest brother, glared down at me from the main hall. His face was all hard planes and angry lines in the cool, blue-green light. Amazingly, a sword hung from his belt.

"It's a nasty habit," he said. "Listening at doors." Joshua had a long face, with dark eyes, like Mother, but there the similarity ended. His brown hair, already thinning, lay flat against his scalp, and a perpetual scowl and sharp, angry jaw dominated his long, clean-shaven face. He was twenty-one, a man, who hadn't lived at the house for years, practically a stranger to me. I knew he'd joined the Royal House Guard and he looked it—tall, lean and powerfully built, wearing a red broadcloth suitcoat, black pants, and tall black boots. There was no sign of the helmet, and the suitcoat and pants were dirty and rumpled, as if he'd been sleeping in them.

"I've been here for days," he said, seeing the direction of my gaze, "after being arrested and dragged here by Father's little raiding party."

"Arrested?"

"Dragged in chains out of our homes, carried out into the country and then imprisoned here. What would you call it? We're being watched, too. I can feel it." He had a soldier's stoic cadence, as if he were talking of enemy troop movements, everything important and hostile and none of it personal.

"It was you talking in her room," I said. "Wasn't it?"

"It was."

"Why won't she let any of us in?"

"Because she doesn't want to see any of you, obviously," he said. "I saw you testing the door." He pointed at the iron doors in the stained-glass window behind me. "You know we're trapped here, too. I've been around the entire house, examining the windows and other doors. I was going to put a chair through one of these windows, but we're being watched." He walked past me, the sword jingling, passing so close I had to step out of the way. Joshua pulled off his heavy glove and put a hand on the glass.

"There's more danger here than you know," he said. "I can feel it."

"Danger?" Then I gasped as I saw something shift behind the colored glass.

His smile was bleak, with no warmth in it. "You see?"

Now, more than ever, I wanted to get out of the colored shadow, but somehow couldn't get my feet to start moving right.

"They've gone," he said, "to a great deal of trouble to make sure you can't see outside, haven't they?"

I frowned. We hadn't gotten any kind of look outside when Mr. Sands had come in, had we?

"It's the work of that magician," he said. "I know it is."

"Mr. Sands?" I said. "He saved us from the storm, didn't he? He and Father both."

"Did they?" Joshua said. "I wouldn't be so sure. I think the storm was part of some trick. Staged, for our benefit. We're like rodents in a trap. They're watching us to see what we'll do."

"Father wouldn't hurt us," I said uncertainly. I was starting to wonder.

"Wouldn't he?" Joshua said, sensing my doubt. He walked back to the other side of the foyer and up the three steps to the front hall. Then he turned and put his hand on the hilt of his sword. "Like this? They wouldn't let me keep my own sword, of course, but I found this in one of the rooms upstairs." He drew the weapon out with a cold rasp. "It's quite sharp."

Something in his eyes made me keenly aware that with the front doors locked, I was in a dead-end. Joshua blocked the short flight of stairs, which was the only way out. I really didn't know this man at all anymore. Being brother and sister wasn't going to matter here. I could see it in his face. He'd remove any obstacles he could to gain his freedom, related or otherwise.

"I have to give Father credit," Joshua said. "He took us by surprise with this little stunt of his, but it won't matter. He can't hold us here forever. Play dumb, if you like, but we both know better. Father's too experienced a commander to swoop in like that without doing reconnaissance first. He'd need information, and I think that was you."

"I didn't have anything to do with it," I said.

"Fine," he said, clearly not believing me. He leveled the sword at me with a quick swish. I stepped back involuntarily. His smile was a cold, dead thing. He stepped down the short stairway and I retreated until my back was against the iron and glass of the doors behind me. Despite the warm sun, they were chilly against my back.

"Tell Father," Joshua said, "he can't keep us here indefinitely."

"All right," I said quickly. "Fine. But he's still our Father. Whatever he's doing, he's not trying to hurt us. We're family."

"No," Joshua said. His face was fierce, still bathed in greens from above. "We're not family. Not anymore."

With that, he spun on his heel and walked away.

# CHAPTER 5

## Guardians of Stormholt—Mother's Decision

After Joshua left, I went up to get Faith and Henry and we all went back down to the locked front door.

I held one of Faith's bobby pins and told myself that I wasn't going to be intimidated by a stupid stained-glass tree, no matter how impressive, but I still didn't like standing in that bottle-green and black shadow.

"What time is it?" Faith asked while I applied the bobby pin to the iron lock. "The light doesn't look right."

She was right. It didn't. "Still early morning," I said. "Isn't it?"

"It's afternoon," Faith said. "I think. Something about this place makes time stand on its head. Maybe because all that food table ever has is breakfast."

"But breakfast is the best meal of the day!" Henry said. Faith smiled thinly at him and he shrugged.

"Well," he said. "It *is*."

"The windows are part of it too," I said. "We never really get to see the sun."

I kept working. Finally, the lock clicked open.

I reached for the handle and then jerked my hand back when I saw the shadowy ripple of movement on the other side.

"What was that?" Henry said. He and Faith were just behind me now.

Something was out there. Father or Mr. Sands returned? A doctor for Benedict? The police?

I turned the handle and pulled open the door.

And screamed.

What we saw, outside the windows. Was cats.

Lots of cats, all turning to look at us. My scream had insured that.

The porch, the limestone steps, and far lawn . . . all covered with cats. An ocean of furry faces and all of them staring enigmatically at us. It was more cats than I'd ever seen in one place before. Orange tabbies, spotted calicoes, black cats, white cats. Cats as far as the eye could see. There was snow on the ground, but that was hard to make out for all the furry bodies.

Every imaginable color of cat. Hundreds of them, thousands, sitting, staring, gathered and packed all together watching us. Thousands of cats meant two thousand luminous eyes, unblinking, staring.

"What are they doing?" Henry said in a hushed voice. "That's just *not* right."

"Don't talk!" Faith said. "Don't even move!"

The cats shifted as a group, with a rippling like wheat in the wind, and I could feel the terrible weight of their yellow-eyed attention. The stress of their unified regard was terrifying.

A resonant yowl began in the army of cats, starting in the twenty or so nearest us, a horrid and ragged sound coming from deep within the animals' chests. A horrible tingling crawled over my skin.

"I think," Faith said, "opening this door might have been a bad, bad idea."

"Don't push!" I said.

"I can't see," Henry said.

I tried to push back frantically, but slipped and fell on my butt with my feet thrust out onto the porch.

All hell broke loose.

A whirlwind of hissing cats surged forward, probably to come tear us to bloody chunks. The closest twenty or so cats leapt right at us, a hissing wave of tooth and claw.

I was yanked back into the house with a suddenness that rattled my teeth. Faith slammed the door and twenty or so fuzzy emerald shapes thumped against it until it shook. The stained glass shook under the impact, but held. The cats all fell to the ground in a hissing, snarling, tangled bundle.

I was on the foyer floor with Henry, who'd been the one to haul me back inside.

"Christ!" Henry panted. "What was that?"

I was shaking all over and couldn't catch my breath. I couldn't get control of my legs, either, and Henry had to help me up.

"That," Faith breathed, "is how a magician keeps you locked up." She sighed happily. "Isn't it wonderful?"

Henry and I both stared at her.

"It's horrible, too, of course," she added, coming back to herself a little. "But it's terribly impressive, isn't it? If he can do *that*, I wonder what else he can do. What would it take to learn how he does it?"

"Christ!" Henry said again.

Faith turned to me. "You really didn't know?"

I stared at her. "Know what?"

"About the cats," Faith said. "About this place." She waved her arms at everything around us. "At any of this? I was sure Father would have told you, of all people, what was going on."

I shook my head. "He said I need to trust him and follow orders, but that he was trying to keep us safe."

"Of course," Faith said. "And you believe him."

"Of course I do!"

"Mother has a secret, too," Faith said. "One she's had for a long time. She won't tell me, but I know she found out something, something *enormous*, about Father. Whatever it is, it's been stewing inside of her. I swear, I think that secret has more to do with what's wrong with her than the brain fever does. I also don't think that Father is truly the person you think he is."

She sighed. "One thing's certain, though. You sure didn't know about the cats. Or else you're the best actress in the world and we both know *that's* not true. But you're still keeping secrets. Your secrets, Father's secrets, Mother's secrets . . . so many secrets." She turned, an expression of worry and yearning on her face as she looked back up towards the second floor where Mother had locked herself up.

I thought of what I'd found in Father's study. He *did* have secrets, too, but I knew that whatever he was hiding, he was doing it for us. I could feel that, a solid core of certainty, in my guts and bones.

Faith turned back to me, clearly struggling internally.

She sighed again. "Mother isn't very clear-headed right now, though, is she?"

"I don't think so, Faith," I said.

"Gone *mad*, Mother has," Henry said.

She glared at Henry. "She's not mad. She's just . . . the medicine muddles her mind sometimes. More than it used to, I think."

She bit her lip and glared at me. "*Are* you trying to break up the family? That's what Mother says. You and Father are trying to break up the family."

"No!" I burst out. "Of course not. I'm only trying to understand why everyone's angry with me. Well, you and Mother anyway. I haven't done anything!"

"Say," Henry said, perplexed. "Are you two having a fight?"

"Been having," Faith said.

"For how long?" Henry asked.

"Almost a year now," I said.

"Christ!" Henry said.

Faith sighed. "Must you keep saying that?"

"Oh, *that's* the problem," I said. "Henry's language. Christ!" A hysterical giggle escaped my lips. Faith glared, which only made it worse. I couldn't suppress the giggle, which threatened to twist into a sob if I didn't keep a lid clamped down on it. I was just trying to breathe with my arms wrapped around me. In. Out. A crying jag might fly me apart if I didn't keep a lid on it.

Faith sat down on the stairs behind us and put a hand on my shoulder, but very briefly, as if not certain what she wanted or meant. We sat a long time without saying anything.

"You might be telling the truth," Faith said finally, "but you're not telling me everything."

She wasn't wrong, but the secrets I held were Father's and I had to trust his reasons. I didn't say anything, just kept staring down at my feet.

"Justice," she said. Something in her voice sounded strange, making me twist around to look at her carefully. "This past year can't have been easy for you," she finished. She didn't meet my gaze.

It was more than the past year, but I let that pass.

"You can't blame me for *all* of it," she went on. "With you being so secretive, sneaking off on your own the way you did."

"I went off on my own because you and Mother shut me out!" I said.

Faith shook her head. "You've always been that way. You know you have."

I opened my mouth to protest, but then shut it again. In my head, I'd always thought of my solitary habits as being Mother's fault, but now I wasn't sure.

"Perhaps," I said slowly, "we should both work on that."

"Perhaps," Faith said, gazing narrowly at me.

"Are we still trying to escape?" Henry asked.

"Definitely," Faith and I said together. A look passed between us. A temporary truce, perhaps more. We'd have to see.

"Maybe we could lure them away somehow," I said, turning my thoughts to our more immediate problem. "The cats, I mean."

"With what?" Henry said.

"I don't know."

"And where would we go?" Henry said. "I mean, this place scares me worse than cranky headmasters, but once we got past the cats and the storm and the hunters and all that . . . where do we go? We can't go home, can we?"

"I think Mother will tell us something," Faith said. "I'll talk to her about you, Justice. Just give me a little time. Things will be different when we all get out of here. You'll see."

I shook my head. "If you say so. But she's been angry with me forever. She barely talks to me anymore. Mostly, she just glares. When she does say something, it's horrible."

"I'm sure it's not your fault," Henry said. "It's not like Mother's right in the head anymore."

"Her head is fine," Faith said. "It's just her medicine. And Father."

"It's not his fault," I said stubbornly.

"He's not exactly acting normally, either," Faith snapped. She waved her arms to indicate the entire house and possibly the strangeness of our ride here and all that occurred with it. "*He's* the one that's gone mad."

"He hasn't gone mad," I said. "He's just trying to do the right thing. I know it. But this thing we're in, all of us, it's bigger than him. Magic, supernatural things like that hunt. He's treading water in a very big sea, I think."

"Exactly," Henry said. "With all of that, what are we supposed to do about it?"

"I don't know," I said. "But there's more to this, and I want to find out what."

"You crazy little adventuress," Faith said, shaking her head. "You're deluded." Her words were critical, but her tone was gentle, perhaps a little wistful.

"You guys act like you haven't talked in months." Henry said. "Haven't you both been in the same house with Mother all this time?"

"Not really," I said.

"No," Faith agreed. "I guess not."

"I'm cold," Faith murmured. "It shouldn't be this cold sitting in the sun this way, should it?"

"It's the glass," I said. "Shadows are always cold, especially through this window."

We got up in unison and turned to go back upstairs. We stopped in the middle of the main hall and stared.

Mother was standing at the top of the stairs.

She stood, just looking down at us. Joshua, still in uniform and still wearing his stolen sword, held her medicine bag and loomed stiffly behind her in the shadows, as if waiting for the next command on a field of battle. There was no telling how much she'd heard.

Then I realized Mother wasn't even looking at *us*. She was glaring at the empty staircase. She didn't even seem to see us down here.

"No, no, no, no, *no!*" she said, marching down. "Filthy beggars! Out of the way!" Her eyes blazed and she beat at the air with a broken, batwinged umbrella. Joshua followed her slow progress dutifully. Faith, Henry and I all stared in stunned silence.

Then Henry looked over at me. "I told you!" he whispered. "Mad! A lunatic!"

Mother made it to the main floor this way, snapped her umbrella shut and suddenly noticed us. The signs of her medication were strong, the brightness in her eyes and the odious orange and licorice.

"Oh," Mother said. "Children, there you are. Well, I was hoping not to have this kind of confrontation, but I suppose it can't be helped. I'm leaving."

"Oh, thank *god*," Faith said. "I don't know why Father brought us here in the first place. But how are we going to . . ."

"Not we," Mother said softly. "I'm sorry, children, but I can't take you with me. Your Father has too many webs around you. Evil. A monster, pure and simple. He's not even your father ..." She tilted her head again, as if pondering something. "Well, that's not true. He is, isn't he? That's the whole point. You may have come out of me, but you are still *his*, not mine. Joshua's all I have left now."

My gut clenched as Mother spoke. Her eyes were bright from the medicine, but her speech was clear. She didn't have the air of someone with a muddled mind. She knew exactly what she was doing. She meant it about leaving us here.

"What are you talking about, Mother?" Faith said. She still couldn't see it. Or didn't want to.

Faith and Mother, standing above us on the steps, were like mirror images of each other, one young and beautiful, one older, but not yet old, and still beautiful.

Faith had Mother's regal bearing, a good deal of her height, her rich, dark eyes and the long, slightly wavy hair, even if Faith's was pale blonde instead of Mother's ember-red. Faith looked as much like our mother as any daughter could, but Mother, Mother didn't see it. *Wouldn't* see it. It broke my heart. Henry and I were stunned, motionless, helpless.

"Faith," Mother said. She reached out and briefly touched my sister's face. "I believe I shall miss you most of all, but I need you to stay here. Watch your Father, watch everything he does, listen to what he says. I tried to arrange things so that I could bring you with me too, but your father has his hooks too far into you for me to feel safe doing that. You're *his*, but perhaps you can get free. Stand watch dutifully and report everything you see to me. I'll send instruction on how later. We shall see."

"I'm *his*?" Faith said, incredulous. "His? Father's a ghost. He's never home. How could I be his? When have I ever done anything except what *you* wanted?"

"Can't be helped," Mother said brightly. "I *am* sorry." She pushed Faith out of the way. "Joshua, we're leaving."

"Why?" Faith sobbed, "why can't I go with you?" Faith's anguish bled out into every word. It seemed too painful a thing, too private for me to see. "Why can't I go back to London, too?"

"London?" Mother said. "Who said anything about London? We're going to Faerie."

"To Faerie?" I said. I staggered and sat down heavily on the steps.

"You can't be going along with this," Henry called to Joshua. "Look at her! She can't even think straight."

"Mother knows exactly what she's doing," Joshua said coldly.

"With *him*?" Faith said, pointing at Joshua. "Why him? He's been gone for months. All of them have. It's been just you and me, hasn't it?"

I tried not to flinch at not being counted, even when I'd been in the house the whole time, but it still stung.

"Joshua has done everything I asked of him the past few years," Mother said. "The only reason he was in the Royal House Guard at all was because I needed him to be there."

She breezed right past us, gesturing peremptorily for Joshua to follow. He did.

Faith followed after, and Henry and I stumbled after her, all of us moving awkwardly as if in a horrible dream.

"You can't leave!" Faith put her hand against one of the pillars, her voice rising in pitch and echoing crazily off the cold marble of the foyer. Mother, without seeming to notice Faith's distress, took a few more vicious swings at nothing with her umbrella. I tried to put a hand on Faith's shoulder, but she shrugged it off.

"You *can't* leave," Faith shouted again. "It's guarded. By magic!"

Mother looked up at us. "It's guarded," she said, "by *cats*. I think I can manage a few cats."

She turned back to rummage in the bag that Joshua held. "Here we are." She pulled out two glass vials of a bright green liquid.

"The medicine's gotten to her mind," Henry said. He still had a grip on my shoulder. "It's like she's not even the same person anymore."

Faith ran abruptly after them, but Joshua had handed the bag to Mother and moved to intercede. His face looked strained but determined. He might not like all this, either, but it was clear his soldier's resolve would carry him through. Faith tried to go around him, but he shoved her back.

Not gently.

Faith skidded across the floor and fell. She lay in a puddle of rose-colored silk, stunned, while Henry and I leaned over the rail and gaped. Mother merely rummaged through the bag, making clinking sounds.

Joshua looked up at us, probably to see if he would have to stop us, too. But Henry and I were both frozen. I still couldn't believe all this was happening. This abandonment felt both impossible and somehow inevitable at the same time. My hands on the railing were shaking with terror, but the rest of me was frozen to the spot.

Faith got back to her feet with a frightening cry of rage. She dashed over and, hauling her clawed hand back as far she could, struck Joshua full in the face.

Joshua's head rocked back and he stumbled. When he lifted his face again, three jagged scarlet lines ran down his cheek. He started to touch the blood on his face, then let his hand fall and nodded to himself, as if accepting some kind of penance.

Henry rushed down to Faith's side. He tried to help her up, but she just lay there sobbing.

Mother had chosen a tiny bottle and handed her bag back to Joshua. Suddenly, the sight of that hateful bag set my blood on fire. I wanted to see it burn. The medicine had to be responsible for Mother's crazed behavior. It had to go, and suddenly my feet weren't frozen anymore.

I rushed down and tried to grab the bag from Joshua's hand. He hung on, barely, as I yanked savagely at it. The bone handles and leather creaked, but I couldn't get it free from his grip. I yanked again. I was on the top of the four steps that led from main hall into the foyer.

With Joshua standing in the foyer, we were face-to-face despite his height. I actually snarled at him and I could see surprise and a touch of fear register on Joshua's damned soldier face.

"Joshua!" Mother said from near the front door. "We don't have time for this! They'll be back soon."

Joshua pulled, putting his weight behind it, but I hooked one arm around the railing, refusing to let go. I gasped at the pain as he pulled twice more, but I held on. I was determined to let him yank my arms right off before I let go and it felt like he was doing just that.

Finally, he put his foot up on the steps, put both hands on the bag and savagely hauled me right off the railing. I flew across the foyer and hit the front door with a sickening crunch. The taste of blood flooded my mouth. My lip was split and the room spun. The tinkling of broken glass falling around me gave me a twisted and black sense of satisfaction. At least I'd broken that damned door, even if it was with my face. Something was burning, though. That couldn't be right.

Then I realized that I still clutched the medicine bag in my hands.

Broken glass knocked out of the door was in there with the broken bits of vial. More of it lay scattered around the marble floor. I tried to get up, but my arms and legs only twitched helplessly and I continued to lie with the left half of my face against the cold marble. The burning was coming from the acrid fumes of the medicine, stinking of oranges and licorice and something vile underneath. The bright green liquid mixed with red stuff that must have been my own blood all over the floor. A lot of it was getting into my eye, but I couldn't lift my head still. My twitching arms weren't listening.

Someone was screaming in the background. I think maybe they'd been screaming for some time now. Hours. But it was a distant thing.

"Damn her," Mother's voice said. "How much did we lose?"

Someone grabbed my arm long enough to drag me through the red and green puddle and out of the way before they let it fall limply. Shoes crunched on the broken glass, then a scrape as someone, probably Joshua, took the bag.

"Some," Joshua said. "Not all."

"This will still work for the door," Mother said. She spoke a word I'd never heard before, in a language I didn't know. It sounded liquid and rich and somehow the syllables didn't fit with each other right.

An enormous explosion of heat went off behind me. Even facing away, the scorching heat flashed across my face, but was over quickly. My arms were starting to work a little bit, but not much.

Someone else was lifting me up, much more gently than before. My eye still burned and I couldn't see out of it at all.

Henry. His voice murmured, "I got you, I got you," over and over again. He sounded even more terrified than I was, which was saying a lot. Faith's voice was still screaming and echoing all over, endlessly, as if she might never stop.

Soft cloth wiped at my eye. Henry's handkerchief. I didn't realize that my hands were working until I levered myself up a little. I needed to see what was going on. Henry kept the cloth on my burned eye, but I could still see with the other one.

The front door was a burned-out hole now. A few smoldering fragments still clung to the hinges on either side, but the rest had been blown all to Hell.

Even the marble was blackened and charred.

Mother stood in the middle of the ragged doorway with Joshua next to her, both of them turned almost to silhouettes against the bright light. A rising wall of hisses and warbles told me the cats were still there and angry, but Mother's stance was merely pensive.

"Well," Mother said. "More of the same, I think." Joshua held out the bag and she plucked two more vials from it. She concentrated a short moment, spoke that same word again, and her eyes flashed green. So did the liquid in the vials. She tossed them casually out the door onto the lawn. Another flash of light and the horrible sound of cats screaming. Mother turned around for two more bottles and her expression of delight was a wicked thing in the flickering glow.

"Oh, god," Henry gasped. "That's . . . *awful*. Mother . . . she . . . set all those cats on fire!"

The burned-out doorway framed them standing on the porch perfectly for a moment, like a portrait, while they looked around.

"Remember what I said, Faith," Mother said. "I'm counting on you."

Faith made a choking sound of fury and grief, clearly not knowing what to make of this.

Mother and Joshua stepped out of view. Another explosion and more cat screams came back to us.

"We need . . . to see what's happening," I said.

"No," Faith said beside me. My vision was growing dimmer. "Here, Henry, give me that." Faith took over carefully dabbing the soaked handkerchief at my eye. "This is useless. It's soaked." She meant the handkerchief, I guess.

"It burns," I said. "Make it stop burning." More explosions came from out front. I was still fighting weakly to sit the rest of the way up, but Henry held me in place. A horrid burnt meat smell was coming into the house and it made the gorge rise up in my throat. Faith put the hem of her dress into her teeth and managed to tear off a strip of silk taffeta.

I struggled free of Henry's grip and managed to lurch to my feet. Ignoring both Henry and Faith's objections, I went through the doorway and out onto the front porch to look at what Mother had done out there.

My vision was blurred, but with my hand covering my damaged eye, I tried to make it all out. The porch was charred and pitted. A sulfurous stench and haze hung over everything, completing the transformation from manicured lawn to ragged war zone. Three blackened craters marred the lawn. Most of the cats must have run off somewhere, but a staggering number of feline corpses littered the yard. Hundreds, at least.

Henry and Faith came up on either side of me, but they didn't drag me inside. Faith handed me the scrap of silk and even put my arm over her shoulder as I swayed in place. Henry immediately bolstered my other side and we watched together. Both of them were sobbing. Probably I was, too.

Mother and Joshua were at the gate. Another flash burst across our sight as another explosion rocked the gate, then another, and the gate still stood. Finally, on the third burst, the lock clanged open, a noise we could hear even this far up.

On the other side of the gate, somebody was waiting near the edge of the snowy woods.

Somebody not at all human.

There were a dozen of them, tall, with a ghostly pallor. They stood so perfectly still that at this distance, I thought them statuary until one of them raised a hand in greeting. They were dressed in the colors of moss and shadowy bark, and carried slender, wickedly barbed spears. But standing next to them was someone I knew well.

Mrs. Westerly. Last I'd seen her she'd been hissing at Father like a wild animal. Father had tried to capture her, too, only she'd given him the slip. No one had been sure how. Never an attractive woman, she seemed grotesque and misshapen compared to the slender figures around her, a crone among swans.

Mrs. Westerly raised a hand at Mother and Joshua as they went through the gate. They spoke some words we couldn't hear and then they all went into the cold, sun-and-shadow dappled woods.

My eyes rolled up into the back of my head on a wave of flaring pain, and then I couldn't feel anything.

# CHAPTER 6

## Benedict and The Ghost Eye

I returned to the world slowly, accompanied by the distant and melancholy sound of a piano. Some memories fade, but that piano stays with me, slow, desultory, and hauntingly beautiful. I lay in a half-world between waking and sleep, just listening to it.

I finally opened my good eye and saw purple curtains, the frigate model and the ship-of-the-line painting on the wall. I was back in my Stormholt room. A small table held clean bandages, salves and pair of scary-looking, needle-sharp scissors. Next to that was the horse chess piece. Someone must have pulled it from my pocket when they put me to bed. I tucked it in my dressing gown pocket.

I put a hand to my face and found a lumpy bandage covering my left eye. The whole left side of my face felt hot and tight. I could remember the feeling of my face on fire, but the skin I could feel felt fine. My entire skull throbbed, though. I was starting to really hate waking up in this bed.

I gently prodded the bandage. How badly damaged was my eye? Was I going to be horribly blind and disfigured? Gruesome images paraded around my brain of white orbs and empty eye sockets.

"Ah, you're awake," someone said from the doorway, and I gasped and twisted around, startled.

My brother Benedict walked stiffly over to one of the stuffed chairs and dropped heavily into it. "I put the bandage on for you," he said. "There's a little light scarring around the eye, but not as serious as it looked, at first. I shouldn't wonder if you make a full recovery."

I was still in shock. Last I'd seen Benedict, Father had just pulled him off the back of Mr. Sands' horse. The time before that had been almost a year ago. Here was another brother I felt I barely knew.

Benedict was short for a boy, barely taller than me, and hardly any heavier. He wore his thick hair in dark curls and was dapper to a fault in a blue and gray suit with a herringbone pattern on the waistcoat. Under that, he had a flawless white shirt and the whole thing was completed with a sapphire handkerchief. I remembered that about him now. He'd always been a fancy dresser, which seemed odd in someone studying in a seminary. But then, that had been Mother's idea, hadn't it? Certainly, it hadn't been Benedict's. He didn't look any more suited to a seminary now than he ever had.

He held a crystal glass still half full of brandy. There was an open bottle of it on a silver tray on the other side of the room. He grinned at me in what he must have thought was a dashing fashion.

"You're all right!" I said. "We thought the worst! They said you got hit by lightning and then we woke up and couldn't find anyone. You *are* all right, aren't you?"

Benedict dashing smile emptied out and he seemed to give this some thought. He shook his head. "No," he said. "Not really. But then, none of us are, are we?"

I wasn't sure what he meant by that, though the sound of it gave me chills. "What about your leg? What did Father say about it?"

"Say?" Benedict let out a bitter laugh. "I awoke by myself in a bunch of empty rooms. The leg feels stiff and I have a lovely set of new scars to impress the ladies with." He gestured at his left leg. The trouser leg was slit, with bandages peeking out through the gap. It looked like they went all the way up.

"No sign of Father anywhere," Benedict continued. "We're obviously fending for ourselves." He stood and approached me, moving with a noticeable limp. "I've been up and about for a few days now, and *still* no sign of him. The Kasrics are really in it up to our brims this time, aren't we? I thought it was just Father in trouble, but what Faith told me about Mother and Joshua leaving a few days ago . . . and with the rest of us trapped here, well, it looks pretty grim, doesn't it?"

Mother's abandonment still hurt just thinking about it. She'd been so inhumanly *cold*. I didn't understand any of this. Then something else registered.

"Days ago? How long have I been out?"

"Well, *days*, obviously," Benedict said. "It's been just the four of us for . . ." He took another healthy swallow from the half-full glass. "Three days now."

Three days! My head spun. So much time lost. Even if I wasn't at all sure what I should be doing, I knew that we had to do *something*.

Benedict walked over to the dresser and poured himself more amber brandy. He hadn't given me a real answer when I asked about his leg, but the heavy limp told the story. The piano music was still going on in the next room, somber and slow.

He drank with the dark satisfaction of someone taking much-needed medicine. Benedict was right about one thing, none of us were the same.

I frowned at him. "When did you start drinking that stuff?"

"About 10 o'clock," he said. "This bottle, anyway."

"That's not what I meant."

He shrugged. "Let's look at your eye, shall we?"

I put a hand to my bandage. "Since when did you start acting like a doctor?"

"I actually studied as much medicine as theology at Hallingtons," Benedict said. "Which took some arranging. Hallingtons doesn't really do that sort of thing. And I certainly couldn't let Mother know I'd arranged for outside tutoring. She'd have fits. Of course, that doesn't seem to matter much now that she's started exploding things and having Joshua bash people into doors."

"I didn't know that," I said. "About you studying medicine at Hallingtons."

"No," he said. "I didn't tell anyone. Except Faith, of course. We correspond constantly, but I knew she wouldn't tell Mother."

"You did? I thought that she told Mother everything?"

"She and Mother were close, yes," Benedict said, "but so are Faith and I. I knew I could trust her to keep my secrets."

I was starting to think that I didn't know anything about any of my family. Faith had been the only one still living at home and even she'd been like a stranger to me lately. A whole family of strangers: Joshua, Benedict, Faith, Henry. Mother and Father most of all.

"This won't hurt." Benedict carefully peeled the gauze off my eye and I flinched when the light hit it. Even with my eye closed, the room was so bright.

"Ouch," I said. "You lied." It was sensitive to the touch, too.

"Yes," he said absently. "We do that. Open it slowly, now . . . Oh!"

"What?" I said. "What's wrong? Am I . . . scarred?" I couldn't bring myself to say the word *disfigured* aloud. "Is there a mirror? There was a mirror here before, wasn't there? Why did you take it out? Oh, god . . . it's that bad, isn't it?"

"I . . ." Benedict didn't seem to have the words.

I brushed past him and yanked the silver tray out from underneath the brandy bottle. It fell with an enormous crash. It didn't break, but it tipped over, spilling brandy onto the carpet. Benedict swore and hastily snatched it back up.

The piano playing stopped and the sound of running feet came from the other room.

I flipped the tray over with shaking hands and looked at my reflection in the polished surface.

No huge scars or cuts stood out, only a small line of stitches on my temple, very neat, barely an inch long. As long as my hair wasn't pinned completely up, any scar would be hardly noticeable. In time, it might fade entirely.

But my actual eye . . .

The left eye gleamed a solid black.

My right eye was the same clear blue as before, just the same as Father's, and Benedict's. But the left eye.

Dear god, my eye!

Black like a crow's eye, like a macabre glass marble, like an unreal, artificial thing. No iris or cornea or any of that, just a sheer, glossy black surface. Nothing would hide this. It didn't even look like my face, with that Devil's eye looking out of it.

"Can . . ." Benedict started, but he had to stop to get his voice under control. "Can you see all right?"

Before I could answer, the door slammed open as Henry barreled into the room. "She's up? She's up! Good. Is she feeling all right? Does she remember . . . ooooo. Justice? What happened to your eye?"

Faith, also running, crashed into Henry from behind. One look at us and she let out a little shriek. She clamped a hand to her mouth.

"Justice?" Henry said again. "What's wrong with it? Oof." This last came because Faith had jabbed him in the ribs with her elbow.

"She hit a door," Faith said to him, "You were there, remember? Besides, I'm sure any damage is just temporary. Right? Right, Benedict?"

Benedict shook his head in wonder. "I have no idea." He hadn't stopped looking at my eye since I'd uncovered it.

"I'm sure it will fade," Faith said weakly. "Only stands to reason."

I was still turning my face back and forth, trying to find an angle where I couldn't see my left eye. Perhaps if I let my hair dangle a bit in the front? No good. There was no way to escape it. The image was starting to get blurred, but that was just from the tears. Whatever else might be damaged in my eye, the tear ducts still worked. I couldn't take my gaze off the reflection. Transfixing, hypnotic. I tried blinking to clear the horrid blackness away, but it just wasn't working. The throbbing in my eye made me pinch my nose before I blinked some more. I could see fine, but that didn't feel like a blessing just now.

"You're squinting," Benedict said.

"It's bright in here," I said. But when I closed my damaged left eye, the light didn't seem that bright at all.

"Sensitive to the light," he said. "Strange. But your vision isn't blurry or anything?"

"I can see fine," I said, again. "But *look* at it."

I let him lean in and peer closely. "Nothing's inflamed or bleeding that I can see. It's not a normal burn, if it's a burn at all. I'm not sure *what* it is, or if it's even an injury."

"What are you talking about?" Henry burst out. "Of course it's an injury! That rotter Joshua *threw* her into a door."

Benedict lifted his hands helplessly. "This doesn't look like an injury. I've heard of the pupil being permanently dilated, but this is something more than that."

"So I'll be like this forever?" I said. A cold stillness coiled inside of me, tight and awful. I couldn't breathe, I couldn't believe any of this was happening to me.

There was a scrape outside the door and it swung open again.

"Justice?" a deeper voice said. Faith and Henry turned and gasped.

Benedict pursed his lips, took one last look at my eye and finally turned, too. "Well," he said. "Look who finally returns."

Father stood in the doorway.

He wore a heavy cloak and muddy riding clothes and no hat. He had mud everywhere, in fact. His hair was a tangled mess and he had stubble on his jaw and bags under his eyes. Wherever he'd been for the past few days, it certainly wasn't indoors. I felt a moment of elation, hoping Father could fix this. Fix my eye. Get Mother back. Make it all right. But one look at his distraught face banished those illusions like a soap bubble.

He looked a man in well over his head with absolutely no idea how to get himself out again. I'd never seen Father so lost.

No one spoke as he clumped into the room in his heavy riding boots. He must have been injured because he limped slightly, an odd, accidental imitation of Benedict's gait. Father crouched by the bedside and put his hands on my face to get a good look at the horror of my eye. Mr. Sands stood back in the hallway, watching.

"I came as soon as I heard," Father said. His expression was carefully controlled, which worried me a lot more than if he'd been openly anxious. "I did all this, put you through this because I wanted you all to be safe. I was so sure you'd *be* safe in here and then your Mother and Joshua do *this*. I didn't think the Faerie could get to any of you here. I thought . . ." His jaw was tight. "I thought you'd be safe."

"You said that," Mr. Sands said flatly from the hallway.

Father sighed. "Sands . . . better come take a look."

Mr. Sands stepped into the room, eyeing all of us warily. Faith tried a smile, but Sands didn't seem to notice. His eyes visibly widened, however, when he got a closer look at me.

"Faerie work," he said. "There can be no doubt."

"We've been," Benedict said dryly, "getting a lot of that lately, haven't we?" He was trying for mildly sardonic, but his tone was forced. He lifted up the slit trouser leg. Blood had seeped through his bandages. Faith and Henry both gasped. They'd clearly never seen it before, either. Father's eyes closed and his head bowed as if a great weight had fallen on him at the sight.

"Is this Faerie work, too, Father?" Benedict said.

Mr. Sands spoke from the doorway. "Unmistakably."

Father opened his eyes and turned to me. "Tell me how this happened." He took my hand. "Leave nothing out."

We did. Mostly, it was me doing the talking, with Faith and Henry adding anything I'd missed. Father, Mr. Sands and Benedict listened with attentive fascination. Sometimes, while the others were speaking, I rubbed the smooth surface of the chess piece in my pocket. It was a comfort, somehow.

"There can be no doubt," Mr. Sands said when we finished. "They got to Martine already. Months ago."

"*Who*, exactly?" Benedict said.

"It's the Faerie, isn't it?" Faith said. "That's where Mother said she was going."

"Like in the stories?" Henry said. "Little people, rainbows and gold and tra-la-la?"

"An ancient people," Father said reluctantly. "Yes, like the stories, but you've probably heard all the wrong ones. Many are wrong, of course, or exaggerated, but not all. They are very dangerous and mostly hostile to human kind. They were driven out, once, long ago. Now . . . they want to return."

"Mother went with them," Faith said. "That was the Faerie? Why was Mrs. Westerly with them? Where did they go?"

Father let go of my hand and moved to stare into the fire. This should have felt like too much to absorb, but it came as a relief to know there was *some* kind of answer, even if it came out of story books.

"We're not sure where she is." Mr. Sands looked at Father, perhaps expecting him to answer. When he didn't, Mr. Sands took a breath and kept going. "Faerie is an expansive place, but there are difficulties in crossing. Wherever your mother and brother are, it's probable that Lady Westerly is with them."

"Lady Westerly?" Henry said. "You mean *Mrs.* Westerly? Mother's maid? What does she have to do with it?"

He was looking at Father, but Father just kept staring at the fire.

Benedict laughed bitterly. "Is everyone in on this? Do we have to watch out for the scullery maid and the butcher, too?"

"We just discovered her identity ourselves," Mr. Sands said. "That's what called us away. Your mother's nurse is a dangerous sorceress from Faerie. Likely your mother has been in her thrall for a long time using Faerie absinthe, the same trick Lady Westerly has used to ensnare kings and magicians before this. Martine never had a chance. She's probably been addicted for months."

"The green stuff in the bottles?" I said. "The stuff that burned my eye?"

"The same." Mr. Sands drew a small bottle of his own out of his jacket pocket and held it up. Even in the well-lit room, the green liquid glowed. How had I not noticed it before? Did it always do that? The bottle was sealed with cork, but still the taste of oranges, licorice, blood, and fear trickled into the back of my throat.

Mr. Sands' eyes seemed to have a light of their own, emerald flickers independent of the fire. His narrow face was suddenly frightening.

"This is the real absinthe that comes from Faerie, not the pale imitation that exists here. One taste can fill you with a consuming craving for more. Repeated use can drive people mad, but many would-be magicians take it as a path to power. It's one of the quicker, but more dangerous, ways to accelerate a study of magic. Lady Westerly wasn't just addicting Martine Kasric. She was teaching her magic—the same magic Martine used to escape, past all of our measures. We weren't expecting an assault from the inside."

He looked at each of us in turn. "Understand this: your mother has gone from you. Separated by distance, but also by the changes inside her. Absinthe changes you irrevocably. She's not the woman you remember anymore."

"I don't believe you," Faith hissed. She was crying now. I knew exactly how she felt, but bit my lip to keep myself together. She turned to Father at the fire. "Why didn't you stop it?" He didn't answer.

Faith's look of utter devastation, mirroring so precisely the yawning pit of despair in my own stomach, undid me. I could feel the same tears on my own face.

"There's much more at stake here than just one family," Mr. Sands said. "There's a host of Faerie marching on England right now. It's war."

"It is," Father said, half to himself. "A war like England has never seen."

"And we need to prepare for it!" Sands snapped. "That's the most important thing."

"I can't believe . . ." Faith said, but the last word came out as more of a choked sob, welling up suddenly from deep inside of her. She fell to her knees. Henry tried to kneel down and comfort her. Benedict just sat there, his face ashen.

Father pulled a thin case from his pocket, removed a cigarette from it and tapped it against the outside of the case before he lit it. His hands shook. I remembered Father facing down the Faerie King in a snowy woods with the steadiest hands I'd ever seen. "We couldn't have predicted the Faerie would have an accomplice in Stormholt," he muttered between puffs.

"A few years ago," Mr. Sands said, "you might have anticipated this."

"Blame me, then!" Father snapped. He stepped forward, towering over the smaller man, but Mr. Sands met his gaze evenly, his face tight but composed.

Father flushed angrily and turned back to the fire.

"No man can predict everything," he said.

"Why would the Faerie care about Mother?" I said. "Or us? Why would they infiltrate our house, go to all this trouble? You're talking about something they *planned* . . . for months."

"Under your very nose," Mr. Sands said.

Father glared at him again.

"It's not just us, of course," Father said. "The Seelie Court has declared all-out war on England, children. I am . . ." He paused. "I've been part of what's keeping them out."

"They aren't exactly *out*, are they?" Benedict said. "They're *here*. I distinctly remember watching a storm cloud filled with riding hunters chasing us. They could have flown right over Parliament, rather than chase *us* through the countryside. Why chase us?"

"There's an organized resistance," Mr. Sands said. He pointed. "Headed by your Father. Eliminating him would remove one of the Seelie Court's largest obstacles."

Father shook his head and stood up.

"Unleashing the Wild Hunt may not benefit the Court the way they think it will."

"What is the Wild Hunt, exactly?" Benedict said.

"Cernunnos' band," Mr. Sands said. "The other gods have links to the reigning Faerie races, and so with the Seelie or Unseelie Courts, who are behind all of this."

"Other gods?" Faith's eyes were very wide.

Mr. Sands chuckled, his eyes bright. "There are many Faerie gods. Cernunnos, Llyr, Taranis, Brighit, Ogma, Arawn, The Morrigna, Lughus. Shades and shadows of them still haunt your stories here, in Ireland, Scotland, Wales, France, Germany."

"But they're not just stories," Benedict said, "are they?"

"That," Father said, "is a more complicated question than you could possibly know."

"They were more than stories, far more, in this world," Mr. Sands said cryptically, "until they weren't. Time will tell if they might be again, at least here in this world. They have always lived in the Faerie world, of course."

"You said something about the Seelie and Unseelie Courts being behind all of this," I asked, desperately wanting to get this conversation on some footing I could understand.

"Light and dark," Mr. Sands said. "The two groups of Faerie. It's mostly the Unseelie Court that moves against England, though members of the Seelie Court are part of it, too. Many of the magicians and powerful Faerie have ties to one of the gods, and so the gods favor them."

"Except Cernunnos," Father said.

"Except Cernunnos," Mr. Sands agreed. "He takes no part in the court wars or politics. His Wild Hunt is just like it sounds, held apart from the other gods and the courts both."

"The Wild Hunt isn't under their control," Father said. "Cernunnos doesn't answer to the Seelie Court or anyone else. Now that they've let them out, they're likely to become a problem later on."

"True," Mr. Sands mused, "but by the time the Wild Hunt turns on them, it'll be too late to do *us* much good."

"It indicates the Seelie Court is desperate, at least."

"It wasn't chasing *us*," I guessed, looking at Father. "It was chasing *you*, wasn't t?"

Father and Sands exchanged a look and Father sighed.

"Cernunnos wants me," he said, "specifically, for reasons that have nothing to do with the war."

I thought again of the Faerie King, if such he really was, that night long ago in the woods. Father had been dismissive, then, almost scornful. Father had always been elegance personified, vibrant, always on top of any situation, but a few nights ago, he was the one firing frantically at an enemy he couldn't touch. It reminded me of that other figure, slumped in defeat with snow gathering on his shoulder and arms. Some invisible tide had turned. Father was on the run now.

"How," Benedict said, "are we supposed to come to grips with something like this?" He gestured at his bloody leg. "With something like *this* inflicted by powers we don't understand? We're supposed to bear this because of something you did?"

Father, very slowly, undid his soggy cravat and let it fall to the floor. Next, he unbuttoned the top three buttons on his shirt, enough to pull it aside and reveal a long, angry, red scar, obviously many years old, that started from his clavicle and ran god knew how far down his chest and back.

"We bear it," Father said, "because we must."

"What about Mother?" Faith said. "Aren't you going after her?"

"That would be a mistake," Mr. Sands said at once. "A mistake they're hoping we'll make, I'm sure."

"I can't just leave her to the Faerie, Sands," Father said. "You said it yourself. It's my fault they got to her."

Mr. Sands blinked. "You can't be serious. I pointed that out to remind you that you can't outwit them at every turn, like you used to. You're vulnerable!"

"Sometimes," Father said, "the hardest thing to do is also the right thing to do."

"You'll be playing right into their hands. They didn't drag Martine off, remember. She *chose* to leave."

"Because the Faerie got to her," Father said. "I *have* to go after her."

"No," Mr. Sands said. "We have the Seelie Court to worry about. They're coming, remember? All of this has taken us away from the center of things at a critical moment."

"My mind is made up," Father said. "You go back to the office and coordinate things."

"You can't . . ." Mr. Sands started, but Father had already stalked from the room.

No one spoke for a long stretch.

"He'll find her?" Faith said. "Won't he? He'll bring her back and this whole thing will blow over and we'll go back to London."

I wanted to trust Father. Trust Father not only to do what he said, but to *succeed* at it. Mr. Sands looked after him speculatively for a moment, then back at us.

"No," Mr. Sands said, his head bowed. "I don't think so."

Faith burst into tears. Part of me wanted to, as well, and I could see from Henry's face that he felt the same way.

"It's all falling apart," Mr. Sands went on, "and war is coming. We're all of us going to have to do our part. But none of us can stand alone. He doesn't see that yet." He lifted his head and shot me a curious glance, then dropped his gaze to where I was worrying the chess piece in my pocket.

"He wants to stand between you and danger," Mr. Sands said, "but Faerie war is going to wash over us all. Stormholt has already proven to be a poor refuge. It might be far better for you to be out and . . . involved." He squared his shoulders and sighed. "But that's not my place to say." He seemed to be trying to read my reaction.

I nodded my agreement. I wasn't exactly sure what I was agreeing to, but I knew I couldn't just sit here if Father was in trouble, no matter how safe Father wanted to keep all of us. A hopeful smile lit Mr. Sand's face.

He followed Father out of the room without another word.

The only sound was Faith still crying. Henry had her hand in his and I envied that comfort.

Benedict tapped thoughtfully on the armrest of the chair for a minute. "Well," he said, "*that* was certainly interesting."

"It's not interesting," Faith said. "It's horrid, and so are you for acting like it's just a foreign play or something."

"It is interesting, though," Benedict said. "What a twisted family we are. I challenge you to find a more interesting one." He pursed his lips. "There's one other thing I don't understand."

I snorted helplessly. "Just *one*?"

"Well, one that sticks out, anyway," he said. "That's Joshua. If Mother was somehow plied with Faerie liquor for months to get her into the Faerie bandwagon, what about Joshua? He's a prig, I'll grant you, more soldier than man, but he's not wantonly cruel. Mother must have something big on him to get him to play along the way he did."

"She does," Faith said.

We all turned to look at her.

"I don't know what it is," Faith said. "But something changed when he was home last holiday. They had a long talk by themselves his first night home and when he came out again, it was like something in him had died in that room. I never found out what it was, but he left London the next day . . ."

"I remember," Henry said. "Sudden orders, he said."

"Only I don't think he had any orders," Faith said. "At least, not official ones. I think Mother wanted him to do something, and she sent him off."

How much more was I going to find out about my family? How much of it might make me wish I could go back to not knowing?

The others must have been having similar thoughts, because we all sat a minute in silence.

Which is why the heavy thump against the window glass made us all jump. I gasped. Something was moving out there. I shivered and cringed away from the window, thinking of a thousand cats hissing all at once. Even through the stained-glass depiction of the woman with a sword, I could make out a large bird perched out there. It pecked against the glass. The tap, tap, tapping was the only sound in the room as we stared at each other.

"It's not like it could get in, is it?" Henry said. "The glass is so thick that . . ."

Tap, tap, tap, tap, *thunk.*

One of the tiny purple panes of glass fell out onto the carpet.

"Lor!" Henry said, grabbing up the fire poker. "It's a killer bird! First cats and now birds!"

"Wait!" said Faith. "It's pushing something through."

Benedict stood up, stepped around Henry, who was still brandishing the poker, and leaned over to take a closer look. Then Benedict pulled a rolled scrap of paper from the narrow hole the bird had made in the glass. The bird cawed once and flew off in a flash of smoky gray plumage.

"Amazing," Benedict said. He read the tube of paper with surprise.

"Justice," he said, "It's addressed to you."

"To me?" I took the paper tube. 'Justice Kasric' was indeed written across the length in large, elegant, and feminine letters.

I opened it and read, "You hold our Father's life in your hands. If you would see him live, meet me at the East India Trading

Company on Threadneedle Street." That was shocking enough, but at the bottom was a signature that gave me chills.

"Father's office?" Faith said. "Didn't he tell Sands to go back there? It's some kind of center for the resistance, he said."

"That makes no sense," Henry said. "If we want to save Father?"

"If he went after Mother like he said he would," Faith added, "he wouldn't go back to the office. Why have us go there? As if he even needs saving. *We're* the ones trapped here! How are we supposed to get there?"

"We can't even leave this house," Henry said.

"Who sent it?" Benedict asked softly.

"That's just it," I said. "It's signed . . . *your sister, Prudence.*"

# CHAPTER 7

## The Escape

The next few hours we did what most brothers and sisters do, even when they aren't magically locked into mansions like Stormholt: we argued.

"We don't *have* a sister named Prudence," Faith said.

"We did," Benedict said thoughtfully.

"She died at childbirth," Faith said. "She didn't exactly have time to grow up and start writing letters. Whoever this is, it's not her. It's someone using her name to rattle us."

We were sitting in the huge drawing room with food and drink scattered all around.

"It's working!" Henry said. "Imagine having another sister all this time and not knowing it."

"It's a fake," Faith insisted. "Some trick of the Faerie. Father didn't tell you anything about another sister, Justice?"

"No," I said. "Father didn't tell me anything."

"Hmm," she said.

"What about you and Mother?" I snapped back, irritated. "We all heard what she said. Are you going to report back to her like she said? Remember, she's counting on you!"

"She left me here to rot, same as you!" Faith said hotly.

"Would you?" I asked. "Tell her everything, I mean?"

"What exactly is supposed to be the big secret?" We were both getting louder now. "And how am I supposed to tell her anything?"

"She said she'll let you know."

She threw up her hands. "You're both crazy! You and Mother! You're talking like we're soldiers and spies, and we're not! We're family. We're not on opposite sides of some secret war here, Justice!"

"Aren't we?" I said.

A silence hung in the air. Benedict poured another drink.

Faith sighed. "I . . . I don't know what to do about Mother. I truly don't."

"You're right about one thing," I said. "There are too many secrets in this family. But we have a way to find some answers." I held up the tiny scroll our sister 'Prudence' had left us. "On Threadneedle Street. That means getting out of here and going back to London."

"Too dangerous," Benedict said. "That storm is out there, waiting for us." He sat back in his chair, refusing to meet my gaze. His hands shook as he poured more brandy.

"You're a coward," I hissed at him. I flourished the rolled message under his nose. "Father's in trouble and the Faerie are coming and I bet whoever sent this, sister or not, knows something about it!"

"If she really is a sister," Benedict said. "She might not be a Kasric at all."

"More of a—" I stopped. I'd been about to say 'More of a Kasric than *you* are,' meaning not brave and competent like Father, only I didn't feel on such firm ground there, what with Father's strange behavior and bleak demeanor lately. I had to satisfy myself a small angry shriek and stomping away.

We checked the front door again, but the army of cats had returned, only slightly diminished by Mother's explosive escape. So, I determined to explore the unlit areas of Stormholt on the first floor. I got Henry and Faith to agree to that much and we each grabbed up a fist full of candles then passed by the large common room, where Henry wanted to grab something off the Everbreakfast table in order to fortify himself.

"Must you eat every hour?" Faith chided him.

"Sure," Henry said.

I was leaning on the doorway, waiting impatiently, when I noticed a small figure coming down the hallway.

I stared. Was I seeing things? There had been no one here with us in Stormholt all this time and now someone just appears?

"Hello?" I said.

The small boy stopped and stared at me in shock, saying nothing.

"Where did you come from?" I said. I was trying to wave to Faith and Henry, but they were picking at the table and paying me no attention.

The boy, around twelve years old, peered at me from underneath a mop of disheveled yellow hair and a grey checked cap. He wore dirty and worn brown pants and jacket, with a shirt that might once have been white. He held a stack of towels. Without speaking, he pushed the mop of yellow hair out of his face and stepped carefully to the left. His eyes shot wide open as I followed his movements.

"Bleedin' impossible," the boy said. I was surprised at the offensive word out of such a small boy.

"She can see you!" another voice said, and I saw a second boy, even younger than the first, peering around the entrance to one of the bath rooms. "It's her freakish eye!"

"She can't see us," said the first boy, still staring at me.

"Of course I can," I said, angry over the nasty comment on my eye. "You're right there." I pointed straight at him.

"She hears us, too!" the boy peering around the corner said. This boy was much smaller and cleaner than the first. His hair was slicked neatly back, and he wore a cravat and shirt with the sleeves rolled up. A very out-of-place but spotless apron was tied across his middle. His English was proper and clipped, very upper crust. Mother would have approved of the accent, if not the apron.

"Of course she 'ears you!" the first boy said. He spoke with the sing-song cadence of the London streets. "You don't never shut up, do you?"

"You're talking, too!" the second boy wailed.

"Where have you been hiding all this time?" I asked, realizing that my questions about hidden servants had suddenly found strange answers.

"Justice, who are you talking to?" Henry said, coming up behind me with a half-eaten sausage.

"He's right there," I said.

Henry shook his head. "I don't see anyone."

The boy with the checked cap edged cautiously backwards.

"Hold on," I said, moving closer. "I just want to find out more about this place. If you've been here, you can help . . ."

"Run!" the boy yelled and made a dash for it. The other boy followed.

I swore and followed them both.

"Justice?" Henry said behind me.

I got to the bath room just in time to see a wardrobe door fall shut. I ran around the claw-foot tub and yanked the door open. Instead of stacks of towels, like I'd assumed before, there was a narrow stairway spiraling down.

I could hear the footsteps of the boys, and rushed down the stairs after them. There was no railing, and the stairs were tricky, especially in the dark. I stumbled once, nearly tipping head first down the steps, but managed to brace myself against the cramped and mildewed walls and keep going. Then light trickled down from above as Faith or Henry opened the wardrobe door above me.

"Justice?" Faith yelled.

"Come on!" I shouted back. "They're getting away!"

Another splash of light opened up beneath me. There must be a door at the bottom of the stairs and someone had just opened it. It was swinging shut as I came around the turn, but I rushed down the last few steps and burst through before it closed.

I was in a kitchen. A large kitchen, to be sure, but otherwise normal enough. The space in the middle was dominated by a worktable covered with dough and flour. There was a small suit coat folded over the back of one of the chairs that had to belong to the smaller boy. If the apron was any kind of clue, he'd been making the bread just before this.

The two boys were glaring at me, completely at a loss now that I'd followed them this far.

The pantry door behind me burst open and Faith and Henry stumbled into the kitchen in a breath of cool air and mildew.

"Amazing!" Henry said. "Secret passage!"

"Ugh," Faith said. She had stains on her dress that she wiped at two or three times before she gave it up as a bad job.

"Who are you?" I said, turning back to the boys. "How long have you been here? How did you stay so well hidden up until now?"

"Who's she talking to?" Henry said. Faith clearly couldn't see them either.

I waved Henry silent with an irritated motion. "Are you Faerie?"

"We're not Faerie," the younger boy said. "We're ghosts!"

I blinked in surprise. "Ghosts? As in . . . walk through walls, rattle chains in the night kind of ghosts?"

"Ghosts?" Henry said.

"Walking through walls is harder than it looks," the younger, neat boy said. "I'm Percy and that's Étienne."

"Oh, Lord preserve us!" Étienne shouted at him. "Are you going to tell 'er everythin'? Mr. Sands told us to keep out o' the way, and don't talk to anyone!"

"Mr. Sands told you?" Justice said. "Then you work for him and Father?"

Étienne shook his head vigorously, until he saw Percy nodding, at which time he threw his hands up in the air and flung himself into a chair, visibly disgusted. "We're really not supposed to be talkin' to 'er!" Étienne exploded. "Some guard you are!"

"I didn't ask to be a guard, did I?" Percy shot back, his little face red. "I got press-ganged into it! We all did! I'm not sure we can trust Sands, anyways."

"'E left me in charge, didn't he, you ninnyhammer!" Étienne shouted.

"Least I'm not faking a stupid accent trying to pretend I'm English!" Percy shouted right back.

Étienne's face went nearly purple. "That's a lie! I was born in East End, I was. Right under the bloody Bow Bells!" He slumped angrily in his chair, finally muttering, "I can't 'elp it if me mum was Frenchie. At least *my* mum didn't make me into a milksop boy in the kitchen."

"Who's a milksop, you . . . mumpsimus!"

"Pillock!"

"Lickspittle!"

"You snollygoster!"

Both boys were going red in the face now.

"Snollygoster!" Percy shouted. "You made that one up! Take it back or I'll knock that apron right off you!"

"Just you try it, you!"

I dashed in between the two apoplectic little boys and they both quieted down and fumed impotently on either side of me.

"Justice," Faith said, exasperated. "What is going *on*?"

"Do they look like ghosts?" Henry said.

"Not really. They just look like two boys."

"We look like ghosts to everyone else." Percy said, still angry but clearly wanting to tell his story. "Or that is, we don't look like anything. Other folks just look right through us! That's why Mr. Sands calls us the Ghost Boys, us being ghosts and all. Here try and touch my hand. It won't work."

Half believing it all to be some trick, I stepped forward and reached out to put my hand out to grip Percy's, but it was like putting my hand into a misty cloud: cold, damp and entirely insubstantial.

Percy gave a sad smile. "See? Ghosts."

I opened my mouth to ask them the obvious. If I couldn't touch them, why had they let me stop their fight? Then I closed it, deciding that if they for some reason thought of me as an authoritative or helpful figure, I certainly didn't want to talk them out of it.

A new idea occurred to me then, an idea about my sudden ability to see them, when clearly they'd been around for a while.

Perhaps my damaged eye?

I held up a hand to my right eye, looking at Percy and Étienne only through my left. They looked right back, plain as houses. I covered my left, and they winked neatly out of sight. Now I couldn't see them anywhere. I let my hand drop and they winked back into sight. That was proof enough for me.

"That eye," Étienne said wonderingly. "That's a Faerie gift, that is. Must be a ghost eye, I guess. Makes you one of the people that can see us."

Some gift. I'd nearly gotten my brains dashed out getting it, but I didn't bother correcting them. Something else was tickling my memory. One of the people . . .

"Obviously, Mr. Sands can see you," I said. They both nodded.

"Father?"

"Yes." Étienne said.

"Mother? You were trying to stop her. She kept shooing at nothing with that umbrella. That was you, wasn't it?"

Étienne sighed. "We did try to stop her, but it weren't no good."

I crouched in front of Étienne. "So you saw what happened with Mother?"

"Yes," he said softly. "And how your brother knocked you around, too. Is that how you got that eye, from falling in that stuff?"

"I guess so," I said. "If it was your Mother that left, you'd want to help her, right?"

Another nod.

"Then help us. Help us find a way out," I said. I looked back and forth between the two of them.

"There isn't one," Étienne said.

"We'll see," I said. "You can at least show us around, can't you?"

Percy nodded, and after a moment's consideration, so did Étienne.

"First things first," I said. I'd been trapped here for only a few days, but already it was starting to make me claustrophobic. Remembering how I'd always escaped when I was feeling trapped back at our home in Soho, I looked up.

"How," I said, "do you get to the roof?"

The roof was only accessible by an iron ladder and a locked trapdoor. Neither Étienne nor Percy had a key and had apparently meant what they said about walking through walls being difficult, because they swore they'd never been onto the roof.

I picked the lock with another of Faith's hairpins. I'd have to start keeping some of those in my pocket.

The roof itself was a tar-colored maze of peaks, slanted edges and crow-stepped gables all mashed into each other at odd angles. The trapdoor sat in the middle of a sort of ravine, with a tall slanted peak on our right and an irregular series of dormers and irregular features on the left. Behind us was another slanted section of roof, very steep, so that walking forward was the only path that didn't require mountaineering gear. Walking a short distance through that path led us to a small open space where we found a shack filled with shelves of wicker cages, all filled with pigeons. There was a waterproof sack of feed next to the cages.

"Well now," I said. "Someone must come up here to feed you."

"Three guesses who," Faith said as Henry threw some seed from a bag on the floor into the cages and the pigeons picked happily away.

"Sands, Sands, Sands," Henry said. "Oho! Will you look at that?"

"Why," Faith said. "It's adorable!"

In the side of one of the gables, facing the shack, stood a bottle-green round door.

"You were awfully eager to get onto the roof. Did you know about this?" Faith asked me.

"No," I said. "I told you."

"All right," she said, lifting her hands, but she still didn't look entirely convinced.

I ignored her and turned the handle.

Inside, we found a cozy little apartment with a round fire pit and chimney in the middle, but not much else by the way of furniture except enough layers of plush carpet and heavy drapes to screen out any noise, a low table overflowing with books, and a ton of cushions. It was eccentric, but very cozy and had Mr. Sands' sense of quirky style all over it.

"Oh!" Faith said. "Look who I found." She was crouching down and looking underneath the book-laden table.

I joined her and peered underneath. A fat, gray cat with fur like new velour glared at me balefully.

"He's cute," Faith said.

"Have you forgotten all the cats downstairs?" Henry said. "This one's probably controlled by Sands, too. He's the enemy! And violent, I bet!"

"He doesn't seem violent," Faith said. Though he didn't seem exactly friendly, either.

"Hello, my fuzzy little enemy," I said.

"Don't get close, Justice!" Henry said. "He'll bite!"

I reached out my hand.

The gray cat whuffed at me and butted his head against my hand until I stroked his back. In less than a minute, Faith and I were petting him together while he flopped and thrashed in completely undignified ecstasy.

"Some enemy!" Faith said, grinning at Henry.

Henry sniffed. "Probably tells Mr. Sands everything. Just as soon as we leave!"

"Are you going to do that?" I asked our enemy cat.

He whuffed again and showed his belly. Of course, there was something to what Henry said, and the cat's behavior wasn't a denial. I rubbed the fuzzy belly just to be sure.

Having placated my adversary, and finding nothing else of interest, we left quickly. There wasn't anything else of immediate interest on the roof except the thing I'd actually come here for: the view. The two Ghost Boys spent the rest of the day showing us through the house, but I returned to the roof several times that evening and it was very early the next morning that I found our way out.

The day after we made plans and before dawn the next day, we all gathered in the kitchen.

It was a dreary time to be awake and the lantern we had lit didn't do much to brighten the dark room.

"I can't believe you're staying here," Henry said to Benedict for the twentieth time.

"I told you, little brother," Benedict said. "It's better this way. My leg couldn't make the run. And we might need to run if the Wild Hunt comes back." He was drinking brandy again. He was always drinking now, though I could never tell if he was actually drunk.

"We could wait a few days." Henry wrapped another loaf of bread in cloth and packed it away into a shoulder bag.

I kept silent and stowed a bottle of milk in my own bag. We'd all had a virtually sleepless night here in order to be ready for my plan, which had to happen at dawn. We couldn't possibly wait another night. But I'd said enough already. Everyone knew what I was thinking. I'd been riding Benedict about it all morning.

Étienne stepped into the kitchen without bothering to open the door and I jumped. I was never going to get used to that. Despite what they'd said before, it sure didn't *seem* like they had any trouble walking through walls.

"Here, Miss Justice," Étienne said. "Mr. Sands left this for us, but I think you'll need it more." Étienne dropped a small bag on kitchen table next to Henry with the tell-tale jingle of coins.

"Lor . . ." Henry said, jumping as the bag landed next to him. It would have appeared out of thin air for him.

"Thank you," I said, taking the bag.

"Percy's got . . ." he turned and frowned back at the door. "'E was right behind me!"

"I'm coming," Percy said, materializing out of the closed door with a bundle of things in his arms so large that he could barely see where he was going. He dumped them on the already sizable mound on the table. The two boys had been carting them down for the last ten minutes. Outdoor coats, hats, scarves.

I still had Father's old black navy coat with me, the one I'd taken with me on the carriage ride here. I'd worn it so often on the roof in London that it felt remarkably reassuring to have it on and couldn't imagine wearing anything else on an excursion like this. It was a short coat for him but came down nearly to my ankles. The treated leather felt like comforting armor to me. I was also wearing a set of black wool breeches that Percy had found for me earlier, which felt far more comfortable than the frock I'd had on before. Faith had already given me many scandalized sidelong glances because of them.

Feeling terribly rebellious, I also chose a black, wide-brimmed hat that was totally unsuited for any self-respecting London woman and put it on with a mischievous grin at Faith. She sniffed and ignored me, refusing for once to rise to the bait.

"I can't wear any of this," Faith said, picking through the second-hand and somewhat scruffy pile of items, but she put on a man's beige overcoat anyway. "We might as well scream 'runaways' the minute we get to London. We'll probably be arrested for vagrants immediately."

"We do look just like vagrants," Henry said happily, "don't we?"

Faith sighed.

Henry put on a checkered cap that might have been a clone to the one Étienne was wearing, though Henry couldn't have possibly known it. Étienne watched him fit it on and shook his head.

The two Ghost Boys had also helped us scrounge a great deal of food, for which I was especially grateful. They'd done a great deal in the past day and night to help us. I hoped that I wasn't going to get them into too much hot water with Mr. Sands. We couldn't have done without their help, but both of the boys looked *so* young that it made me feel a touch guilty. Étienne couldn't have been more than twelve and I guessed Percy a couple of years younger. Being almost sixteen myself, there really wasn't that much of a gap between us, but it *felt* huge. I just wanted to give them a hug and tell them that I was certain it was all going to work out wonderfully, but I couldn't do either, because they were untouchable ghosts and I wasn't that good a liar.

"It's time," I said. I hoisted the small bag of supplies onto my shoulder and straightened the brim of my hat. "Let's go."

Faith smoothed out her coat then sighed. "Horrible." She looked over at Benedict. "I know you think your leg couldn't stand the trip, and that you're afraid of the Wild Hunt. I understand that. We're *all* afraid. But you're not afraid of the same things that we are at all, are you?"

Benedict laughed bitterly. "Dear Faith, you always did understand me a little better than I wanted."

"Tell us," Faith said.

Benedict pursed his lips and looked down. "The Wild Hunt doesn't frighten me. It *calls* to me!" He poured himself another drink. "Something about being struck by lightning from that cloud. It's marked me. I hear the horn at night. In my dreams. The brandy helps a little to drown out the noise, but I think it's really the black iron gate that runs around this place. Here, I can fight that call. Outside the fence . . ." He shook his head. "They'd have me in an instant."

"Have you?" I said, with a dark feeling churning in my gut.

"When Mr. Sands," Benedict said, "was trying to rescue me, do you know what I was doing?"

No one did. We all stared. The sudden intensity and pain in his face was too painful to look at, but neither could we look away.

"I was trying to get up in a tree," Benedict said. "Broken leg and all. I had some idea of flinging myself off the highest one I could find so that I might reach them. The leg hurt like mad but I didn't care. Probably would have just fallen and broken my neck, but I didn't care. I would have taken any chance to try to get to them. Sands tried to talk sense into me, but I wouldn't hear it. I wouldn't let him help my leg, either, and I nearly clawed his eyes out trying to get past him and join the hunt.

Sands had to knock me out, I think, to get me out of there. The memories are muddled. Most of this I didn't even remember until a few days ago."

"If I go out there," Benedict said. "I'll run straight to them." His gaze was very blue, and very wet. "I know I will."

Now I felt like a rat for riding him so much about staying. I'd had no idea, and I could see from their faces that Faith and Henry hadn't, either. It also shed a different light on Benedict's constant drinking. Both Étienne and Percy looked grim, but not surprised.

"Does Father know?" I asked. "About the dreams, I mean. Maybe he can ..."

"He knows," Benedict said. "He's got scars all down his back from lightning strikes. Scars that match the ones on my leg. I'll bet he has the same dreams. I bet he knows exactly what I'm going through now. How he resists, I have no idea."

"Father said the leader of the Wild Hunt wanted *him*, specifically," Faith said. "Remember?" She looked at Benedict. "Do you know why?"

He shook his head. "No, but watching the way they pursue something, I'm guessing they won't stop. Ever. They're not called the 'hunt' for nothing."

"Oh, Benedict," Faith said, softly.

There was so much more I wanted to say, to understand, but we just didn't have the time. Étienne was pulling at my elbow.

"Miss Justice," he said. "It's getting light out. We have to hurry."

Henry embraced Benedict with the total lack of self-consciousness the rest of us had. I embraced Benedict, too, but awkwardly. I was actually relieved we were in a hurry and couldn't draw this out.

"I'm sorry," I said. "I shouldn't have called you a coward. I didn't know."

He smiled weakly. "How could you? But you're right about one thing, Justice. If the Faerie are coming to England, we need answers we're not going to find locked up in this place. You should go. I just can't go with you."

"I'm sorry," I said again, because I couldn't think of anything else to say.

He was pouring more brandy when we left.

⤝⧫⤝⧫⤝⧫⤞

Étienne led the way down stone steps into the cool of a wine cellar, I followed and Faith and Henry came after. Down in the cellar, we helped Étienne push aside two brandy barrels. Behind them was an opening of soft, dry, brown earth.

A tunnel.

The two younger boys went in, but when I moved to follow, Faith grabbed my arm.

"One more thing," Faith said. "I know you think Father walks on water, but you must know he needs help, or you wouldn't be doing this."

"Yes," I said. "Of course he needs our help."

"I'm just saying," Faith said, "we might not want to count too much on *him* being able to help *us*. Just try and remember we don't have that safety net anymore."

"Fine," I said. "Are you coming or not?"

"I am," she said, "we're not doing any good sitting here and at least you have a plan. It's hare-brained, but it's better than any plan I have. So I guess I'm right behind you."

"Thanks for the support," I said dryly.

Faith grinned. "Don't mention it." Then she sighed and looked at the tunnel entrance. "I just wish your plan didn't involve so much crawling through the dirt."

It was my turn to grin. "Come on, princess."

We crawled through, moving slowly and awkwardly through the dirt to keep our candles from flickering out. We followed the tunnel for sixty feet or so, until it curved around and met with a brick wall. Étienne carefully worried a slice of brick loose with a soft grating noise.

"Put the candle out," Percy said. "Cats see everything. Even ghosts."

We did, and Étienne slid the brick the rest of the way free.

"Come on then," he said. "Look." I had to grope my way over and he talked me through finding the gap with my fingers and peering out.

Dawn was just starting to pour gray into the world, so it took me a full minute of staring to understand that I was looking out of the house and onto the front lawn. Indistinct shadows milled restlessly about, and the paired fireflies of cats' eyes when they looked our way. That didn't happen much, though. Something interesting was happening near the gate and all their attention was there.

"We got 'ere just in time," Étienne said. "Always 'appens just at sun-up."

"What's happening?" Faith whispered. I hadn't given Faith or Henry the full details of my plan because I wasn't sure they'd agree if they knew.

I peered through the opening with just my ghost eye because everything was a little brighter that way. The gate was opening and a cart was coming through. Someone, I couldn't see who from this distance, closed the gate behind them and the cart started up.

A choir of mewing started to rise.

"'Ere they go," Étienne said. "Emily brings the fish cart every mornin'. They're magicked guardian cats, but they're still cats, ain't they? You was brilliant to think o' this, Miss Justice. It's the perfect time, it is."

"Fish cart?" Faith said.

"Shh . . ." I said.

The mewing was louder now, much louder. Now it rose to a cacophony of plaintive, demanding cries from hundreds of cats like the Devil's own orchestra.

The cart picked its way slowly and creakily up the gravel drive, pulled along by a single, weary, piebald horse. Two figures sat in the driver's seat, one larger and one smaller.

The back of the cart was filled, literally to overflowing, with an innumerable quantity of fish. The trail of feeding cats led all the way back to the gate. A shift in the wind carried an overpowering wash of fishy odor with it.

The light was a bit brighter now and I let Henry push me aside so that he could take a look.

"That," whispered Henry excitedly, "is a *lot* of fish."

Faith wrinkled her nose. "Ugh. I can smell it."

The horse pulled gamely, plodding on without any regard to the milling carpet of cats around it. Miraculously, cats ran under the horse and wagon both, but none got stepped on or ridden over. They were everywhere now. Cats crawled over the back of the cart like swarming locusts, fighting and clawing for their fishy treasure.

The hissing, spitting and outraged cat wails hurt my ears. The fastest cats sprang off the cart with prized morsels in their jaws, but the crowd milling around the cart didn't seem any smaller. A constant press of furred bodies swirled around as it passed through the drive and towards the corner of the house.

I could see the people on the cart better now. The driver was a bearded man, barely visible for the heavy oilskin hood and coat. Only a gray beard poked determinedly out.

He was grimly slapping the horse's reins to urge him on faster through the frenzied crowd. I couldn't see that his urging made any difference, but he kept at it. A young, red-haired girl of about ten sat next to him, talking excitedly, though I couldn't hear what she said at this distance. The cats crawled about the man's shoulders, but the girl was untouched.

I switched eyes on a hunch and saw that I'd guessed right. With my right eye, I could see the bearded man, the cart, the horse, and all the cats, but no girl. She was a ghost, too.

"That's Emily and her da," Percy said. "They come every morning to feed them."

Henry put his hands to his ears. "How did we not *hear* this every morning?"

"The house keeps out sound better than you'd expect," Percy said over the noise. I relayed his words to Henry.

"Cart's goin' around the back way," Étienne said. "Are you sure you can get past that lock? We ain't got no key for it. Emily can open it, but she never won't tell us 'ow."

"We'll manage the lock," I said. Even that little bit of light was causing a throbbing pain in my ghost eye, making me pinch my nose.

"All right, then," Étienne said. "Remember, don't stop for nothin'. They won't pay attention while they're eatin' but the minute they finish . . . well, just 'urry, that's all. Now 'elp me push on this wall. Right 'ere, that's it!"

A three-foot section of the brick wall fell out when we pushed at it.

"Go!" Étienne whispered. "Go, go!"

I scrambled over the fallen brick slab and immediately tripped over two cats fighting over a chunk of mackerel. I got to my feet, ready to run, but they didn't even notice me. They were too busy with the fish and each other.

"Oh, god," Faith said as she came out. "Maybe this was a bad idea."

"Christ does that stink!" Henry said.

He wasn't wrong. The reek was tremendous, but there wasn't any help for it.

We picked our way through a whirling field of feeding and hissing and bickering cats, leaping from patch to patch of empty ground like crossing boulders in a stream. Glistening fish were lying everywhere. Twice, I tried to go too fast and got a bloody scratch on my leg for it from the nearest cat, but mostly the cats were too engrossed in the fish to pay me any mind.

I kept looking for the cart. They weren't too distracted by fish to call some alarm, I was sure. But they were still behind the house and shouldn't have any idea we were even here. Certainly they wouldn't hear us with all this wailing and mewling. Twenty feet behind us, Étienne and Percy were already struggling the bricks back into place. They had to do it from the outside, but that wasn't a problem. When they finished, they waved at us and disappeared through the wall. Being a ghost had its advantages.

I wasn't watching where I was going, and stepped on the tail of a yellow tabby. It hissed and bit me on the calf. I staggered, but Henry caught me.

"I'm all right," I said. Blood already soaked my stocking, but we kept on.

That's when the cat landed on Henry's shoulder from the roof.

Henry shrieked and waved his arms and the cat, a tabby, jumped off immediately. It headed for the cart, ignoring us now that Henry had provided a landing spot, but it left a trickle of blood down Henry's forehead.

"It's nothing," he said gamely. "I'm fine." Both his eyes and Faith's were wide. Probably mine, too, or at least one of them. We were all sweating despite the cold.

"They're running out of fish," Faith said. "Hurry!"

Twenty feet from the gate, a path opened at last and we broke into a run. I had to jump over a quarreling pair of Siamese, but Henry just barreled through.

"Sorry," he yelled back, but they were too busy fighting among each other to care.

I ran into the gate hard enough to rattle teeth. Quickly, I yanked a spare hairpin out of my pocket.

"Why don't you just keep them in your *hair*?" Faith yelled. "Like a normal person?"

We were all panting and out of breath. The wet, unsettling sounds of a thousand cats eating came from all around.

I worked at the lock, but it wasn't moving.

"Hurry," Faith said. "The cart will be back any minute!"

"I'm trying!" I snapped.

Thirty seconds crawled slowly by, the wet, lapping sounds of the cats started to fade.

"Justice . . ." Henry said. "Can you get it?"

"I don't know," I said. I could feel the tumbler, but it wasn't responding to pressure.

"Justice . . ."

"Shut up! I'm trying!"

"Maybe we can make it back to the house?" Henry said. "Christ. I think some of them are done eating."

"Mmmmmrrrrrr . . ." There was a rising feline growl coming from the nearest dozen cats, who no longer looked so distracted.

"We won't make it back to the house," Faith said. "It's too late for that! When Father opened it, he sang a song, do you remember?"

"No," Henry said. "I don't remember."

I banged the lock with my fist. "It won't turn!"

Henry groaned. "They're coming, Justice. Can we climb the gate?"

I looked up at the barbed hooks on top, and swallowed with some difficulty. "We can try."

I looked back. The number of cats looking and growling at us had risen to fifty or so. None of them were eating anymore. They regarded us menacingly. Some of them stalked our way, their hackles rising.

Even worse, I could see the horse and cart coming around the corner of the house now, too.

"I think it went like this," Faith said. She sang a quick, wordless melody. Four notes.

The lock trembled in my hand, but didn't open.

"That's it," I said to her. "That's close. Try it again."

"Oh, god," Henry said. "We're going to *die* here!"

Faith sang again.

This time, the lock snapped open.

The gate swung in when I pulled and we stumbled through as quickly as we could. Henry slammed the gate shut behind us just as twenty or more cats came running up. For a moment, I was afraid they would just slip through the bars and keep coming. They certainly could have, but once the gate clanged shut, they seemed to lose interest.

"Faith," I panted. "How did you do that?"

Faith shrugged. "I don't know. It just came to me."

Henry puckered his lips and tried to copy the same tune. I smacked him on the arm, afraid the gate would open and we'd have another rush of cats, but nothing happened.

"Huh," Henry said. "Didn't work."

"Good," I said.

"Forget that," Faith said. She lifted her arms and spun around. "Look at us! We did it!"

It was true. We were dirty and bloody, but we'd done it. We'd gotten out of Stormholt. Faith and I exchanged a look, understanding that we'd both had to work together to make this happen.

I stared at the long shadows Stormholt threw to the west. Father had thought we'd be safer in there and expected me to go along with that like a good little soldier, but I'd chosen to break out instead, against his wishes. But hadn't Father himself raised me to think, to judge, to look and observe? He'd never advocated a blind obedience. I just hoped he understood my reasons when this was all settled.

# CHAPTER 8

## Victoria Rose and the Soho Shark

It was already noon by the time we stepped out of the trees into a cold, but brilliant snow-covered meadow. On the far side, past the dazzling white, lay the gray lines of the railroad tracks. We'd only been trapped in Stormholt for a few days, but so much had happened that it felt like weeks. The bright light hurt my ghost eye a bit, and I had to pull the brim of my hat lower to shield it. Even so, simply being out in the sun was a lift to my spirits that pushed my fears about Father, Mother and the Faerie to the background.

That is, until we followed the train tracks over the next rise and saw the field littered with corpses.

Suddenly it didn't seem right that the sun was shining anymore, because here it fell on still, darkened frozen humps that had once been men. Some women, too, though they'd all been dead for some time and the differences were less. The uniforms weren't the English reds and blues, but rather a green so dark as to be almost black, which didn't look familiar until I saw the cord on the back that looked like a string of barbed thorns. I found another uniform with the same cord pattern that looked even more familiar, being of the deep indigo I'd seen before, on Caine, the officer with Father. I realized that I hadn't thought about Caine since he'd been lost in the storm. I hadn't known him well and what I knew wasn't exactly charming, but he could be dead now, like these people, and that meant something.

"Father's men?" Faith said.

"Father's men," I said.

I moved on to some others in painted armor that I didn't know. I kept looking at a man with a short blade protruding out of his eye. Someone had shoved that blade in there, on purpose, knowing what it would do.

Large groups of men and Faerie were all uprooting their lives, marching or sailing to travel great lengths for the express purpose of shoving knives into each other's eyes until one side or another ran out of people willing to die. That was war, wasn't it? Right now, it seemed too horrible to contemplate.

Most of the bodies were human. Young men like Benedict and Joshua. Even a few who didn't look any older than Henry. There was a large hairy mound in the middle so matted with mud, frost, and dried blood that I couldn't even imagine what it had looked like in life.

Henry stopped. He bent and carefully pried something off the frozen ground and turned to show us.

It was another corpse, only a very small one.

I felt a shiver of recognition when I saw the tiny shape. It was a girl, about the same size as Henry's hand, with oversized claws and brown fur running down her back. I'd seen another just like her in a jar.

"The Pix," I said, remembering the card. I told him about what I'd seen in Father's study. I couldn't tell them much about the Faerie besides that, though. I didn't know much.

"Fifty-two," Faith said suddenly and I realized she'd been silently counting as we passed through. "Someone needs to know this is here. Father or someone. It doesn't seem right to just leave them lying here like this."

"We'll tell someone," I said.

"When Father said a Faerie war," Henry said, "I guess I really didn't think he meant *war*. I thought there would be a few glorious charges and heroes and stuff. I didn't know it would look like *this*."

"War," I said. It was just a word before. Now, it was a whole lot more. I looked over at Faith. With the reality of war suddenly made more real, something she'd said before hit home. Not only was this a war, with real battles and real lines drawn, but our family was on both sides of it. There was no denying that anymore. Did Mother mean what she said about contacting Faith later? How would she do it? What would Faith do to get back in Mother's good graces? Was Faith going to become a traitor in our midst—and what could I do about it?

I couldn't think of one bloody thing.

"We should be on the lookout for more Faerie," Henry said. "If this kind of thing is happening everywhere, there could be Faerie coming for us."

"Father's Faerie," Faith said with a tremor in her voice, "Or Mother's? How would we even know the difference?"

Henry shrugged. "We don't even know what most of the Faerie look like."

A shiver of premonition came over me. "We will," I said with certainty. "We will."

None of us had much to say after that. We walked on in silence. We climbed the hill on the other side, the breath clouding in the cold air, our feet crunching in snow and frost-covered ground. It didn't seem right to have the sun on our backs, but the sun and the sky didn't care.

"Do you really think," Faith said, "there's any chance we're going to find a long-lost sister in London?"

"*Someone* sent that note," I said. "Someone who knows us well enough to use that name, and knows the situation well enough to send that message."

"That could be Mother," Faith said. "Or one of Father's enemies. Someone in Faerie. I just hope we don't end up regretting it."

"I'm just glad," Henry said, "to be outside instead of in that stuffy mansion."

The walk hadn't looked like much from the roof of Stormholt, but actually walking it took several hours, and I was worried we'd somehow gotten lost.

Then we found the train tracks that I'd seen. From there, it was a short distance to the incline that Étienne had told us about. This was a good place to try the next step of our plan. Well, my plan, really. It wasn't a steep grade, but it was a long one and we were tired and sweaty and footsore by the time we reached the top.

We were going to try and jump onto a running train.

"This," Henry said, "is going to be amazing."

Faith shook her head. "If you had any sense in your head, Henry, you wouldn't sound so happy about it."

"Can't walk to London from here," he said cheerfully.

"We're just in time," I said, pointing back the way we'd come. It was too far down the hill to see the actual train, but the clouds of black smoke coming closer were clearly visible and we could just make out the *chuff-chuff* sound in the distance.

We'd gotten into position just in time. Now we only had to crouch in a clump of scrub brush and wait. That was just enough time to get cold again.

"Oh, god," Faith said as the black iron monstrosity came into sight, large and bulky and belching coal smoke as it labored up the long shallow slope.

"Stay under cover while the engine goes by," I said. "We'll make for one of the box cars near the back."

Henry grinned and nodded. "It's moving so slowly! It'll be easy!"

"Right," I said. "Easy." I wasn't thinking at all about any of the bad things that could happen to someone who tried to jump on a moving train and missed. This was my plan and the only way we had of getting to London in under a week. What choice did I have?

The engine took eighteen or so days to work its way up to our position. At least it felt like it. We stayed behind the scrub brush as the front part of the train crawled by, car by car.

"Not yet," I said. We'd had a brief look at the engineer going by at a stately pace, but after that, no one.

Down near the end of the slope, I could see the last car, the caboose, come into view. Still no sign of anyone in the nearby cars.

"Now!" I said.

We broke cover and ran for it. Henry was the fastest and quickly got out in front, with me following him and Faith trailing behind me. The train had gotten very slow coming up the slope and it was surprisingly easy to angle closer to the train and match its speed. We'd even lined up nicely with an open freight car.

Henry caught hold of the ladder rungs and hauled himself up onto the ladder and into the car as if he'd been born to it.

I half expected someone to shout out some kind of alarm, only no one did. I followed Henry, first grabbing the ladder and hauling myself up, then swinging my leg so I could jump off the ladder and into the darkened opening of the rail car. I landed with a loud clang that made me cringe. But Henry was right there and still no one was raising any kind of alarm.

I reached for Faith to help her up.

"It's speeding up," Henry said. "Hurry!"

He was right. The engine must have crested the hill and the entire train was now picking up speed. I swore, realizing I'd been too careful and waited too long.

Faith was running alongside, reaching out for the ladder, getting her hand on the rung but not getting a good grip. The train was still gaining speed now and Faith was running full-out just to keep up.

"Come on!" Henry shouted.

Faith got her hands on the ladder rungs with a little jump, but couldn't pull herself up. Her feet were still mostly on the ground and she was trying to run and hang on at the same time, her feet flailing frantically.

"Hold on!" I shouted. I leaned out to try and grab her other hand, grasping desperately, but it was just too far and I nearly toppled out of the car trying to lunge for her.

Faith tripped.

Her feet flew up and she just barely hung on, coming back down onto the ladder with a jarring impact that hurt just to watch.

One of her hands slipped. She was sobbing now, clinging with one hand on the ladder and the other flailing out.

"Reach for me!" I shouted, but she shook her head, refusing to even lift her head enough to look at me, sobbing pitifully.

I reached out again, nearly falling myself trying to get a hand on Faith and pull her over. The tips of my fingers just brushed her shoulder.

"Don't let go!" I shouted. The patches of snow and frozen ground were flying by now underneath us, dangerously fast. The clickety-clack of the train was getting faster.

"Look out," Henry said. "Let me do it!"

But there wasn't time! Henry wasn't any bloody taller than I was anyway.

Then a massive shape reared up behind us and my blood froze. We were caught for sure!

It came from the dark interior of the car, a huge shape. A hand the size of a soup plate grabbed my shoulder and yanked me out of the way. Henry, too. We both went sprawling back into the railway car.

Faith was sobbing as the shadow leaned out and seized her. I couldn't see her from this angle, but she screamed. The shape hauled her into the freight car then dropped her negligently next to us in a heap on the dusty slat-board floor of the car.

"Oh, god," Faith sobbed. "Oh, god!" She clutched at me as if floundering at sea.

"It's all right, Faith," I said, though I didn't at all know if that were true.

Our rescuer was a burly, bow-legged man with a bristly mustache and a battered bowler hat.

Just as I was trying to get a better look at him, a line of elm trees flickered by outside, blocking the sun so that I only had a nightmarish impression of heavy, dangling claws, saber-tooth fangs and a single glowing eye.

Faerie! It had to be!

Then the train whistle screamed and the trees cleared and he was just a man again, albeit a disreputable-looking one. Behind him, the freight car was packed with crates that shifted and swayed gently with the motion of the train.

I squinted carefully at the man, closing first my ghost eye, then the other, to try and see what the flickering shadows had briefly revealed, but the man remained unchanged. His face was very wide, with black matted hair, small black eyes, and that large black bristly mustache. He had on a frayed suit worn to the color of old newspaper with a bright yellow pull cord dangling from the vest in place of a watch chain. He limped forward, revealing one foot that twisted at a permanent angle.

Still, my instincts clamored while the three of us huddled together, stunned, on the freight car floor.

While we stared, he swept the bowler off his head in a rough parody of a gentleman's manner.

"Well," he said, "there's a bit of a caper for you, eh?" I realized from the voice that he wasn't a man at all, but a boy about my age, even with that scraggly mustache. He'd seemed older at first just because he was so huge.

The huge boy leaned over us. Underneath the mustache, he gave an oversized, jagged smile that was about the least comforting thing in the world, but then he jerked his head back in surprise.

"Devil be damned, girl!" he thundered. "What's wrong with yer *eye?*"

"Nothing!" I blurted out, which wasn't going to do for an answer at all. "Childhood accident," I finally mumbled.

Henry scrabbled to his feet and stood protectively in front of Faith and me, his hands clenched into fists.

It was a patently ridiculous thing to do. The other boy was huge. Henry barely came to his chest. The steadfast courage of it took my breath away and even Faith stopped sobbing. I scrambled to my feet, too, and Faith, after a moment, followed suit.

The boy's grin twisted even larger, but his eyes glittered dangerously and his hands flexed menacingly at his sides. No one said anything for a long moment. There was just the creaking of the boxcar, the swaying of the crates all around, and the rattling of the wheels below us on the track.

"Just you stay where you are!" Henry said.

"There's no need for all this," said a girl, stepping out from behind a stack of crates. "I assure you, you're quite safe 'ere." She was also about our age, very pretty, with wild hair the color of ripe cherries and a mouth painted to match. She had large green eyes, but also a long nose that twitched and a mouth that, like her companion, had more predator in it than anything else. She wore an oxblood dress that hung in tatters, revealing far more leg than fabric, as well as gloves and boots of the same reddish color. A scandalous perfume wafted off her, filling the boxcar with the scent of petal blossoms, cheap alcohol and something dark and metallic that might have been blood. The scandalous look would have been disconcerting enough on a woman, but on a girl, it was even more so.

"Don't mind the bruiser," she went on. "'E don't mean no 'arm, despite 'is looks."

"Well, o' course I don't mean no 'arm!" the boy roared indignantly, seemingly confused why anyone would ever think otherwise.

"Why should we believe that?" Henry said, trying to be stern, but the effect was ruined when he glanced down at the girl's naked legs, blushed furiously, and looked away.

The girl saw his embarrassment and giggled, a strangely girlish sound from someone who'd clearly left her childhood and innocence long behind.

She draped herself insouciantly along the huge boy's side the way someone might lean against a wall, which had the same effect on the boy that it would on your average wall. He didn't budge an inch.

"Well," said the boy, "I shouldn't wonder if your nerves is a bit jangled. Now where are me manners? A bit of a shock, I'm sure, us comin' up on you like that, so . . . this 'ere is Victoria Rose, and every moocher who does the Mary Blaine calls me the Soho Shark."

"Every *what* that does the *who* does what?" Henry said.

The train whistle split the air again and Victoria Rose and the Soho Shark both grimaced.

"Rattlin' over metal rails like a shuttlecock," Victoria Rose said passionately when it had finished. "It jars my senses, it does."

"The Rose 'as got the right of it," the Soho Shark said. "Perhaps some of the bottle to calm the nerves a bit? Come . . . 'ave a sit." The huge boy gestured towards a gap between the stacks of boxes, where a small empty space was cleared out, with a few smaller boxes arranged for seating.

"I don't think . . ." I started.

But Victoria Rose had already taken Henry's hand and led him away, and there was nothing for Faith and me to do but follow.

"So," Victoria Rose said as we arranged ourselves. "What brings you pets to London?" She handed Henry the bottle, then watched happily as he drank.

Hours later, by the time the train slid into London, Henry, Victoria Rose and the Soho Shark were all a bit tipsy and fast friends. Faith and I kept exchanging looks, and she clearly had the same sour opinion I did of our new acquaintances, but neither of us had a way to pry Henry loose from them.

Even worse, Henry was telling Victoria Rose and the Soho Shark *everything*. Henry told them that we were originally from London and going back, but not to our home. He told them that our Father was in trouble and that we were going to try and sneak into Father's office at the Far East Trading Company, on Threadneedle Street, in order to help him.

"Investigating a strange piece of business," Henry said for the third time, clearly liking both the sound of it and the look of approval that an older girl like Victoria Rose gave him every time he said it.

"We'd be happy to show the way," Victoria Rose said.

"Out of the goodness of your heart?" I sneered.

Victoria Rose gave me a ferrety smile. "Why not?"

"Because no one goes out of their way for nothing," I said.

Victoria Rose shrugged. "Why not?" she said again.

"Wonderful!" Henry said as if that decided everything. He waved the bottle so expansively that he fell off his crate and the Soho Shark had to haul him back up.

Slipping off the train just before we arrived at the station was a tricky bit of work, jumping at a near run, but even Faith managed it without mishap. The Soho Shark led us between two buildings and we quickly found ourselves on a dirty street, squalid, cold, and deserted, with the railway track out of sight behind us.

An enormous stench lay all around us, thick as dust. The whole street stank of blood and chemicals and gleamed like an oil slick from the foul runoff from a tannery that mixed with an earlier rain.

"Oh god," Faith said.

"That's better," Victoria Rose said, seeming to take no notice of Faith's comment or the foul stench. "I can breathe a bit better now that I'm out of that infernal boxcar."

Faith and I, and even Henry, stared at her.

"Now then," the Soho Shark said. "I think we goes this way." He pointed around the corner of the tannery, where brownish wisps of fog curled around the wet bricks.

"Right!" Henry crowed, following eagerly.

"Good boy." Victoria Rose said, smiling with red-stained lips.

Henry beamed. He and the Soho Shark led the way, chummy as thieves, while Faith and I followed, with Victoria Rose shepherding us from the rear.

We left the tannery behind, at first for the alleyways behind a slaughterhouse, then through a neighborhood of dilapidated Georgian apartments. Then we left the cobblestones of the smaller streets for the macadam of a main road and I saw that the Soho Shark had indeed been right as we joined the crowds heading for the London Bridge. Henry dodged around a shellfish cart and through a line of men wearing haberdashery sandwich boards, and we followed.

A few people picked out my black eye, but their gazes slid away again an instant later. I'd expected people to point and shout, but my eye seemed barely worth comment. Certainly I saw worse, blemishes and scars and amputations that made my mark seem almost trivial by comparison. The crush of people around us on the walkway was simply astonishing and I was so pressed by the crowd that it became a struggle to keep Faith and Henry in sight. I was actually glad for the Soho Shark's massive bulk to follow, or we might easily have been separated.

When the flow of the crowd jostled me closer to the railing, we could see boats of all shapes and sizes fighting their way through a dreary wash of yellowed fog below us. The fog grew thicker and even the people on either side of us dimmed to whispering apparitions.

A cool wind tore a tattered hole in the fog and revealed a long, twisted black root that ran for at least fifty feet along the stonework of the bridge.

"What in the world?" I stammered.

"What?" Faith said, clearly not finding anything alarming. She didn't see it.

An enormous tree root, splayed across London Bridge like a massive hand.

And no one seemed to notice anything about it except me.

The cart traffic navigated around it, while the pedestrians clambered over. Dozens of people going out of their way to avoid it and yet *somehow* not seeming to notice it at the same time. How could that be?

Then the fog cleared some more, and I saw the rest of the tree.

I couldn't take it all in, at first. No tree could be so big. Massive fingers of root and moss clung to the far side of the bridge and a great black eldritch mass rose up, up, taller than the Parliament building, taller than St. Barts. Unsavory things *lived* up there, too, for I saw the occasional flicker of burning eyes way up in the boughs and limbs, but never for more than a heartbeat.

The shadow the tree cast covered everything like a darkening storm. London Bridge, the Thames, the City proper. All of it lay in shadow. I looked down at the spiral of cracks from where the roots dug into the stonework of the bridge. The bridge was being torn apart. When it finally collapsed and the tree settled in, who knew what that would do to the river? Threadneedle Street could well be underwater after that.

The press of the crowd had brought me right up to the root, a waist-high barrier. I half thought my hand might pass right through it, but it didn't. Still more people were climbing over, in a daze.

I reached out and touched the root. The bark was rough and cold to the touch. It was real. It wasn't a ghost, like Étienne and Percy. So why didn't anyone acknowledge it?

I realized then that the battlefield full of bodies we'd seen on the way here was just the beginning. If the Faerie Father had told us about could do something like *this* (and who else could it be?) then London had no hope. How could you fight something like this that could tear London apart and not even be noticed?

This, *this*, was how the Faerie made war.

"Justice?" Faith said. "Why have you stopped?" She nudged me to keep going forward.

The Soho Shark and Victoria Rose exchanged a surprised look. I couldn't tell what they saw and what they didn't, but they clearly knew something was going on when I stopped.

A seething anger welled up inside me as I stared at these two schemers, who I was sure were Faerie spies. I needed to do something about all of this, starting with them. But now wasn't the time. I thought about maneuvering around the root, but impulsively changed my mind and started climbing up. It was a good ten or so feet up and over and the others followed me without comment. Their eyes took on an odd glazed look while they climbed, even the Shark and Rose.

I rolled this last bit of information around in my head for a bit. I was certain they were Faerie, and the idea that the Faerie could fall prey to their own illusions struck me as an important one.

I was the first one to clamber down the other side, which afforded me an opportunity to turn and cover my left eye. I wanted to see what things looked like with just my normal eye.

The bridge looked completely unfettered when viewed that way. No tree, no roots, nothing untoward or exceptional. Just the London Bridge on a wet, foggy London day.

I tried looking with just my ghost eye and the roots, tree and shadows were all back.

I gave the Soho Shark and Victoria Rose the same treatment.

With just my normal eye, they both appeared less garish, far more ordinary. Odd and shiftless, certainly, but only in a mundane, non-magical sort of way. Not at all dangerous.

Viewed with my left eye, they were something else altogether. It was different than with the tree, which was just hidden, or not. With the Shark and the Rose, whatever enchantment it was that changed their appearance, it had layers in it. They didn't just look dangerous, they looked *inhuman*. I'd tried the same trick, at least with the Shark, on the train, and found nothing. Why was it different here?

But it was, and I was sure that *this* version of our two guides was far closer to the truth.

The Shark's face looked far more savage, his mouth overlarge, the eyes flat and lifeless and cruel, with one eye of gold, and slit vertically, like a goat's. The other was missing entirely, showing just an empty socket. An enormous pair of curved ram's horns protruded out of the top of his head. His hands were enormous talons.

Victoria Rose also looked cruel, dangerous, and feral viewed this way. A fox-woman with a vicious mouth filled with pointed teeth, she had tall ears and a reddish-furred face. Her hands were also talons, though far smaller than the Soho Shark's.

So there were layers to Faerie illusion. There were also degrees to which my ghost eye could penetrate that illusion. It wasn't like a switch and probably by no means completely foolproof. I filed all this away and began to plan.

On the other side of the bridge, I saw more signs of the Faerie incursion. A lot more.

Thick roots possessed the curbs and pushed up through the macadam. Woodland streams ran through the brickwork of shops, police stations, banks, and apartments without human impediment or response. Everywhere I looked, the city was crumbling away, pushed back, and eroded by the intruding world of the Faerie, and no one could see it but me.

# CHAPTER 9

## Widdershins

For another hour, we walked in the shadow of that massive tree. We crossed London Bridge and past Fishmonger's Wharf and up King William Street and into the city proper, passing through a pedestrian crowd that couldn't see that the statue of William at the Cannon Street crossroads was choked and crumbling under an ivy assault. King William Street angled left, which eventually carried us past the post office, which was smothered in brilliant green mushrooms. Even St. Mary's Church was covered with briar and thistle.

Finally, as we turned onto Threadneedle and passed the mammoth Royal Exchange, we got out from under the malignant shadow and I breathed much easier.

There was no Faerie overgrowth here, as if it required the shadow of the tree to thrive. Everything, like the Royal Exchange, was just as I expected it, no matter what eye I used to look at it. The Romanesque columns of the Exchange were brilliant in the sun and I'd never been so happy before to see them.

The Far East India Trading Company was ensconced in a great limestone building, between a high-end shop that sold watches from Switzerland and a lawyer's office that boasted a clientele that included royalty. Luxury apartments sat above, pristine and lovely. None of the overgrowth had made it this far.

We hid ourselves in the narrow crevice of an alley formed between a theater and more luxury apartments. It wasn't ideal, but it overlooked the street directly across from the office. There was some sort of construction happening further back in the alley, only it had apparently gotten late enough in the day that all of the construction workers were gone. The top of the alley behind us was covered with planks forming a temporary and rickety walkway ten feet above us, supported by upright boards lining the alley. A potent and unpleasant smell of the outhouse clung to the bricks.

"Ugh," Faith said. "Lovely."

"So this is where your Father holes up, eh?" The Shark said. "When he's not at Storm . . . what did you call it?"

"Stormholt," Henry said. He looked at me. "Aren't we going in?"

"No," I said. "We watch and we wait." I leaned against the theatre corner where I had some shelter from the street but could still see Father's office. Evening was starting around us, turning the already bleak sky above us dark.

"Oh," Henry said, crestfallen. The Soho Shark and Victoria Rose shared an uneasy glance.

"Just wait, then?" the Soho Shark said.

"Just wait," I said without looking around.

The Far East Trading Company was larger than the other shops, but there was nothing else to mark it as extraordinary. I would have expected a big office like that to have visitors, but the door never budged.

Perhaps our supposedly-dead sister Prudence was waiting inside, like the note said, or perhaps she wasn't and it was some sort of lure. Either way, if we wanted to find out what was going on, this seemed our best lead.

But before that, we had to find a way to shake off the Faerie watchdogs.

In the end, this was a problem the Faerie were going to solve for me, but I didn't know that yet.

Faith leaned against the side of the building next to me. "What are we going to do?" she said in a low voice. "What if Father's *in there*? It is his office. We have no idea if this Prudence will be there, or why she wants us there."

Victoria Rose stepped closer to us, a sly smile on her face, and opened her mouth to say something, probably something I didn't want to hear . . .

But nothing came out. She staggered and her hands flew to her head.

Then a hammer slammed into my mind.

I sagged against the wall as it hit. I couldn't think, couldn't breathe. I could see through watering eyes that everyone around me was staggering and moaning. Henry, Faith, Victoria Rose, even the Soho Shark.

The pressure in my head increased, like a cold, gloved hand in my brain, squeezing, squeezing.

I saw, through the pain, a man dressed in black step out into the square of light down at the end of the alley. He was thin, not tall, with a suit, cloak, and top hat all of deepest black. Most of his face lay in shadow, throwing the silver disks of his spectacles into sharp prominence.

Those silver discs burned as the grip on my mind increased. Blood dripped on the pavement stones beneath me. My blood. Seeping out of my nose. He lifted his hands, encased in two pale gloves. I could feel those chill gloved fingers sifting through the images of my mind as if they were old photographs, tearing and discarding with a casual brutality.

I shook my head, fighting this profoundly intimate violation, but it was like swinging at shadows. There was no way to fight it. Even lifting my head was an impossibility.

The white gloves pushed deeper.

I was barely aware of the Soho Shark trying to crawl feebly towards him. A broken moan tore out of me. The others must have been suffering the same way, as a chorus of moans and sobs surrounded me. Then . . . tentatively at first, a song.

It was Faith.

Faith sang, very softly. Her voice slid through the darkness, a knife through a curtain, and the pressure in my head slipped, just a little.

Then, a second voice joined the song. Except there wasn't any second singer. Faith opened her mouth and two voices came out. I didn't understand how, but I knew my sister's voice. Voices.

Then a third voice came out of Faith's mouth, interwoven with the first two like the sweetest, most pure trio of sopranos you ever heard. Moonlight on clear, clear water. The song was wordless, lovely, glorious.

The pressure in my head was gone. The pain stopped and I could think again.

Faith sang *at* the shadowy gentleman, who staggered, gave a thin cry that echoed off the bricks, and fell against the wall. He waved a hand weakly in our direction. "Silence . . . her . . ."

Several shaggy creatures dropped down from the construction platform as we all struggled to our feet. Scabrous Irish wolfhound faces snarled at us, gray and dead. They growled and the smell of wet wolf filled the alley. Underneath lay the sickly-sweet stench of carrion.

Faith's face went white and her song faltered.

"I want the children alive!" the dark gentleman screamed. "Alive! I don't care what happens to the other two."

I was sure that the dark gentleman, the cadaverous wolves, and our unwanted guides all *had* to be Faerie. What else could they be? So why weren't they working together? But there was no doubt that they weren't as the wolves came in for blood.

The first two wolves hit the Soho Shark while he was still getting to his feet. They bore him down, howling and tearing at his throat and face.

With a twelve-foot bound, Victoria Rose darted forward. She had a blade in her hand, though I hadn't seen where it came from. But it was there, about two-and-a-half feet long and brilliant in the half light. Silver. It flashed and one of the wolves staggered. The other lifted its muzzle from the business of trying to get at the Soho Shark's jugular and lunged at her, but Victoria Rose jumped sideways out of reach, nimble as a mongoose.

That respite was all the Shark needed.

One massive hand seized the throat of the wolf still on him and a fist the size of a cantaloupe smashed into its face. The wolf went down and the Soho Shark was up, the boy's massive barge of a body blocking the corridor.

"Come on, then, little puppies." The Shark's hands flexed eagerly. "Come to Sharkie."

The wolf Victoria Rose had wounded was back up, dragging a rear limb as it snapped its huge jaws repeatedly, forcing Victoria Rose back. She slashed open two gashes on its muzzle. But the beast faltered only briefly and kept coming. None of the wounds bled.

"Run!" I said. "We have to get out of here!" I grabbed Faith and Henry and tried to haul them back into the street away from danger.

Too late. One of the other wolves had leapt clear over the battle and now loped towards us.

Then Henry did a surprising thing.

My little brother wrenched free one of the two-by-four planks supporting the walkway above and swung it as if it weighed no more than a cricket bat. I couldn't believe what I'd just seen. Faith's magical voice, my eye, and now . . . this? What was *happening* to us?

Henry's blow came down on the wolf thing with crushing force. The heavy plank broke across the creature's back and the wolf swayed. But then it stood up again. Henry's astounding blow would have killed full-grown oxen outright, this thing was just dazed.

Henry swung again, but the shortened beam had even less effect this time, and the beast backhanded the board to one side and fell onto Henry with a wicked howl. They both went down hard enough to take out another support beam.

The ceiling groaned ominously as the wooden walkway above us threatened to give way.

Victoria Rose was suddenly moving past us. "Run!"

"Henry!" I shouted. "I'm not leaving him!"

But I couldn't even see him anymore because two more of the wolves had moved between us and Henry's struggle.

Victoria Rose whirled and slashed with her blade at another of the support planks. Amazingly, her knife went clean through two inches of wood. Dust trickled down as the walkway groaned above us. I couldn't even *see* Henry.

"Run!" Victoria Rose said again, and shoved. Faith and I stumbled into the street, followed by Victoria Rose.

The walkway collapsed down into the alley in a great avalanche of broken boards and dust and splinters that covered everything and everybody behind us. I couldn't see Henry, the Soho Shark, any of the wolves or the gentleman in black.

The ground seemed to drop out from underneath me.

"No!" I sobbed.

Victoria Rose had both Faith and me by our wrists now, hauling us across the street towards Father's office at a near run. Her grip was shockingly strong. We dodged a cabby and a few pedestrians, all of whom were slowing to see what kind of disturbance was going on in the alley.

"No," I said again, struggling, but Victorian Rose held on tight. "Henry! They've got Henry!"

"He's gone!" Victoria Rose snapped. "You can't help him anymore, and more of the Cu Sith will be coming. That won't hold *them* for long."

"Cooshee *what*?" I said.

Victoria Rose towed us across the street and into the opposite alley behind the Far East India Trading Company. Faith was sobbing uncontrollably again, and I kept saying, "No, no . . ." and trying to turn around, but she got us there anyway.

"Wait!" I said, and this time managed to get my arm free. We were behind Father's building now near a door with a heavy chain and padlock. I pulled a hairpin out of my pocket.

"No time," Victoria said and knocked the lock open with a sharp blow from the handle of her sword.

Howling came from down the street. Victoria Rose wasn't wrong. The things she'd called Cu Sith were going to be here any second from the sound of it.

We all rushed through into the building. Faith and I struggled to close the door, a heavy thing made of wood on the outside but lined with metal on the inside.

"Wait," Victoria Rose said, blanching white. The Faerie girl swayed in the middle of the room, looking very sick.

Snarling came from the other side of the door, but very distantly.

Then I looked around and realized just how lucky we'd gotten. This was no ordinary room.

The room was a fortress, heavily fortified. The walls were sturdy brick, with long black metal strips laid across the walls and hammered into place with black railroad spikes. The floor was made of packed dirt, with more railroad spikes hammered in every five feet or so. More iron covered the door so completely that I couldn't even see the wood underneath except in one patch about five feet off the ground to be used as a peephole. I touched the rough metal. Black iron. This place was protected from the Faerie in the same manner Stormholt had been.

I didn't think we had to worry about the Faerie getting into this place any time soon.

There were piles of crates stacked against the righthand wall, labeled as various food items, next to several barrels. The nearest one was open and I could see it was filled with railroad spikes and I remembered the barrels of the same spikes that the sailors had brought to our townhouse in Devonshire Terraces.

Lanterns hung from the ceiling every six feet or so. Oil lanterns, not gas-lit. On the other side of the room was another door of black iron with another peephole.

I went back to Victoria Rose, who had sunk to her knees in the hard-packed dirt. She looked up at me. "Where have you brought me?" she said.

I stared down at her for a moment, feeling a cold space open up inside of me. Henry, my little brother, had just been killed or taken prisoner by the Faerie. Even if this Faerie and those Faeries weren't working together. It was the Faerie who took them. It was the Faerie that had Mother and Joshua, too, and the Faerie that were trying their hardest to get Father and all the rest of us.

Now we had one of the Faerie and it was time to get some answers.

Victoria still held her blade, but could barely lift it. I kicked her arm and the silver weapon dropped to the dirt floor. I picked it up. Silver and black iron. Both seemed to have useful properties for fighting the Faerie. Victoria Rose made a feeble protest, but I ignored that.

"Justice?" Faith said. "What are you doing? She just saved us!"

I ignored her, too.

I pushed on Victoria Rose's shoulder and she toppled from her kneeling position to sprawl on her back. She hissed when the bare flesh on her upper arm (above the long, red gloves) hit one of the spikes. When she tried to yank her arm back, I stepped on it, pinning it to the metal spike. Victoria Rose hissed gratifyingly in pain.

"You're Faerie," I said to her, letting up on her arm a minute.

"Justice," Faith said, "Stop it!"

"No," Victoria Rose gasped. "I'm just . . ."

I used my foot to pin her arm down again, holding it until she said, "Yes! Yes! Curse you, of course I'm Faerie."

"What did you want with us?"

"Your Father asked us to watch over you," Victoria hissed. "To protect you."

"A lie," I said. "Father wants us back at Stormholt and you were happy to traipse around London with us. You didn't even know where Father *was*. You were trying to find out." I leaned hard on her arm. The fox-like girl moaned, a long and tortured sound. Her arm made a sizzling noise, like rashers frying. My stomach twisted at the sound, but I tried hard to keep that out of my face.

"Justice!" Faith said again.

The Faerie girl shook her head, then groaned. "Yes! Yes, it's true! We were sent to spy on the Lord o' Thorns." Her other hand tugged ineffectually at my boot, but she was too weak to stop me.

"Who?" Faith said.

The Faerie girl had a laugh like a hissing cobra. "Oh, you know him, sure enough."

"Our father," I said, "he's this Lord of Thorns?"

"Yes," Victoria Rose nodded.

I lifted my boot.

Victoria Rose's arm came away from the metal with an ugly black burn exactly the shape of size of the head of the railway tie. A sickening smell of cooked meat filled the room. She glared up at me, her brown eyes seething with hate. If she ever had a chance to hurt me, the desire to take it was written plainly on her face.

"Why were you on the train?" I said.

She frowned, not wanting to answer, and I lifted my foot again. Victoria Rose's face went very white.

"We were followin' the Lord o' Thorns," she said hastily.

"We already established that. Why?"

She glared at me. "Our general is tryin' to track 'is movements so they can make a guess as to 'is defenses, only we never could. We think 'e's got some way of movin' about that we can't follow. Our thought was to follow *you* instead and see what we'd learn." She looked around the room. "You should let me go. It's not too late for me to forgive you. But if you don't . . . well . . . this black iron won't *always* be 'ere, you know. All the black iron in the world won't stop us anyway. Not forever."

"We'll see," I said. "What about Henry? Where are they taking him?"

Victoria Rose actually shivered and seemed for a second to forget all about Faith and me. "If 'e's lucky, 'e's dead. Even my people fear Widdershins. The Black Shuck 'as some control over 'im, but even 'e can't keep 'im in check all the time."

"Who's the Black Shuck?" I was starting to feel out of my depth. So many names I'd never heard of.

"'E commands all our forces," she said. "Our general, though I don't know as that's the right word."

"If you both work for the same commander, why are you fighting each other?"

"I don't know!" she said. "The Black Shuck ordered *us* 'ere, I swear it! I don't know what game Widdershins is playin'. 'E's mad! 'E always 'as been. I would 'ave said 'e was unstoppable, but you . . ." She turned to look at Faith, curiosity warring with fear in her face. "But, you. You stopped 'im, didn't you? I won't pretend to understand 'ow."

She looked at Faith with a curious awe on her expression. Faith and I exchanged a look, but didn't say anything, because we didn't want to let on that *we* had no idea ourselves how Faith had pulled off that particular trick.

I couldn't get any more out of Victoria Rose after that. Her fear of the black iron was potent enough, she just didn't know any more. After another fruitless half an hour of questioning, the Faerie girl passed out. She didn't look like she was going to go anywhere, but I used the belt of my coat to lash her hands behind her back anyway.

Next, I wanted to see what else was in this building.

"Faith," I said. "Help me move one of these crates." We wrestled one of the crates over and, getting up on my toes, I was able to peer through. No indication of any kind of Faerie plot in the Far East Trading Company offices that I could see, just a normal-looking room with desks and chairs. If someone had gone to enormous lengths to put together the most ordinary office imaginable— almost extraordinary in its ordinariness—it would have looked just like that one.

But checking out the rest of the room, we found something much more extraordinary.

A small gate sat in the corner, hidden before by some of the stacked boxes. Behind that was the strangest-looking door I'd ever seen.

It was round and very yellow in a way that reminded me of Mr. Sands. An ornate border of reddish cobblestones ran around the rim. Someone had nailed a copper coin resembling an extremely old penny near the top. A wooden handle carved like a mermaid and a dolphin swimming together was fixed on the righthand side. The more we looked at it, the more the peculiarity of it stood out. The wood was actually yellow, for instance, and the stones were really red. None of that was paint or stain. Red stones I could imagine, but I didn't know any tree that color of yellow.

I reached for the handle.

"Wait, Justice," Faith said, but I pulled anyway.

I was more than a little surprised when it opened. Inside the door we found another surprise: a mirror.

The mirror was strange, too, the glass finer than any I'd seen before, unbelievably smooth. I tapped it gingerly with my fingers and gasped when the mirror *moved*.

Ripples spread outward from the place I'd dipped my finger in, lapping after a five- or six-second delay at the red stones on the outer edge. It was like a forest pool stood up on edge.

"Why doesn't it slosh out all over the floor?" Faith said in wonder.

"No idea," I said.

"What is it?"

"I don't know, but I'd bet my new hat this is what someone wanted us to find."

"I wish you would," Faith said. "It's a terrible hat."

"Shut up," I said with a grin. "This hat is amazing. I wonder . . ."

"What?" Faith said.

"Well, it *looks* like a door," I said, "and Victoria Rose said that Father has a way of moving around that they can't track. Maybe it's a door to Faerie."

"Oh god," Faith said. "You want to go through it, don't you?"

"Maybe we can go through and find Father," I said, talking more quickly now. "We need to find him, tell him about Henry. He can do something."

"If he's even our Father," Faith said suddenly. "That's what he says, but how do we know that's true?"

"What are you talking about?"

"You've seen what Faerie magic can do," Faith said. "Illusions, disguises, hidden ghosts. I remember the stories. All of Faerie is tied up in illusion and glamor and all sorts of mind games. Those things *are* Faerie."

"I guess."

"So what if the man posing as Father is being controlled by the Faerie, same as Mother?"

"He's been protecting us," I said. "That doesn't make sense. Would the Faerie do that?"

"Who knows?" Faith said. "But if you weren't so busy believing everything he said, you might pay attention to a few other things. Maybe there's a reason Mother got bitter. Mother's always said the Crimean War made him a different man. What if it's because they have some control over him?"

I didn't know what to say to that. Faith turned to stare at the Faerie door, so I couldn't see her face.

"We should have told you our concerns about Father before this," she said. "I know we should have. Benedict and I talked about it. But it was our secret together, and somehow it seemed right to keep it between us, even after Father dragged us out of our beds and all this happened." She touched the wooden door thoughtfully.

"What kind of concerns about Father? Why?"

She turned towards me but kept her gaze locked on her hands, which were picking at the material of her shirt. "All those times I accused *you* of having secrets. Well, I have one, too. Actually, it's one that Benedict and I have together."

"All right." I tried to keep my tone even. I could tell this was something enormous to Faith.

"It was two years ago, just before Benedict went to school. The night before your birthday, actually. Benedict and I were both up very late, talking. Neither of us were very happy, and we heard music coming from outside. This was before Mother moved us here to London, so, you know, the country house. Well, Benedict and I went out, in our nightclothes, and saw Father walking out into the wood. That's where the music was coming from."

"So we followed," Faith went on, "and instead of the woods we knew, there was a dance hall among the trees. A grand spectacle with what must have been a hundred torches and a whole mess of people dancing. Only they weren't really people. I didn't know what they were at the time, but I do now."

She pointed at the unconscious Victoria Rose. "They were like *her*. Faerie. I know it sounds ridiculous, but it was *there*."

The room felt odd, canted. My head not right. All this time, I thought that my dream in the forest *was* just a dream, but also, somehow that it was my secret, and mine alone. I let out a deep breath, as if something terrible trapped inside of me for all these years was finally let free.

"No," I said. "I believe you." I couldn't help but imagine my own walk through the woods that night years ago, when I followed Father. I could *still* feel the weight of holding that secret in. I'd never dreamed for an instant that anyone else might have had a similar secret of their own.

She gave me a funny look.

"Well, the cherry on the cake was Father. He was there, too. Only he wasn't dancing. He was in the center playing chess with this . . ."

"The Faerie King," I said. "He has horns like a stag, one hand larger than the other, and a cloak of moss and dirt."

Faith looked at me. "You saw them, too. I thought we were the only ones."

"I thought I was the only one. I didn't see a party, or the dancing Faerie. Just Father and the Faerie King out in the woods. The Faerie King is just what I called him in my head. I don't know his real name. When I woke up the next morning, I thought it was just a dream, sort of. I didn't believe it, exactly, but I believed *in* it. I didn't think it was real, I just knew it was important. Recently, I found this, and I realized it had really happened." I pulled the horse chess piece from my pocket and showed her. "It's the chess piece from the game when I first saw the Faerie King. I *know* it is. But I found it in Father's study a week ago. The morning he came back."

"So you took it from Father's study?" she said in wonder. "You little thief!" She took the piece gingerly, holding it like it was a religious relic. "It feels . . . important, doesn't it? I don't know how an object feels important, but this does."

"It does," I said. "Somehow I feel like he's been holding onto it for me all these years. Like he meant for me to find it."

"Like he meant for you to steal this *one* thing from a room you weren't even supposed to be in?" She looked doubtful. She handed it back.

"That's why I think we should find Father," I said. "He knows about the Faerie. He'll know how to get Henry back."

"What if," Faith hesitated and then blurted it out. "What if Henry's *dead*?"

"He's *not* dead! But he might *be* dead in a few days if we don't find some way to help him, and we're not going to be able to do that here."

"You're missing the point of the story I told you," Faith said. "Didn't you see Father back at Stormholt? Something's happening to him. He used to the be the most amazing man I'd ever seen when we were little. He could do anything. Maybe all children feel that way about their Fathers, but . . . I don't think that any more. He's not what he used to be, if he ever was. He's been caught flat-footed by *all* of this. You heard him and Mr. Sands arguing, same as I did."

She took me by both arms, leaning close. "Justice," she said, "If *I* could see that Mother was unhappy and looking to leave, he should have seen it, too, and if she's really gone to Faerie, I don't think Father's going to be much help. He just wants to put us all back in Stormholt, which might be a good idea, except . . . if we can escape because cats like fish, it's not much protection, is it? You really think that's going to keep the Faerie out after what we saw in that field?"

"So who, then?" I said. "Mother?" I still felt Father was our best option, but I wanted to hear what she had to say.

"No," she said, "Mother's . . . I don't know who she even is anymore. Joshua, either. They left us. At least Father's *trying* to help us, even if he's woefully overmatched. I'm just saying we might be on our own on this."

I looked back at the door to the alleyway, thinking of the monster tree and the moving wolf corpses that had taken Henry. "There's more. London's not safe. There's Faerie plants and trees all over that no one else can see but me. I don't think the Faerie are going to invade. I think, somehow, they're already here!"

Faith gasped. "How?"

"I don't know," I said. "But we can't stay here. Besides, this is the only thing I can think of to help Henry."

Faith thought about that and reluctantly nodded. She looked at the door. "So, we see if this thing really goes to Faerie?"

"I don't see that we have much choice."

Faith looked over at Victoria Rose, unconscious and still with her face twisted in unconscious pain. "We can't leave her here. This place might kill her."

Looking at the Faerie girl's face, her labored breathing, I had to concede that it might.

"I guess we don't have much choice there, either," I said. Sighing, I retrieved Victoria Rose's silver sword from the floor. We couldn't carry her outright but managed to each hold onto one of her arms near the elbow. Hopefully, we wouldn't have to drag her too far. Holding her with one hand and the sword with the other, I faced the door. Faith did too.

"Ready?" I said.

"No," Faith said.

We stepped into the pool anyway, dragging our prisoner of war behind us.

# CHAPTER 10

## Henry: Interrogation

H enry groaned in the darkness. He was lying on his side, holding his head in his hands and praying his head wouldn't split. The rattling of the police wagon went straight through his battered head and jostled every ache in his back and wrists. His wrists hurt because of the manacles, which jangled with every bump, making his head ache more. The rhythm of the wagon changed as it slowed, turned, became muffled by passage over wooden planks, and then finally came to a stop.

A bolt slid back somewhere behind him and the doors opened up with a rusty groan. His legs wouldn't work right so two constables had to climb in and drag him out. Henry was about to beg the constables to release him, telling him that there'd been some kind of mistake, before the reek hit him. Underneath the blue, domed, constable helmets, even shadowed as they were, Henry could see they were dead. Dead like the wolves that had attacked him and his sisters in the alley, only these were men. Men long dead, with ghastly, bloodless gray skin and sores all over and dead mouths filled with rotting teeth, but somehow still moving around in a ghastly parody of the living.

The rain felt cold on Henry's face, and turned the gas streetlights into blue and yellow halos. The light gave Henry a better look at his captors' faces and he wished they hadn't. Their necks, all of them, were horrid tatters of gray ribbons, ripped open long ago. Somehow, Henry was certain these had once been real constables, until the dead wolves had murdered them, ripped their throats out to a man. Fear and the reek all around him made Henry's stomach rebel, and he emptied it onto the cobblestones of a small courtyard.

A short distance away, several of the undead wolves sat or paced as they watched the dead men drag Henry out. The wolves had the air of being in charge of the entire affair. One of them barked and the dead constables hastily dragged Henry to his feet again.

Henry realized, as he saw the forbidding building, just exactly where they were. It was built of heavy blocks, expressly for the permanent purpose of shutting the light of day out, and the inmates in. They were at Newgate Prison.

There was no one else in sight but the rotting things and him. The sounds of a cat yowling came from somewhere up near the roof. The metal-reinforced door swung open and the dead constables hurried him through into blackness. The wolves padded behind, and then the door, without any visible assistance, closed behind them with a heavy boom and ponderous finality.

They all stood in a long hall. One entire wall was covered with an extensive collection of chains, manacles, and shackles hung from metal pegs. Small blue gas lights burned in each corner without shedding much light.

The reek of the place, even more sickening than the dead flesh of men and beast all around, made Henry felt the need to vomit again, but there was nothing left. Henry knew, then and there, that even if he managed to survive the night, the week, the year, he would forever have the stink of them in his nose and throat.

The men stepped back, as if this place was no longer in their domain, and the wolves drove Henry forward by snapping at his heels. Henry screamed and scrambled away from those yellow teeth, which sent him through an open door and deeper into Newgate.

They herded him, them snarling and him screaming, through a wide corridor and many turns, past iron-bound closed doors, finally turning into a little-used, narrow staircase leading up. There was an iron gate and another undead constable at the top of the stairs. His neck was shackled to the wall, but he also acted as turnkey, as if he'd been imprisoned there specifically for the use of his human hands. This shuffling corpse, too, had his neck torn out, cementing Henry's certainty of how they'd become corpses in the first place.

The wolves drove Henry through that gate and into another dark corridor. There was another ridiculously superfluous gate and shackled turnkey at the end of this hall before they got to the next one. Henry was nearly screamed out by now, his throat raw from it, but he still gasped and sobbed as he stumbled down the hall.

The main source of light there was a dull and lurid red glow that came from a stove down the hall. All down the left side were identical heavy doors that led to the cells, the way inadequately lit with faltering candles. They chased Henry down to the door at the very end.

These locks weren't to be trusted to a human-shaped warden, it seemed, because one of the wolves used his teeth to seize an oversized key from a hook on the wall and managed, clumsily, to unlock and open the door.

Henry's cell was a stone dungeon barely large enough to pace in. A small high window on the back wall, crossed with double rows of heavy iron bars, admitted very little moonlight or breeze. His manacles were removed and Henry fell onto the naked bench under window, shivering uncontrollably on the hard wood.

They left him there. He slept like the dead.

◄◄◊►◄◊►◄◊►►

He jolted awake later with a shout that echoed off the stone walls. He sat gasping on the bench for a short time, then got painfully to his feet.

His door had a large, heavy grate. He looked out into the hallway and flinched when he saw that his wolf wardens were standing watch over the door. They sat, two dark shadows in the faint candle light, facing his cell as if there were no other prisoners in all of Newgate to attract their attention but him.

They didn't pant like wolves, or even breathe as far as Henry could tell. They sat entirely still, like foul machines gone suddenly inert.

The high window behind him was still dark. More gates clanged down the hall, this time closer. Henry's hands gripped the grate hard enough to cut off the blood to his fingers. Someone was coming.

The two sentries stirred themselves suddenly, whining and slinking down to their bellies. This frightened Henry even more. What creature struck fear into wolf corpses?

The farthest candle in the hall, flickering all this while, guttered out.

Henry had the impression somehow that the light might still be burning, but obscured by . . . something. The next furthest candle winked out and one of the wolves whined and Henry gripped the grate harder to keep his hands from shaking. In the weak light, Henry could make out black smoke rolling down the hall towards him.

The candle directly across from Henry's cell door was the only light left now.

The darkness shifted and *it* came out.

Another zombie wolf.

No. This was bigger, lots bigger, a *huge*, shaggy beast the size of a cart horse that walked on all fours. Henry sensed somehow that this wolf shape was the primal source of the other wolf creatures. This, *this* was the real monster.

It crossed the open space in absolute silence. Nothing that huge should be able to move without making any noise. The other two wolves slithered out of its way.

It sat in front of Henry's cell and regarded him from the other side of the grate. It was a gruesome regard, Henry realized with a cold pit opening in his stomach, because it had *no eyes*. Only empty sockets. There was also a ring of hairless pink flesh running around its neck from where someone, long ago, had tried to hang the beast and failed.

But as horrific looking as the thing was, that was as nothing compared to the terrifying presence of the thing. A nightmarish panic rolled off the thing in waves. It hit Henry like a sledge hammer to the gut and he cringed back from the door.

He flung himself into the farthest corner from the door and even crawled frantically under the hard bench. It was as much as he could do not to pass out. He lay, shivering, under the bench and tried not to scream. Little whimpering noises were escaping from him and he could not control them.

Someone else was approaching now.

Henry could distantly hear the clicking sound of boot heels. It was the gentleman in black. Somehow, Henry just knew it. Damn! Damn, damn! A heavy clang and the lock of his door snapped open. The door creaked and boot heels walked into the room. There was a walking stick, too, tap tap. The bench creaked as the Gentleman sat, but still Henry cowered under it, unable to open his eyes. Unable to do anything but whisper to himself: "Please, please, just go away. Leave me alone. Please."

"Now then," a thin, aristocratic voice said. He rapped thoughtfully on the bench with his walking stick. "Let see what you know, shall we?"

The Gentleman crouched and dragged Henry out from underneath bench with one white-gloved hand. Henry got a flash of white gloves before the Gentleman got a fistful of Henry's hair and hauled his head back, before settling comfortably back on the bench.

The white gloves were in his mind now, rifling through an old box of intangible photographs. They sorted through memories of school, home, early childhood, things Henry barely remembered himself. Shuffling, discarding, looking for something. Images of family dinners when he was young, Father holding a glass of wine, Henry playing at pirates with Joshua when they were both little,

Mother laughing, a Christmas dinner at the country house before they came to London. Too many pictures to count . . . The gloves were systematically digging for information, but they paused every time they found a picture of Mother. Why?

The fingers in Henry's mind paused, hesitated, as if overhearing the question. Widdershins. The man's name was Widdershins, and he was suddenly very nervous. Henry was supposed to be in mental shambles by now. Henry could feel all this, and the sudden knowledge sluiced Henry's own terror away.

"What does he know about the Lord of Thorns?" the wolf thing's voice grated. "Why are you taking so long?"

"It's nothing. He's more . . . resilient than I'd expected," Widdershins said, his voice straining. "Like *her.*"

"Forget her! What does he know of the Lord of Thorns?"

Widdershins grunted softly and leaned forward on the bench. He still had Henry's hair in his grip. He probed deeper, but it was costing him something.

More names drifted down to Henry. The monstrous wolf was the Black Shuck, the general of the Faerie Army, and it was one of the few creatures that frightened Widdershins. More frustration. Widdershins wasn't just taking information, but helplessly scattering it throughout Henry's mind in a messy uncontrolled manner. It was, Henry knew, entirely by accident, and it was making Widdershins furious. Henry wasn't just resilient, he was *fighting.*

His body was still paralyzed by fear, helpless at Widdershins' feet. But inside, Henry could push back. Henry felt torn and bruised inside, but otherwise intact. Most of Widdershins' victims were not so lucky, he now knew. Henry felt the barrier that he'd formed inside of his own mind, amazed something like that could come from inside of him.

"What does he know?" the Black Shuck said again.

"Nothing!" Widdershins snapped, his voice tight. "He knows nothing about the Lord of Thorns. Less than we do. Not even the name. There's nothing in here whatsoever about any defensive plans."

Interesting, Henry thought. Widdershins had been supposed to be looking for something else, but instead, he'd spent all that time on Mother.

"Then we're done," the Black Shuck said.

"As you wish." Widdershins let go of his grip on Henry's hair and stood up.

Then he swayed in place.

Widdershins tried to withdraw from Henry's mind and found that he couldn't. He couldn't seem to break his gaze away because *Henry wasn't letting go*. He was caught in Henry's grip now.

"What are you doing?" Widdershins said, suddenly very frightened. Henry plucked a whiff of real fear out of Widdershins' scattered thoughts.

"My turn," Henry croaked. He *pushed*.

He reached into Widdershins' mind and lashed about with vengeful fury, tearing, kicking, shredding whatever images he could find. Widdershins fell with a loud cry of pain.

Both of them lay panting on the dirty stone floor like exhausted boxers who couldn't get up.

"What just happened?" The Black Shuck demanded. "Is he a magician?" Henry suddenly noticed that the waves of fear coming off the Black Shuck no longer affected him like before. He could look at the beast squarely now without his insides turning to jelly, even if he couldn't stand up yet.

"He's nothing." Widdershins said, climbing slowly to his feet. "A nobody within an important family. Resilient, but otherwise unremarkable. Still, best to kill him." Widdershins snatched his fallen cane from the bench and yanked the handle free to reveal a long silver blade. He moved the blade to cut Henry's throat on the spot.

Henry shifted, tried to get out of the way, but his hands and feet still weren't working right.

The blade came closer.

"Stop," The Black Shuck said.

Widdershins hesitated, the gleaming sword swayed back and forth. "But . . ." Henry could still taste Widdershins' fear, and knew that the Faerie had deliberately lied to the Black Shuck about how much Henry was capable of, only Henry didn't know why.

"Not yet," the Black Shuck growled. "I promised someone else they could visit, before the end." He sounded cross having to repeat himself.

"As you wish," Widdershins finally said. He put the sword and cane scabbard back together with an irritable gesture and a sharp click. "The rope will have him soon enough."

❦❦❦

The early light trickling through the high window found Henry still lying on the cot, staring at the ceiling, wide awake. Henry had been lying here for hours, nursing a headache and waves of dizziness. Mostly, though, he was trying to sort out the new things rolling around in his head.

Henry knew so many new things.

Widdershins' powers allowed him to tear into the minds of others and reap their memories and knowledge. Which meant that some of the memories Henry had pulled from Widdershins hadn't actually happened to Widdershins, but to someone else.

Widdershins had stolen them from others, and now Henry had stolen them from Widdershins.

Which was how he knew that the Black Shuck wasn't any kind of dog or wolf, not really. He'd been a London man and a murderer who'd killed, hundreds of years ago, and been caught. After a swiftly casual trial, he was hanged. But the soul of the Black Shuck hadn't passed on to the realm of the dead, as it should have. The body passed, but the spirit remained, gradually taking the monstrous wolf shape. The Black Shuck straddled the area between the dead and living now, and he both remembered and hated the city of London that had condemned him to death, and all the residents in it. He'd vowed to see London burn and fall. This hate was the source of his palpable, malignant aura of fear, and the means he used to shepherd the Faerie army.

Widdershins was the key to this control. His powers combined with the Black Shuck's haze of fear were a formidable combination, far greater than the simple sum of the two. Men and women who might have recovered from one or the other never did from both.

It was with the increased power that Widdershins and the Black Shuck gave each other that the two of them started capturing and binding the hateful spirits of other hanged criminals, which was where the undead wolves, the Black Shuck's minions, came from.

Widdershins, too, had once been a man and a murderer. Widdershins had enjoyed killing. Lustful and bloody images lingered in Henry's mind. A scalpel in the dark. Women screaming. When a chance attack in the back alleyways had taken his own life, he lingered there, formless but unwilling to depart the filthy corridors where he'd felt most alive. He'd been only a shadow of a thing until the Black Shuck found him. It was this common origin and purpose that bound the two together.

Henry saw this, too: the invasion that Father had warned them about wasn't just a real possibility: it had *already begun*.

The images plucked from Widdershins' mind were haunting. The Faerie had already infiltrated large sections of London, like Newgate, and their main force had yet to arrive. There were many, many more coming.

Their only real obstacle: the Lord of Thorns.

Father.

There was even a game within a game. Generals and armies, yes, but there was a smaller but more powerful struggle going on, and it was both the Black Shuck's and Widdershins' opinion that the smaller battle, seven versus seven, would actually decide the entire war.

Seven was a sacred number for man and Faerie both and symbols meant a great deal in things like this. Seven special emissaries to strike at the world of man and seven to defend it. Somehow—and this confused Henry most of all—Father had had a hand in creating both sides.

Seven magical powers stood arrayed against London and mankind, which included the Black Shuck and Widdershins', of course. Henry knew some of others, too, including Lady Westerly. The Soho Shark and Victoria Rose. (Henry lamented his own role in falling so easily under their influence. Justice had tried to warn him, hell and damnation! No help for that now.) The other two of the Faerie Seven, the Changeling and the Goblin Knight, were names with vague images to Henry.

Of course, Widdershins had about as much respect for the Faerie Seven as he had for everything else and had nearly killed the Soho Shark and Victoria Rose trying to apprehend Henry, Justice and Faith. Widdershins hadn't meant to, he'd just forgotten who the other two were in the heat of the moment. That happened to Widdershins a lot, Henry knew. The Black Shuck was the only power that Widdershins remembered always.

The seven defenders were mostly just names and general impressions to Widdershins. Some names Henry didn't have faces for: Temperance, Love, Hope, Charity. But he knew they were daughters of the Lord of Thorns. Sisters of his, alive in Faerie. Or half-sisters, anyway. Also, Prudence, who had supposedly died before he was born, but hadn't!

Which meant that the letter Justice had gotten, signed by Prudence, had to be real. Henry wondered what it meant and what they might be finding there, even now, without him.

Of course, the last two defenders of England and mankind he knew well: Justice and Faith Kasric. He knew now, too, that they were Faerie, which meant *he* was too.

But knowing the facts didn't mean that Henry had any idea of how he was supposed to come to grips with them.

What did it mean if he was Faerie?

That would explain how he could resist Widdershins. And the strength Henry had shown back in the Alley. Henry had very nearly forgotten about that. Did it mean he had a role to play in this war? Widdershins didn't think so, and neither did Father.

But, if Widdershins' memories were to be believed, Father had carved out a prominent role for Justice and Faith and a number of other sisters that Henry had never met. That was likely because while there were a few powerful male enchanters in Faerie, all the *truly* destructive ones were women. Widdershins had meant it when he called Henry a nobody.

And what was Henry supposed to make of Widdershins' obsession with Mother?

This much Henry understood: the Black Shuck, Widdershins, and Lady Westerly had targeted Mother more than a year ago with a plan to addict Mother to the Faerie absinthe and make a hostage of her. Henry could taste the absinthe on Mother's tongue, just as he'd smelled it when Justice had fallen down the stairs. Except he was having a hard time remembering when he was himself in these memories, or when the memories had actually been experienced by someone else. Widdershins, Mother, Lady Westerly . . . flashes jostled each other for space, much of it incoherent.

He knew this: Mother had turned the tables on them all. He could feel Westerly's panic, Widdershins' confusion and anger and finally, his acceptance. Widdershins didn't know how Mother had pulled it off, so Henry didn't either. Lady Westerly had become the addict, and Mother had somehow traveled to Faerie and taken extreme advantage of the fact that time, in some places within Faerie, moved much faster than in England. As a result, Mother had been able to spend a full decade in Faerie honing her skills, which only amounted to the last *four days* for Henry. After that decade, she'd come back to England as a newly-budding magician, an ally to the Faerie invasion. She was the one who knew another way across to England from Faerie besides the bridge. She'd been sending Faerie across for some time now, which was how the Faerie had gotten so far ahead of Father's defenses. She was an ally that the Black Shuck and Widdershins had to accept, but a dangerous one, with her own agenda.

It was a lot to absorb.

But he might not have to worry about that for very long, because the clearest memory of all had been Widdershins' relief when he could leave Henry in his cell with one last consolation: he'd meant what he said about the rope.

Henry was scheduled to be executed.

# CHAPTER 11

## Benedict: The Hussars

With Justice, Faith and Henry gone, and Stormholt mostly empty, there was little for Benedict to do. He'd had some brief thoughts about trying to contribute to the war efforts going on around him. There were always priests with the fallen, but he shied away from that. That required real faith, something he knew he lacked.

He had a fair amount of medical knowledge and field medics were always needed. With this possibility in mind, he spent the day over papers and maps that Father and Mr. Sands had left all over the library. Stormholt was removed from the fighting, but it served as a hub for information. So Benedict read. The war was the only thing happening, and what else did he have to do?

Some of it was interesting: ship deployments, platoons of Winged Hussars and Faerie Outcasts moving to cut off the invasion forces, planned raids and barricades and the difficult nature of crossing from the Faerie world to this one. All of it cataloged and relayed by Mr. Sands' elaborate spy network of cats and Ghost Boys. Benedict learned a lot, but notations of Jötnar, Pix, Fomori, Barghests and the like just left him feeling out of his depth. A room full of books, but none of them could tell him what a Fomori *was*, let alone how to field dress an arrow wound for them.

There wasn't really anyone to answer his questions. He discovered, after a great deal of written interrogation, that the Ghost Boys didn't really know much. They collected the reports, but they didn't understand most of them. Father or Sands must have come regularly—he often saw fresh notes in Mr. Sands' curved, tidy writing, or Father's more ornate script—but Benedict never actually saw either man.

He spent the evenings exploring the rambling and twisting ways of Stormholt by candlelight. There was an abandoned aviary still littered with feathers, a massive skylight-fed indoor garden, complete with topiary, and a museum-style armory, among other strange places. Once, he heard snatches of violin, but saw no other sign of Mr. Sands and when Benedict tried to follow the music, he got lost again.

He was brave and foolish enough that night to follow Justice's lead and climb up the iron ladder that led to the roof. Stormholt's roof was a jumble of slanted angles just made for sliding off to your death. He'd intended to wait for a storm and try and throw stones at anybody he might see riding around the sky, and even caught the sound of the Wild Hunt's horn, drifting on the wind as if it had to travel a long distance to get to him.

Benedict shouted an obscenity back, stumbled on the wet roof and slid partway down one of the slanted sections. He managed to stop himself before tumbling over, but his mishap had taken him close enough to the edge to see down onto the moonlit lawn.

All the cats were gone.

Staring down on the dark and empty lawn was such a shock that Benedict nearly slipped again. He decided that brandy and rooftops were a bad combination, especially for someone with his Storm-touched condition, so he went back down the iron ladder and drank himself to oblivion. When he dreamt, he still heard the horn, but at least the iron gate kept the Wild Hunt out.

The following morning, when he asked about the missing cats, Percy's written answer was short: "On Spy Detail." One self-imprisoned and useless Kasric didn't rate the same precautions as the entire family had and Father was deploying his eccentric resources elsewhere. Either the black iron gate would be enough to keep the Faerie out, or it wouldn't.

After lunch, which was even more breakfast, Benedict sat in the library underneath a stained-glass window all done up in red and gold that pictured some kind of Faerie infantry crossing a bridge at sunset. The books in the library had an abandoned sort of feeling to them. Clouds of dust billowed in the red-gold air whenever he disturbed one, but the maps and piles of reports scattered all over the larger table were in constant use and free of dust.

There was another tool, Percy wrote to him, a special chess set that Father and Sands had somewhere that they could use as some sort of magical gauge of the war. According to the set and the reports both, the main thrust of the war hadn't really started yet. There'd been some battles and already there were many Faerie in England, but the serious engagements were pending. Still, the smaller skirmishes were shocking enough. Three Faerie killed in Suffolk. One man lost in Norwood. People and Faerie fighting in London and neither the Queen nor any other part of the British government knew anything about it.

(Back in London, *I* was just discovering that Father was very, very wrong about how far the Faerie had come and could have given him a good idea as to how they were hiding such an enormous incursion, but Benedict and I had no way to communicate with each other.)

Benedict was bent over another report about Faerie spies being ferreted out of an abandoned belfry in Camberly when the library door flew open without any visible signs of anyone opening it. One of the Ghost Boys bringing more brandy, hopefully. This one was getting low.

A few seconds of delay and a pen near Benedict's right hand jumped up and wrote in the margin of the report Benedict was holding.

*Hussars*, it said, *Hurry!* It was Percy's writing.

The Winged Hussars were some of Father's crack troops, a cadre of human soldiers specifically equipped to fight the Faerie and do it well. Heavy cavalry that wore fabricated wings on their backs, though Benedict could not imagine why.

But the Hussars were supposed to be miles away from here.

"Why would the Hussars come here?" Benedict said to the empty room.

The pen wrote: *??? Hurry!*

By the time Benedict got to the front door, the distant cracks of rifle shots were already drifting up the hill. He paused a moment on the porch, looking out into the drizzling rain, still not used to a cat-free lawn. He kept expecting a drove of cats to slink out from around the edge of the house or drop down from the roof in hordes.

He limped as fast as he could down the wet gravel drive, holding his hand to shield his face against the light rain. He was freezing already. He should have brought a coat.

Benedict walked down to the gate and hit it hard, but it didn't budge. Whatever spell Father had on the gate, it wasn't taking requests. He might be able to climb over, but there were those barbs at the top to discourage that and what good would he do out there? All he could do was grip the bars and peer through.

The metal arch of the gate sat on a ledge of dirt and stones. From there, the dirt road swooped down a long incline so Benedict could see all the way to the bottom of the hill and to the heavy, green darkness of the woods on the left.

Twenty-odd men or so were riding up the slope as fast as their mounts could climb in the rain. They were shouting in Polish and lashing their mounts with febrile energy. The rifle cracks were constant as the rear guard kept shooting behind them, but Benedict couldn't see any of their targets through the black haze of gunpowder and the drizzling rain.

The Hussars were heavily armored, heavy plates over the green and black uniform. Ostrich feathers streaming gloriously from a wooden framework of wings that were their trademark.

The rearmost horse screamed and fell, taking the rider down with it. The horses wore some armor, but it was minimal at the rear. Two long arrows protruded from the horse's back legs. It whickered once pitifully in the rain, lifted its head and then let it fall again.

The rider had lost his helmet in the fall and when he tried to lift himself up in the heavy mail, another arrow flew into the back of his neck from the direction of the woods. The man fell to the wet road and neither man or horse got up again.

Benedict realized that the Hussars were riding for their lives.

Neither of the Ghost Boys could open the gate. They didn't need to. Not being Faerie, they could just slip right through. Benedict realized he didn't have any idea what they were doing right now.

Looking for a key? Sending Father a message somehow? There was no telling. He bit his lip in frustration. Another horse and rider went down as Benedict gripped the cold gate bars and watched, helpless.

He still couldn't see any archers, but they had to be back in the woods. A hell of a shot, to hit the unarmored horses so precisely. A few of the arrows missed, but not many. Benedict didn't understand any of this.

The Winged Hussars were supposed to be Father's crack troops and capable of handling any of the minor Faerie that had made their way into England.

The Hussar in the lead forced his mount up the last bit of the incline and rode up to the gate.

"Open the gate!" he bellowed. "For the love of god, open the gate!" His English was heavily accented. Polish, perhaps. His seamed face on the other side of the bars was white and strained. This close, the archaic bright uniform, complete with streamers, tall helmet and epaulets, all of it stained with blood and dirt, was the picture of fallen grandeur.

Benedict hauled at the gate, hoping against hope that he could somehow wrestle it open now, but it still didn't move. "I can't!" he said, desperately. "I don't have a key. No one here does! You'll have to climb over!"

Two more riders brought their horses up behind the first. Both the men's and horses' eyes were white with fear. The stamping hooves were churning the wet ground outside into mud.

"Open the gate!" the first man shouted again. His voice cracked on the last word.

"Romuald!" the second man said, pushing up his armored face-plate. "Romuald can open it!" He was a thin, spare-faced man under the helmet. A priest's collar was just visible under the mailed gorget. He spun his horse with a twitch of the reins then lifted his rifle and fired off two shots, all without relinquishing the reins in his left. An amazing maneuver that meant nothing. Immediately after the second shot, an arrow flew from the forest and appeared in the rider's open mouth. He screamed, a horrid, gurgling noise around the arrow, and fell with a loud clanging noise.

Benedict stared, his heart pounding, as the man struggled in the mud to pull the arrow out of his own mouth. Then he sagged and went still. Benedict wanted to throw up or scream or do something. He'd never seen death this close up before. Who could shoot with accuracy at two hundred yards and uphill, with a bloody bow and arrow?

The first Faerie archer stepped out of the woods at the bottom of the slope. Tall, pale figures in dark green leather with ornaments of bone. They didn't look like much from here. Clearly, that didn't mean anything.

If they could shoot a man in the mouth, it meant they could shoot Benedict right through the iron bars, couldn't they? Benedict flung himself down on the ground.

"Open the gate!" the man on the other side screamed.

"I can't!" Benedict cried out with his face still in the dirt. He could taste acid in his throat. He could hear the thunder of more men riding up to the gate. Another horse screamed and fell with a wet sound in the mud.

Benedict lifted his face for a quick look.

The archers were slowly walking up the hill, firing as they came. Benedict saw another man take an arrow right through the face plate. The Hussars returned fire with rifles, but the archers made poor targets in the rain, flickering unnaturally so that it was hard to tell precisely where they were.

Yet another Hussar crested the ridge and rode up to the gate to join the rest. His helmet was missing and blood trickled down from his forehead.

"Romuald!" one of the men shouted. Several men pointed at the gate and said something in a stream of Polish. Benedict didn't know the words, but the meaning was clear. *Locked.*

Romuald urged his mount through the others and sang three notes. The sound of his voice hung in the air a moment while everyone waited.

The gate lock snapped open.

The moment they pushed the gate open, the noise of a horn rose up and Benedict's world lurched and spun while the Hussars hurried through.

It was the Wild Hunt's horn, distant but powerful. It surged up, held so long at bay, but now blaring in Benedict's ears so that it drowned out the shouting and screaming of men and the pounding of hooves. Benedict froze in place the way prey does when it knows its last moments have finally come. He felt the weight of it on him and peered at the lead-gray sky with both longing and dread.

The Wild Hunt would find him. Soon. They were up there in the sky just over the horizon and now they could sense him, defenseless . . .

Then the gate clanged shut.

The commander, Romuald, guided his mount away from the gate and Benedict found he could think again. He stood, stupidly blinking up at the mounted men moving away from the gate. Romuald bellowed orders to get his men further up the lawn. One of the men leaned down from the saddle and got hold of Benedict's collar, dragging him up the slope. The rifleman got into defensive positions behind the poplars while the rest took shelter further back. The horses, with surprising alacrity, lay down flat on the wet ground. There were less than twenty men and horses left.

The man flung Benedict down behind another of the trees just a few feet from the commander.

"What defenses are in place here?"

It took Benedict a second to realize that the commander was talking to him because the man never took his eyes off the slope below.

"None," Benedict stammered. "At least, I don't think so. No one expected the battle to reach this place."

"Nieh," Romuald said. "I was afraid of that."

"The arrows have stopped," said the man who had dragged Benedict.

"For now," Romuald said.

Benedict peered around the tree. Maybe the archers were playing some cagey game? Or maybe the gate somehow stopped the arrows, even though the bars had gaps plenty wide enough to shoot through. He couldn't see the archers from here, which meant they could be doing anything now.

"It's over, right?" one of the riflemen said. This close, the Hussars' rifles looked older, like working antiques. "They can't get through the gate."

"It's over," another man said hopefully. "Black iron burns them. They can't touch that, can they?"

Romuald laughed bitterly. "That's what we said yesterday at the camp perimeter. And the night before that at the bridge."

Down by the gate, a man climbed up the ridge, looming suddenly into view in the rain. He was tall, wearing a heavy cloak and a helmet with huge ram's horns curling at the sides.

"Sweet mother in Heaven," one of the riflemen said. "It's *him*." There was a nervous murmur from the others.

In some ways, the man looked surprisingly . . . normal. Not at all what Benedict expected and didn't have that otherworldly feel the archers had, even at a distance. He was large and heavily built, with crude leather armor. His features were masked by the helmet, but grey hair poked from underneath the bottom.

The commander spit at the ground and peered over his rifle. When the man with the ram's horn helmet reached the gate, he jammed a large round shield into place for cover and crouched behind it.

The riflemen were firing constantly now, and distant *pok-pok* of hits on the shield came in between the louder cracks of the rifles themselves. There was a gap between the shield where they could see that he was peering closely at the hinge. Then he took a deep breath and blew slowly on the hinge.

Rippling waves of heat distortion billowed out from the man's open mouth. The hinge of the gate smoked and grew red. The riflemen kept shooting and Benedict was sure the man was hit at least once, because he jerked in place. But he kept on working on the hinge anyway, which was glowing a deep molten red.

"What is he doing?" Benedict said, "Is he *breathing* on the hinges? Who *is* that?"

"A devil in human skin," Romuald said. "There's no stopping him with black iron, Faerie or not."

The man in the horned helmet placed gauntleted hands on either side of the red section. He yanked and the bottom part of the gate swung loose.

Behind him, Faerie archers stood up out of shallow valleys in the snow that Benedict would have sworn couldn't hide a cat.

Their faces were almost beautiful, in a cruel, severe way that chilled Benedict to the bone. A head taller than most men, slender, with fair hair, stern faces that held pale almond eyes, and a breathtaking grace in every motion. This close, Benedict could see their outfits were actually a very dark green, with bone slivers three or four inches long stuck horizontally through the tunics, possibly the finger bones of something very large. Their bows, nearly as tall as they were, were made of equally pale wood, inlaid with bone, each clearly a deadly work of art.

"There's shelter in the house," Benedict said. "It's enormous. You could hide an army in there."

The commander eyed him with disdain. "Those are archers from the Seelie Court, boy. We've been dealing with the disorganized riff-raff that stumbled their way across before this. But not now. Playing guerrilla warfare with this lot is like hunting fog."

"The devil is with them, too," one of the riflemen said. It sounded like an ominous mantra, often repeated.

Romuald coughed and spat blood with matter-of-fact contempt. "There's that, too. We'll not shake them while *he* leads them. We didn't shake them across three days of forest and the mist, we're damned well not going to lose them in a *house*. I'm sure as Hades not going to leave our horses to them." He pitched these last words so that all his men could hear them and there was a murmur of assent.

Romuald stood up and went to where one of his men held his horse down on its side. He took the reins and the horse whickered happily as it stood up. Romuald checked the saddle briefly and nodded. The other Hussars were standing up now and exchanging dark and serious looks while they checked their own horses and gear. Several were hefting long lances with pennons flapping from the tips.

Benedict looked back down the snow-covered lawn. The man with the horned helmet twisted the gate back and forth, trying to get the last hinge to give. The Faerie archers moved up close behind him, waiting as if they had all the time in the world.

Benedict knew that the Hussars were going to stand and fight, and the Faerie knew it, too. There was a terrible weight of inevitability in the air. Benedict wanted to run, to hide, to slink back into the house, but he didn't do any of those things.

The other hinge to the gate gave with a loud, metallic snap and man in the ram's horn helmet heaved the gate to one side. Stormholt was open to the Faerie.

Instantly, the call of the Wild Hunt hammered at Benedict's skull with renewed force. He was braced for it this time, which didn't help much. His vision turned blurry with the fury of the horn's call in his head.

The man in the horned helmet stood just inside the gate waiting while the archers came in through the gate and started up the hill, spreading out slightly as they came. They didn't look to be in any hurry.

Romuald mounted up and one of his men handed him a lance. "Let's see these bastards take a full hammer! I'll be damned if they won't pay at least some blood for what they've taken from the Winged Hussars. Mount up! We ride!"

"Don't," Benedict pleaded over the din. "This is madness. You'll get butchered!"

"We ride," Romuald said again. The riflemen were discarding their rifles with contempt and taking up lances.

"Yes, sir!" several men shouted back, a resolution now rang out in their voices and shone in their faces that hadn't been there before.

The men stood their horses up, sliding smoothly into the saddle so that horse and rider rose up together. They were all of them ready in seconds. The wind picked up and the pennons and feathers of their winged backs made an eerie hum.

"We ride!" the commander said, a third time, his voice heavy with the weight of ritual.

Benedict sagged against the wall. The wail of the Wild Hunt's horn thrummed all around him and cast a haze of disorientation over everything that followed.

Commander Romuald turned expressionless eyes to look around him. Even haggard and pale, with his polished armor spattered and torn, he carried a ponderous dignity. Benedict realized with a shock that the commander was only a few years older than Benedict himself. The uniform, mustache and beard had hidden that until now.

Another man took an arrow in the chest. At two hundred yards, the arrow went right through the chest plate. A second man went down with an arrow in his eye. Benedict turned in horror. The Faerie archers walked up the hill slowly, easily, firing in rapid succession as they came. They looked relaxed and confident. It might have been an archery exhibition.

That left only fifteen mounted Hussars, who kicked their mounts into motion and started down the hill, slowly picking up speed. Three horses and riders went down before they went twenty feet.

The Hussar charge *was* a terrifying thing to behold. Horses and men coursing down the incline, a massive front of heavy plate armor and protruding iron-tipped lances, a moving engine of war. The wind picked up their streamers as the horses thundered, the ground shook, and the hum rose to a terrifying buzz. Benedict could well imagine the devastation they must have caused, falling on the flanks of an enemy army, any enemy army. He could understand why Romuald had made his choice. The charge was their ultimate weapon.

For a brief moment, it looked like the Hussars might actually succeed.

At full speed, with helmets down and shields lowered, the charging Hussars presented a united and heavily armored front. Several arrows pinged off of the heavy shields and metal helmets.

But then a few more arrows found their marks and by the time the Hussars had traversed the eighty feet downhill, their numbers had dwindled to half.

When the charge reached the Faerie archers, the line of archers melted effortlessly and the lances pierced only thin air as the Hussars charged harmlessly by.

The archers rose up from their crouches, still firing at the backs of the charging Hussars.

From behind, without the shields or the most heavily fortified part of the Hussar's armor to deal with, far more arrows found their mark, even through the armor. Horses and men screamed and tumbled, their charge turning into a bloody tumble down the slump. The commander himself, the last to fall, took four arrows that buried themselves halfway into his back before he slumped in his saddle, dropped his lance and fell when his mount screamed and toppled.

Their bodies landed, rolled a few more times, and then came to a stop about ten feet from where the man in the ram's horn helmet waited. Everything fell silent around them, with only the echo of a thunderous charge still ringing off the stonework of the house.

Benedict stood alone at the top of the hill with his hands at his sides, hearing the horn of the Wild Hunt and watching the Faerie archers as they moved among the fallen now. Would they kill him, too? All the attention of those golden eyes was on the wounded. They put arrows into anything, horse or man, that still breathed. Benedict turned his own eyes upward, looking for the Wild Hunt through the continuing drizzle, but there was nothing to see in the overcast sky.

The man with the ram's horn helmet strolled casually up the drive towards Benedict. His eyes and nose and mouth were barely visible through the slit of the helmet, but it was clearly a human face. He stopped ten paces away from where Benedict stood alone by one of the trees.

"Don't worry," the man said. This close, his eyes were a clear blue. "You will be taken prisoner, of course, but treated fairly. I haven't descended so far as *that*."

Benedict had always been quick, and of course, even with the Wild Hunt horn wailing in the background, he knew that voice very well.

The leader of the Faerie raiding party pulled off his helmet to reveal long hair that had once been brown, but was now shot through with gray. His face looked older, too, astonishingly so, and seamed with years spent outdoors. It was as if a decade had passed since Benedict had last seen him, and not an easy decade at that.

Joshua Kasric looked across the bloody snow and smiled.

"Hello, little brother," Joshua said. "Mother will be *so* glad to see you again."

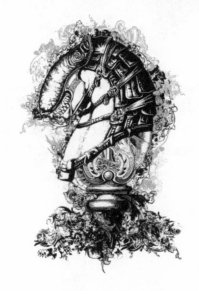

# CHAPTER 12

## The HMS Rachaela

Using the Faerie door wasn't what I expected. Jumping into a pool of water should be wet. Even a vertical pool should be wet. But what I got instead was a cool velvet wind in my face and then . . .

. . . falling.

I hit bare wood hard enough to knock the wind out of me and force Victoria Rose's sword out of my hand. If there had been some kind of danger, fat lot of good I would have done to prevent it. Then the water came, a ton of it. A frigid lake dumped all over us in a big splash, leaving Faith, Victoria Rose and I dripping and shivering and very much awake, thank you much. At least Faith and I were. Victoria Rose groaned, but remained unconscious.

We were in a small, now very wet cabin. Climbing to my feet, heart hammering, I felt the unmistakable rise and fall that could only mean one thing. Even before I turned to look out the stern windows at the blue horizon, I knew.

We were at sea.

But not any sea on Earth. The four large gallery windows looked out on an unnatural, lemon-cream sky filled with glittering white clouds. A small skylight above showed the same. That was no sky I'd ever seen before and all I could think was that we *must* have made it to Faerie. The water of the sea rose and fell, a clean, reflective blue under the peculiar light with a long furrow from our wake.

The sun itself was an even whiter light high up in the sky. That took a moment to sink in. Evening had been upon us when we'd left London just a few minutes ago, so the days and nights of the Faerie world and our world must not be in sync. Or we'd lost time crossing over. That presented a chilling possibility I hadn't considered. We might have lost days, months. Years? That bizarre sky made the impossibility of it all sink in. Anything could be true.

The room sang of the sea all around us. The floor had already gone from being an inch deep in water to merely wet as the water from our arrival seeped away through the planking. The slap of water outside and the groan of shifting wood brought me back. Distant shouts and thumps came from the deck above us. I forgot all about my temporal concerns as a huge grin came to my face.

Faith wrinkled her nose. "Ugh. Do all ships smell like this?"

"Oh yes," I said happily. The salt was the strongest, but the smells of standing water, moldering wood and sweat were here, too.

"Well," Faith said with a sigh of resignation. "I'm glad one of us is having fun."

We were in the captain's cabin. A chess set sat on a small table, which seemed a colossally foolish thing on a rolling ship, but there it was. The same chess set I'd seen in the woods and then later again in Father's study, and from the looks of things, it was still in the middle of a game. Maybe even the same game.

It was missing one of the black knights, too. I gripped the piece in my pocket.

There were also maps on the table, covered in Father's writing. I looked down at one of England with the railroad lines highlighted. Curious.

I wondered what Father would do when he found we'd escaped. Probably send us right back to Stormholt. I wanted to find him. He might be the only one who could do something about Henry. But I didn't want to go back to Stormholt. I couldn't. Not now.

Behind us stood another round door like the one we'd just come through. Or perhaps it was the other side of the same door. Who could tell with magic doors?

"At least," Faith said, "we can get back when we . . ." She pulled the door open and we both stared blankly at the rough wood of the cabin wall. Whatever magic was in the door, it had gone inert now. This had been a one-way trip.

"Oh," Faith said. "Well that's just *wonderful.*"

I looked down at our prisoner, Victoria Rose, who was still unconscious. "Help me get her up in the hammock."

Then I took a better look. Victoria Rose was something of a surprise. She looked different now.

Faith gasped. "Her ears!"

I felt a weight lifted. I'd gotten so used to being the only one to see magical things that it was an unbelievable relief to realize she could too. Maybe it was being in Faerie that made the difference.

Victoria Rose's ears were nearly a foot long, delicately pointed, with russet fur like a fox's. Victoria Rose's hair looked different now, more like a lion's mane.

Her face was even sharper now, with long, slanted eyes and a mouth filled with sharp little teeth. She looked feral, even unconscious, but alarmingly pretty for all that. Her hands still had the scarlet gloves on, but I could see the shape of claws underneath the leather.

"Is this what you saw all along?" Faith said. "Why didn't you tell us?"

"She was odd-looking," I said. "But not like this. I guess my ghost eye only gave me a hint of this shape."

Faith tentatively lifted Victoria's ankles, and we wrestled her into the hammock. The Faerie woman weighed hardly anything. I checked the belt around her hands. It still felt secure and the gloves would keep her from bringing the claws into play. I retrieved her silver sword from the floor but decided not to take it with me. Instead, I hid it behind the chests that lay underneath the cot. I might regret leaving it with her if Victoria Rose got free, but I didn't have any decent way of carrying it and something told me that appearing on the deck of a strange ship waving a sword around wasn't such a fantastic idea.

"She's not even human," Faith said. She couldn't tear her eyes away.

"Come on," I said. "We need to find Father."

"I still don't understand how you can be sure he's here, or why you think he can help Henry."

"If I think that," I said, "then we have something we can do. A plan. If I don't, we have nothing. I'd rather do something than nothing."

The cabin door had a name burned into it: the HMS *Rachaela*. I opened it, and the whole deck lay in front of us. I went up three stairs and out onto the deck with a feeling of awe and sublime joy.

We were on the main deck facing forward with the raised quarterdeck right behind us, which would be where the officers were. Their moving around had made all the thumping in the cabin. Probably Father and Mr. Sands, among others.

There were people everywhere, running, shouting, climbing all over the deck and swarming up in the rigging. Officers were shouting commands underscored by shrill whistles. I would have been surprised at the number of girls and women in the crew—something unheard of in the British Royal Navy, or any navy—except for the even more amazing thing: of the hundred or so people running around, most of them weren't even remotely human.

I thought about the HMS in front of the *Rachaela*'s name on the door behind me and wondered if good Queen Victoria knew about her newest subjects. Somehow, I doubted it.

A pair of green ragamuffin children ran up the quarterdeck stairway, one boy and one girl, each of them with clawed, webbed hands gripping a curiously shiny cannon ball. Copper, maybe? That had to have something to do with the Faerie aversion to iron.

A quartet of British sailors in front of us ran out one of the cannon with a rumble I could feel through the deck. Further amidships, more crews pushed more cannon into position, but many of these were not men at all. At least, not Englishmen. They were stout, bearded persons only half the height of regular men, but more than burly enough to make up the difference. A good half of them were bald, while others ran to wild, bristly hair. Nearly as wide as they were tall, they didn't have any difficulty with handling the bronze cannon, hefting the massive weight around as easily as the largest of men.

Dwarves!

Up above us, a sail crew scuttled from spar to spar. Made up of mostly of squat and fuzzy misshapen critters about half the size of the Dwarves. With batlike ears, brown tufts of fur, sharp noses and grins filled with pointed teeth, these could only be Goblins! I laughed out loud at the sheer joy of it. Creatures of all shapes and sizes, men and women, Faerie and Englander, all clearly preparing the ship for battle. Being on a ship by itself was magnificent, just as I'd always imagined, but having it happen in Faerie, with such a fantastic and unimaginable crew, made it all the more delightful.

The *Rachaela* was an older style of ship, a triple-masted war sloop rather than one of the new ironclads. She was a smaller ship, square-rigged as she might have been in the last century, running with her sail trimmed and close-hauled on the starboard tack, but this was no merchant vessel. It was a fighting ship. She was sailing into the wind as much as she could, which kept the deck at a hefty tilt to port as the ship heeled over. The slanted deck combined with the yaw and pitch of the sea made it seem as if the ship must flounder onto its side and go down at any minute, but clearly whoever guided the helm knew their business.

Unlike a British ship with Englishmen, we were hardly out of place at all and to this day, when I look back, I still feel that if I'd simply secured a loose line near the bow or made my way up the mizzenmast with the sail crew, I might have joined the crew of the *Rachaela* with barely a ripple and still be there to this day.

I saw another of the Dwarves conferring with a gun crew, but this one wore the uniform of an officer of the same vivid blue as Caine had worn, frogged across the front in gleaming white cord, with collars and heavy cuffs to match. There was an ornate pattern of white cord on the back, too, rendered like a winding bit of thorned ivy, and I remembered the name Victoria Rose had given Father: The Lord of Thorns.

Twenty or so Faerie soldiers—marines, by their uniforms and armament—lined the opposite rail near the bow. Their uniform was much the same as the officers', only it was of a green so dark as to be almost black. The same uniform I'd seen on all the dead soldiers outside Stormholt. The light caught the brilliant white cord that ran over lapels, mandarin collar and sleeves. White cord also formed the pattern on the back. Long barbs didn't seem like a very friendly symbol. The Lord of Thorns didn't sound like such a friendly title, either, now that I had time to think on it.

The marines here stood slender and tall, with recurve bows as tall as they were. I realized with a sudden shock that these were unmistakably the same kind of Faerie as those that had escorted Mother, though the ones who had taken Mother hadn't worn uniforms.

I stayed close to the quarterdeck wall, wanting to avoid being seen by anyone on the quarterdeck itself, which was where the captain would be.

That was where I expected to find Father, but I wanted a better look at the rest of the ship before he saw me. Amazingly, none of the crew gave us so much as a second glance.

I edged forward a few steps to get a closer look at the nearest guns. Faith stayed right behind me. These guns were 'long nines', smaller guns that shot nine-pound cannonballs, known for their excellent range and accuracy fifty years ago when they had seen more common use. Only these cannon had curious glyphs on the side that didn't look like any writing from our world.

I could see all the way forward on the forecastle. Probably they had two more cannon behind me on the poop deck and a whole lot more below on the gun deck. There was a lot more rumbling and shouting coming from down there.

I moved over to the rail now and basked in the rolling glory of the sea itself. Something difficult caught in my throat just looking at the heavy rollers sweeping past.

I tugged the brim of my hat lower to protect my ghost eye from the sun's glare, but the light here didn't seem to bother it as much. The ship's bow rose and dipped into the waves as white foam sprayed up and drenched my hands on the rail. I could feel a wild grin on my face.

"Blast it!" a voice roared. "Where did you come from?" The Dwarf in the officer's uniform had spied us from further down the deck. He had a brilliant red mustache and beard, but almost no hair above except for an equally red top knot. He looked ready to burst with anger like an overheated sausage.

"We've no time for this!" he shouted, crossing the deck, passing us and starting up the quarterdeck stairs. "Avonstoke! Yer never doin' anythin' useful. Secure 'em! Find out 'ow they got 'ere! Shoot 'em or lock 'em up if you 'ave to, but keep 'em out o' the way!"

One of the Faerie Marines turned from the rail. "You bellow and I obey," he said cheerfully. Avonstoke turned and regarded us. He wore a black mask shaped like a predatory bird of some sort, but what I could see of his face lit with a wide smile.

Yet another officer next to him, a woman marine with ornate epaulets and a feathered hat, grabbed Avonstoke's arm and he nodded as she spoke a few curt words that I couldn't make out. Her attention was focused entirely on something out at sea, aft of us, but the quarterdeck blocked my view.

Avonstoke moved across the deck with breathtaking grace despite the angled deck, the irregular motion of the ship, and the need to weave around the bustling gun crew.

"Oh," Faith breathed. "He's gorgeous."

I glared at her, but she wasn't wrong. He was tall, with long, straight hair tied into a long rope of tawny goldenrod down his back. His face underneath the mask was tan. Unlike the others still at the rail, he wore a long, dark cloak which should have snagged on a number of hooks or cleats as he passed, only it never did. What he didn't have was any military insignia on his uniform, or even the spear and long bow that seemed to be mandatory with all the other marines.

"Forgive me, ladies." Even Avonstoke's speech was beautiful, curiously accented with a lilt that made his words almost a song. "My commanding officer has instructed me to find out if you have come to blow up the boat. If so, I'm supposed to shoot you."

A small black and silver pistol he hadn't been holding on his way over now glittered suddenly in his hand. It seemed anachronistic in his hands, but he leveled it at with a precision that suggested he was very familiar with its use.

"Are you going to shoot us?" Faith said in soft, coquettish voice.

"I sincerely hope not," he said.

This close, I realized that Avonstoke's mask wasn't a mask at all, but a black tattoo. It was shaped like a bird, possibly a raven, so that his pale yellow eyes regarded us from within the darkness of outstretched wings. They were disconcerting, those eyes, completely without irises, both of them a gold parody of my black ghost eye. Or was my ghost eye a black parody of the Faerie?

"You're not, going to blow up the boat, are you?" he said.

"No!" Faith said, "Of course not."

I'd been staring without saying anything and when I finally got my mouth working all I said was, "Ship."

"What's that?" Avonstoke said. "Beg pardon?" This close, those enormous, golden eyes were even more unsettling. They weren't featureless like I'd first thought, more a swirling mist you could get lost in for days at a time. Two errant golden curls had escaped the tie that kept the rest of his hair back and lay on his forehead in a way that made me want to push them back into place. He was, at that moment, the most unsettling man I'd ever met.

"It's a ship," I said, feeling more and more like an idiot. "Not a boat. We're not here to blow up the *ship*." I was still watching the gun, too. That and the back of my mind was worried about the impending combat. You didn't run out the guns unless you planned on using them. I didn't see any sign of the enemy, but that was certainly what all the marines at the rail were staring at, at an angle I couldn't see.

"Yes, of course." He stepped back and lowered the pistol. "Ship. Excellent. Now that that's settled." He waved the pistol around as he talked, as if it were no more than a gentleman's cigar. The wide mouth looked as if it might always have some version of that sardonic smile on it. It certainly had one now.

"We're not enemies," I said, "though we have a prisoner unconscious in the captain's cabin. And we need to report someone taken hostage back in London. Our brother."

"Ah," he said. He turned abruptly and walked back to the quarterdeck stairs. We waited while he exchanged a few words with the Dwarven officer.

Finally, he came back. Behind him, the officer was sending two men down to the captain's cabin. Avonstoke was still pointing the gun. "My full name is Raythe Avonstoke," he said, "a humble bowman assigned to the Crow Whisper Brigade." He gestured back that the group of marines as if the uniform didn't give him away.

"I'm Faith Kasric," Faith said before I could stop her. "This is my little sister. Our brother is Henry Kasric and the Faerie have him back in London. If he's not killed, that is."

It was hard to read his face because of the strange eyes, but our names didn't seem to mean anything to him. The gun was still very much in evidence.

"Does little sister have a name?" he asked me.

"Justice," I said grudgingly.

Faith got a sudden calculating look on her face, then she stumbled. The motion of the ship pitched her directly into Avonstoke's arm.

"Oh," Faith said breathlessly. "I beg your pardon."

"Do you?" he said lightly. The gun had disappeared. He steadied her with an arm around her waist.

"Good Lord, Faith!" I snapped. "Now? Really?"

"Delightful," he said. "I can think of no better introduction." He drew Faith's hand up in his, still maintaining his other arm around her waist. He brought her hand to his lips like a courtier of old. Pressed as close as they were, they might have been lovers dancing. "It's Lord Raythe Avonstoke, actually," he murmured against the back of her hand. "But we're well past that kind of formality already, aren't we, my peach?"

"Well, I..." Faith blushed and tried to pull away, clearly overcome with second thoughts now that the danger of being shot was further away. Avonstoke's grin had an edge to it now. On her second tug, he released his grip and Faith tumbled back, past me and into one of the Dwarves dashing past carrying a bundle of rope.

The Dwarf growled something that might have been, "Pardon, miss," but didn't stop running. Faith got her arms tangled in the hemp coils and the Dwarf would have dragged her and rope away together in his rush, but Faith shrieked and wrenched herself free of the rope. But her violent motion so unbalanced her that Avonstoke had to catch her again or watch her pitch right over the railing. She gasped, stunned.

"Get your hands off her!" I said.

Avonstoke kept hold of Faith's hand to steady her, but stepped a careful pace away so that they were no longer in that farcical embrace. She tottered unsteadily.

Avonstoke's smile remained, but it had a touch of wry humor in it now. "Ah, yes, you would be the serious sister, I take it? I meant no harm, it only seemed interesting to carry out the part I was cast in your sister's play. I apologize. I would sooner cast myself into this sea than offend you."

"Oh please," I snapped.

"You wound me, serious sister."

Faith hooked her arm through the railing, and he made a grand show of finally releasing her hand.

"Land!" a voice shouted from above. "Land off the starboard bow!" It was the lookout in the crow's nest far above us.

"Ah," Avonstoke said in an entirely more serious voice. "We've come to the bridge."

He pointed towards the bow and we all stared at the shape slowly coming into view. It didn't look like a bridge. No bridge could be that big. This looked more like, say, Russia, if Russia had been pinned up in the sky and left hanging there. Except it was impossibly straight, like a ruler supported by large masonry arcs, each of them large enough in themselves to stage fleet maneuvers under.

The top of the bridge was far above us, but I could still see siege weapons of some sort. Ballistae, I thought, lined up at the edge like a bunch of enormous crossbows. If there was some kind of fort up there, or a traveling army, I wasn't sure.

"What bridge is that?" I said in wonder. It looked the same with either eye, too. Belatedly, I closed my right eye and checked everything around us. Ship, crew, bridge, . . . even Avonstoke remained stubbornly unchanged.

"The Bridge of Sorrows," Avonstoke said softly. "The road through the Borderlands from your world to ours." There was no sign of the mocking humor of seconds ago, but his voice was filled with deep regret. A muscle worked underneath his ear, but otherwise his face was empty of all expression.

"Send out the leaf riders," a voice shouted from the quarterdeck behind us. It still didn't seem like Father's voice, but I couldn't believe that Father wasn't here. Not after seeing the chess set in the captain's cabin.

There was a bustle up near the front of the ship, and a green cloud of leaves rose from the forecastle. On each leaf rode a tiny, pale mushroom-cap figure. They held the reins as their leaf steeds pawed the air with serrated edges and climbed up in defiance of the prevailing wind. They disappeared quickly in the direction of the bridge.

More orders were coming from the quarterdeck as the ship began the intricate and often tricky process of bringing the ship about on the port tack. That was something I desperately wanted to watch in action, but we needed to find Father first. Henry's life might hang in the balance, and I had delayed long enough. I didn't want to be sent back to Stormholt, but balanced against Henry's life, there wasn't any question what the right choice was.

"The captain will likely have you thrown in chains as stowaways," Avonstoke said. His melancholy was discarded as quickly as it had come. "Just when things were getting so entertaining. How sad. But at least we can put that off while I interrogate you. I've told you about the bridge, Serious Sister. Now it's my turn to ask a question. Back and forth is how we shall go, yes?"

"Fine," I said, thinking that this didn't sound so bad compared to normal interrogation methods. The delighted look on his face gave me second thoughts. There was a formality to the way he'd just outlined this game of questions that gave it the weight of ritual. I didn't fancy fencing words with this smug and self-serving Faerie, but he clearly knew a lot I needed to know and anyway, I was in it now.

Avonstoke watched me, stroking his chin in a great show of pondering. "You clearly came through the Round Door. So I don't need to ask how you got here. You don't seem like the enemy to me, despite Mr. Starling's assumption. So I'll ask why you came here." He seemed to expect the answer to come from me, and for once Faith had gone silent. The ship had finally entered the actual turn, coming neatly around.

"We're here to see the Lord of Thorns," I said, using the Faerie name for Father that Victoria Rose had used, since 'Kasric' didn't mean anything to them. "Where is he?"

"Our esteemed leader returned from London seven days ago," Avonstoke said, "and then immediately went deep into Faerie on a venture that did not, I would say, end well. He came back last night injured and alone."

"That can't be," I said, "he was just in London a few days ago."

Faith gave me a serious look. Father's attempted rescue of Mother clearly hadn't gone well.

"Time moves differently in different worlds," Avonstoke said. "The Admiral is on the *Seahome* now, but shall be returning to the *Rachaela* tonight." He pointed at the ship that came into view as the *Rachaela* swung around and we could finally get a look at what was behind us.

It wasn't a ship so much as a floating city made of hundreds of rafts lashed together and bobbing in the water. It had to be the most unseaworthy vessel I'd ever seen. I couldn't imagine how such a thing could possibly stay afloat, let alone manage at sea. Even more perplexing was the nonsensical arrangement of sail. They seemed to be pointing every which way, with nothing like a jib or staysail to guide direction.

Looking at the thing gave me a strange disorienting feeling, because I could clearly see some of the sails billowing in the wrong direction compared to others and contrary to the prevailing wind. Some kind of magic? It had to be.

*Seahome* followed in the *Rachaela's* wake with both ships closing slowly and carefully on the enormous Bridge of Sorrows.

The call came from the quarterdeck to open fire on the bridge.

The bellowing from the gun deck below reached a fever pitch. The two port cannon on the main deck crashed at once, followed an instant later by an even mightier crash from below that shook the entire ship as the *Rachaela* let loose with a broadside at the bridge.

The wind carried away the cloud of foul black smoke in time for me to see the distant line of dust clouds that blossomed partway up the bridge, nowhere close to high enough to reach the line of ballista at the top.

"Don't have the range," Avonstoke said. The holes blown in the side of the bridge were probably large enough to stand in, but they looked like no more than pinpricks from this distance. The *Rachaela* could blast a thousand holes like that and have no effect.

A ponderous series of distant crashes came from the bridge as the enemy returned fire, like twenty enormous doors latching shut. Huge javelins shot from the Bridge of Sorrows, returning fire with siege engines. My stomach lurched as I watched the mast-sized missiles arc out towards us. But we were still out of range for them, too, it seemed. The nearest javelins slid silently into the water a quarter of a mile off the *Rachaela's* starboard bow.

"Don't worry," Avonstoke said, "Captain Caine hardly ever gets within range. The ballistae crews are just hoping for a lucky shot like last week."

"Caine?" I said. "Caine survived the Wild Hunt?" I craned my neck to see back up to the quarterdeck but couldn't see anything from this angle.

"Much to our admiration and dismay," Avonstoke said.

"What happened last week?" Faith said, clearly terrified.

"Main sail wrecked," Avonstoke said offhandedly. "Five of the crew killed outright, three hands lost overboard. Nearly sank. Five more died in surgery after." He shrugged. "Such things happen in war. My turn. Why would the Lord of Thorns help you?"

I ground my teeth and glared at Faith for using up one of our questions. I hadn't wanted to give *that* information away, at first, but maybe it was time to do so, if only to prevent being clapped in irons. I briefly considered lying, but decided against that, too. There was a weight of ritual to this that reminded me of what I knew of the severity of breaking Faerie bargains and promises.

Finally, I said, "He's our Father."

"*Is he?*" Avonstoke said. I'd surprised him with that. His handsome face was deep in thought.

But what question he might have asked next, I'll never know, because his gaze shifted upwards and his yellow eyes shot very wide behind that black mask.

Faith and I spun and saw distant winged shapes, like enormous bats.

"Are those," Faith said, "what I think they are?"

Avonstoke's voice was very hoarse as he said: "Dragons."

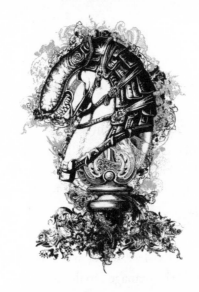

# CHAPTER 13

### Battle at Sea

They might have been only olive-green seagulls at this distance. But I knew they weren't. We weren't that lucky.

"Blood and bones!" Avonstoke was staring, openmouthed. "Dragons don't fight in wars. They're . . . they just *don't*. How does the Black Shuck get them to *do* that?"

"Dragons?" Faith said. "Actual dragons?"

I squinted up into the sun, trying to make out the distant dots. Yes, there they were. Enormous winged lizards, far more graceful in flight than I might have expected, if I'd ever gotten around to expecting dragons. One quick look at the relatively fragile expanse of sail and rigging made me feel sick at the idea of trying to repel attacking dragons from a sailing vessel. Sea captains shouldn't have to factor dragons into their defensive planning. How could they? Dragons!

"The Black Shuck must want us dead in the worst way. Captain!" Avonstoke didn't bother with the stairs, but sprang at the side railing. He seemed barely to touch it before he sprang off that and caught hold of quarterdeck rail above us, hauling himself up with astounding grace. He disappeared with a flash of shadow green cloak.

I ran to the quarterdeck stairs without thinking, dragging Faith with me before she managed to flounder over the rail or into another man's arms again.

Avonstoke was pointing out the spot in the sky for Captain Caine, who was every bit as alive as Avonstoke had said. He pointed a spyglass and erupted into cursing fit to blister my ears.

Caine looked much the same as the last time I'd seen him: tall, thick but not quite fat, with grizzled muttonchops and a heavy scowl. I didn't see any sign of injury from the carriage crash until he lowered the spyglass to reveal a diagonal scar near his right eye. He glanced at us briefly, clearly dismissed us, and put the spyglass back up.

"Whatever they're bloody holding," he growled, "pounds to pennies says they're going to be dropping it on *us*."

A large man with green skin and a mane of black, weedy hair held the tiller with webbed fingers while a small knot of officers stood deferentially to one side, including the red-haired Dwarf we'd seen before. Behind them, on the raised poop deck, two more Dwarven gunner crews manned the shorter carronade guns.

"The Shuck hasn't bothered about our little scouting missions before this," Caine was saying, almost to himself, "but today, he goes to all this trouble. Dragons. There's something up on the bridge he very much wants to keep us from seeing." He handed Avonstoke the spyglass. "Can you see what the beasts are carrying?"

Avonstoke squinted through it. "I can't tell."

While they were doing that, I tried again with my left eye only. The light was curious here, like being out in the country after years spent in the rowboat gray of London. I knew the three dragons had to be more than a mile up, but if I looked very hard, I could make out the dull, greenish tint of their scales and the lighter shade that ran along the underside from neck, to belly, to tail tip with only a little difficulty. I wasn't sure how this could be true, but something about the Faerie light made it so.

The dragons were each clearly carrying something bunched in their claws. Nets filled with something ponderous and heavy.

The Dwarven officer stepped in front of us to block our way. His red mustache, beard and top knot all quivered in rage. "Get them out of the way, I said! Get them off the deck! In chains, if necessary!"

"No! Wait!" I called still looking up. "They're carrying nets filled with something. Cannonballs, I think."

"Are they now?" Caine said.

The Dwarf turned on Avonstoke "I said . . ."

"Avast that," Caine said, cutting him off. "As you were, Mr. Starling."

The Dwarf looked ready to chew his own beard. "Aye . . . captain." He said grudgingly.

"Mr. Lacon, broaden our reach a bit."

The green man at the tiller answered. "Aye, captain."

"We've come as close to the bridge as I dare," Caine said. "Can't play cat and mouse with those ballistae and watch the sky at the same time. Prepare to wear the ship and run full with the wind, north by north west. Mr. Starling, signal the other ship, in case they haven't seen what we have. Have the crew man the braces." His tone was perfectly calm, as if dragons weren't preparing to drop cannonballs on us at all. I could feel my stomach churn. That many cannonballs could turn this entire ship to kindling in addition to pulverizing everyone on board. *Seahome* wouldn't fare any better.

Mr. Starling began shouting orders, getting the crew ready to make sail, human and Faerie figures swarming like monkeys in the rigging to get to their places in preparation for the shift.

Only then did the captain favor us with a glance. "Well, then. You're a far cry from being tucked away in Stormholt, aren't you?" He went back to the spyglass.

"Yes, sir," I said.

This was it. Caine was going to have us clapped in irons and sent back to Stormholt. After we all got killed. Faith still hadn't made any kind of noise. She just kept looking up.

But Caine kept squinting through the spyglass up at the dragons, far, far above. Mr. Starling was still bellowing orders up to the sail crew, preparing to reef the sail with the turn.

"Cannonballs, you say?" Caine said. "I don't know how you got here, girl, but you've just been pressed into service. Come, stand here in the corner. Take the glass and keep watch on those beasties. Give a shout if they let go of those cannonballs. Or do anything else, for that matter."

"Aye-aye, Captain," I said, taking the spyglass with amazement and relief and moving to the spot he'd indicated by the rail. I dragged Faith along and she let me, too bewildered to make any fuss.

"Mr. Lacon, make our turn as soon as she calls the drop," Caine said with a pleased nod. "With the wind, north by northwest. Don't wait for my order."

"Aye-aye, sir. North by northwest."

The ship's crew had suddenly gone still. The guns were run out, the sail where Caine wanted it. We continued cutting through the sea with a regular rhythm. No one spoke.

I kept the spyglass trained on the dragons overhead as they effortlessly drew closer to a position far above us. The black claws released their bundles, so that the contents spilled out, black dots against the yellow sky.

"They're dropping!" I hollered.

Each dragon had dropped at least a dozen cannon balls. That made almost forty deadly missiles falling down.

"Mr. Lacon!" the captain said, but the man was already spinning the tiller and calling out orders to switch the headsail. The *Rachaela* entered into her change of direction with alacrity. The crew clearly knew their business, but it was nerve-wracking maneuver to be done while the cannonballs fell. There was the threat of the siege engines on the bridge, too. If we drifted too close, they'd have us.

The sails hung limply for an uneasy moment as the ship faced into the wind and the sails filled out backwards, then the *Rachaela* heeled over towards her new course and the sail caught in the proper direction.

I could feel it in the deck and hear when the wind through the rigging changed. Everything I'd ever read in Father's nautical books sprang alive and sang around me.

Mr. Starling hollered for the crew to pull the sail tight on the port side, then to reef the top foresail. Caine was desperately trying to get all possible speed out of the wind. But the captain himself said nothing, only watched the cannonballs fall.

We all did. Any second now . . .

An ominous whirring sound swelled, then the first cannonball hit the water with a resounding slap, shooting up a column of spray three yards aft, then four more shots immediately behind it. Our turn, perfectly timed, had taken us out of harm's way. A thirty-second delay and we'd have been right in the thick of it. I tried not to think about what a cannonball at speed does to a person, or a ship.

The sound of splintering wood drifted across the water, followed by screams. *Seahome* had not been so lucky as the *Rachaela*.

I tried to peer over there and still keep an eye on the dragons, but shots falling into the water raised a thick white mist between the two ships, blocking out the Faerie ship entirely. All I could see was a plume of smoke rising up from the back.

Father could be dead right now, crushed by a cannonball. Or lying with a limb shattered, dying. Mr. Sands, too. Either could be dead or dying and there wasn't anything I could do about it.

High above, the dragons banked lazily, admiring their handiwork, perhaps. "They're coming back around!" I called out.

"That was just the opening salvo," Caine said. "Those lizards will be coming down here next."

Avonstoke gave the Captain a shocked look. "No! Do you fire your saints out of cannon?"

"What's that?" Caine said.

Avonstoke answered with reverence in his voice, still gazing upwards. "Before the gods gave birth to the world of Faerie, they gave birth to dragons. It is through the dragons that the gods give us magic. There are only twenty-one of their kind left in all the world. No more new dragons are born. These dragons will be the last. When they die, *magic* dies. A part of the gods forever lost to us, and all of the Faerie realm with it. Not even the Black Shuck would risk that."

Captain Caine made a growl, deep in his chest. "We'll see." He shouted across the deck. "Ready your archers, Swayle. If those things come in, I want to make sure they take as much fire as we can dish out!"

"Sir?" the female marine that had spoken to Avonstoke called back, in much the same voice as if he'd told her to stick her own head in the cannon and fire. She had dark hair, short, underneath a silver gilded helmet.

"You heard me," Caine bellowed. "You knew what this war would mean." He added in a low voice, "We all did. Mr. Starling, you'd better have the carronades ready, too. It might be the only chance we have of actually hurting one."

Mr. Starling's expression was shocked. He finally nodded and said, "Aye." Clearly Avonstoke wasn't alone in his reverence towards the dragons.

"No one told me there'd be bloody *dragons*," Caine growled, while Avonstoke looked shocked and slightly offended.

"If they do come down here," Faith said, "what chance do we have?"

Avonstoke just shook his head.

"Doesn't sound like much of a risk," I muttered. "Not for them." I didn't know if these breathed fire, but the thought of uncontrolled fire on a ship was catastrophic. Of course, looking at the size of them, dragons probably didn't even need the fire.

The danger felt like a dream to me. Less than a week ago, we'd been safe in an outrageously non-magical London. Now, after midnight carriage rides, escapes, train rides and a magic door, it would almost be too laughable and ridiculous to die ten minutes after I'd finally gotten to sea. My heart started to race as I saw the dragons furling their wings.

"They're diving!" I said. "All three of them. Coming fast!"

The Dwarven crew on the poop deck were following orders, but clearly with great reluctance. They operated a winch on the trunnion unlike anything I'd heard of before, levering their carronade up so that it could fire at nearly a forty-five degree angle. I couldn't imagine that working well for very long. The recoil would probably break the wood planks of the deck underneath the carronades after a few shots, and that was assuming they didn't accidentally tear half the rigging away with grapeshot if they pointed it anywhere amidships. Not to mention the sail crew.

"All three dragons are coming for *us*?" Caine said. "None for the Faerie ship?" He sounded hopeful.

"It's us," I said.

"Firing at dragons," Avonstoke said bleakly, pulling his ridiculously small little pistol out. "Highest forgive me. It's not permitted, shooting at divinity. *You'd* better do it." He pushed the gun into my hands.

"Me?" I said. Now that I held it, I could see it was a revolver of stunning beauty, all chased silver and black onyx, but I couldn't see it doing much to dragons unless it shot lightning bolts. I held it at the ready anyway.

I watched them come, their forms swelling as their dive brought them closer and closer. Each of them was half the size of the *Rachaela*. So beautiful, so deadly. So fast. I held the gun, waiting . . .

There was a collective gasp on the deck below. Some of the sailors pointed.

Two familiar figures stood on the highest platform of the Faerie raft. A tall man with dark hair and a shorter one with blonde and tousled hair. Father and Mr. Sands!

The strains of a violin came across the distance. Fiery shapes formed. Mr. Sands' firefly dragons. I remembered them slowing the Wild Hunt, briefly, but couldn't imagine them stopping dragons.

I had more hope in the archers. There looked to be about thirty here on the *Rachaela*, and I could see more than three times that on the Faerie raft. Some of the archers had opened fire already, though how anyone could expect to hit at such a range, I didn't know. I was still waiting for a decent shot to fire.

Only the archers *did* hit them.

It was a glory of Faerie archery, hitting anything while firing straight up. The arrows glanced off the dragons' rocky hides. With their wings tucked mostly in, their eyes narrowed to the barest of slits, the dragons presented no real targets. Or so I thought. I saw the closest dragon twice duck or jerk its head to avoid what would otherwise have been a shot to the eye.

The dragons bore down on the *Rachaela*.

I held the pistol at the ready, knowing how useless it would be. Maybe at close range the archers could do some good, but something told me that by then, it would be too late.

"Prepare to wear the ship," Caine said. Running with the wind might make the *Rachaela* a harder target to hit.

But being attacked by dragons seemed to have done something to the crew.

The British sailors were screaming and flinging themselves over the sides. Nothing in their tour of duty in the Navy, it seemed, had prepared them for anything like dragons. The Faerie weren't much better, stunned and cowering. Even the Crow Whisper Brigade scattered like startled pigeons. Only a few of them were standing their ground, but those few, including Swayle, were firing rapidly, despite the fact that their arrows weren't doing anything whatsoever.

The green helmsman, Mr. Lacon, screamed, let go of the tiller and ran at the railing. He didn't fling himself over so much as hit and rail and keep going, his limbs thrashing all the while. His pained scream, so high-pitched it hardly seemed to come from a person, faded out of earshot.

The tiller spun and the whole ship lurched.

"Damn you, Lacon, you gutless worm!" Caine grabbed the tiller and spat at the railing where Mr. Lacon had gone over. There was no time to turn the ship now. Caine was barely keeping the ship from laying over into the water.

Avonstoke gripped my arm. "Look!" He was pointing at the Faerie ship. "Look at the sail!"

"Who cares about any bloody *sail*," I snarled, which would have been laughably ironic coming out of *my* mouth at any other time. "Get your hands off me and *oooohhhhhh!*"

The largest sail on the Faerie ship, a massive black triangle, was *moving*.

It wasn't a sail at all.

A horned ebony head rose up above the boat, and the black triangle—a wing!—drew itself out, revealing itself to be yet another dragon, and a huge one at that. A dragon on the Faerie boat?

It ducked low behind the dozens of large sails that had helped hide its own bulk. Then the Faerie ship lurched up, relieved of a huge weight, as the new dragon slipped into the water. It had gone, perhaps, retreating to safety.

The enemy dragons drew closer. They were nearly on us.

"This is madness!" Faith sobbed. "We're not even meant to be here!" She and Avonstoke crouched next to me. Faith had one arm hooked around the railing. The other hand clutched Avonstoke's belt. Avonstoke still had a grip on my arm and I used that hand to grasp his arm and steady myself. We could all die here, today, now. Faith, Father . . . all the other people around me. I *had* to do something.

I lifted the pistol and gave it a quick glance. I didn't know much about pistols, but this, with all the silver and black, was clearly a beautiful and deadly piece of art. A combination of human craft and Faerie magic, covered with glyphs like the *Rachaela's* cannon. I had no doubt that it could be deadly with somewhat smaller targets. But this? I cocked it, and the glyphs on the black metal started glowing a deep and serious red. I aimed for the eyes and squeezed the trigger. The pistol went off with a sharp crack.

I wish I could report a fantastic dragon-slaying shot, but the truth is this: I emptied the revolver at our enemy and to this day, I still have no idea if I hit anything or not. In any case, the dragons didn't waver from their course.

"Brace yourselves!" Caine shouted, as the foremost of the diving dragons fell on us, wings dropping a black shadow on us like the touch of doom.

The dragon pulled gracefully out of its dive as it hit, spreading its wings and bringing those claws to bear. The thing's wingspan covered the main deck. The dragon plucked two sailors off the staysail rigging as an eagle takes fish from the sea. Most of the rigging went with them and the sail tore loose and fluttered away as the dragon glided past.

The two men screamed like the damned. Then the claws flexed and they went horribly silent. The dragon dropped bodies and bits of torn-away rigging into the water with equal contempt.

Now that we could see them better, I understood both the terror and the reverence they inspired in the Faerie. The dangling claws, olive-green batlike wings and long, powerful body were terrifying enough, but then the dragon banked to face us. A crown of ragged horns covered the brow and skull and ran along the back to the heavy, spiked club of a tail. Arrows glanced off the dragon's hide continuously, doing nothing. The eyes were unlike any eyes I'd ever seen, gateways to a white-hot incandescence not found on Earth, like the interior of a star.

The first dragon was still turning when the second dragon struck.

It hit the forecastle carronade on the other end of the ship, scattering the crew that had been trying to load it. The impact ran through the deck. The dragon dragged the carronade across the forecastle and through the bow railing, mauling and dragging one of the unfortunate gunners in the process. When the dragon let go, gun, railing and man all disappeared over the bow and down into the water.

Part of the jib and staysail had come loose during the attack and Caine was doing all he could just to keep the wind from putting the *Rachaela* over onto its side. The ship had already gone too far off course. The mizzenmast boom swung over our heads as we caught the wind from the other direction. Caine struggled desperately to haul the wheel over and bring the rudder into a position that wouldn't capsize us.

Both enemy dragons were banking now, getting ready to come back and make second passes, but that was nothing compared to the third green dragon, the largest of them, which bore down on us from above.

The quarterdeck carronade roared, deafening from only a few feet away, but the gunners had fired too soon, at long range. The smaller grapeshot that would have scoured an enemy deck free of men didn't so much as make a mark on the dragon's hide, especially since the crew had angled the cannon away to avoid raking the sail or sail crew. The deck splintered under the pressure. It wouldn't take many shots like that for the carronade to crash right through.

The last green dragon had held back, letting the other two strike first. Now it braked as it fell on us, looking for a killing blow. Its wings were fully extended as it reached out talons that would tear off the main mast and cripple us once and for all. It was so close, now. I felt I could reach out and grab it. An arid wind came with it, foreign to the sea.

Frantic, I tried the pistol again. All I got was empty clicking.

A second shape rose from the surface of the sea in a colossal spray of water.

The black dragon from the Faerie ship!

It passed over the *Rachaela* like a breaching mountain, glistening black all over and sheeting water down on us as its arc took it past the masts and sails, where it intercepted the other dragon. The black dragon was enormous, more than twice the green dragon's size, which meant it dwarfed the *Rachaela*. The water from the dragon's breach alone hit the *Rachaela* like the crest of a storm. Two of the Goblins shrieked as rigging snapped and the main topsail tore into two raggedy pieces, each of them flapping uselessly.

The enemy dragon's pained scream tore through the air with enough force to bruise my ears. The writhing bundle of dragons, black and green, tumbled down, and both of them fell into the sea thirty yards off the starboard railing. The last part to disappear was the black dragon's long and sinuous tail, which smashed the quarterdeck railing next to us to absolute bits before it slipped down into the water and out of sight.

That much dragon hitting the water was like an instant tsunami.

The ship bucked and heaved up like a god's plaything. With a sickening motion, the ship fell. I heard the wood planking tear and we hit something with a crunch. Then the cascade of water came down on the quarterdeck, battering us to the planks like a massive hammer.

The ship tipped and Faith slid towards the gap in the rail, screaming and thrashing.

She would have gone right through the gap in the railing with the water and foam if Avonstoke hadn't held on to her.

He gripping my hand, too, and I hooked my other arm around the railing near me. Even with this support, Faith's legs went off the quarterdeck and the rest of her nearly followed. I could feel my shoulder joint being pulled right from its socket, but held on anyway. Finally, Avonstoke managed to haul her back on the deck and she clung to him, sobbing gratefully.

I was just struggling to my feet when a broken spar hit Caine on the back of his skull. He crumpled to the deck like so much wet laundry. The tiller he'd been holding spun wildly, and the ship lurched.

Without thought, I rushed over and grabbed at the moving tiller. The spokes bashed my hands hard enough to split the skin, but I got a hold and kept it. The ship rolled, groaned and shook as if it might break apart at any time. I couldn't pull the tiller back over, and the *Rachaela* was getting ready to lay right over to port. I screamed in frustration and dug in my heels, pulling, pulling . . .

Then Avonstoke was there, holding the other side of the tiller amidst the spray. He followed my lead and together we forced the tiller slowly back around. Suddenly the weight on the tiller got easier and the ship got some headway and I breathed a sigh of relief as the deck straightened out underneath us. I bawled at the two nearest people I could see, the two green-skinned, web-fingered children I'd seen before. They were staring, amazed, past the rail where Mr. Lacon had gone over.

"He just . . ." the girl said.

"Help him!" I said nodding at Caine. They both glared at me but dragged Caine's limp body off the quarterdeck, hopefully to surgery.

The battle around us was far from over, but it looked like nothing was going to further pulverize us in the next few seconds.

Distant strains of Mr. Sands' violin drifted across the open water. Above *Seahome*, a dozen of Mr. Sands' magical firefly dragons chased one of the enemy dragons like bees on a bull. The dragon snapped and bellowed angrily as it flew, trying to angle around towards *Seahome* and lose his pursuers at the same time. The other dragon was climbing. It looked like a few of the Faerie archers had done some damage. The shafts of two arrows were stuck in the dragon's eye and the light in it had died, even if the dragon itself was still very much alive.

*Seahome* was burning. It was only one corner, but with oiled sail and tar and a hundred other flammable items, fire could engulf a ship in seconds. *Seahome* didn't have long. Despite arrows and Mr. Sands' firefly dragons, both of the real dragons were banking to come back in and finish it off.

A quarter mile off the port bow, the water broke and the enormous black dragon breached out of the water again.

This was my first real good look at our savior dragon, and was it a sight! This dragon moved differently than the others, not mere raw power but a sinuous black waterfall, dangerous and deadly swift. The eyes burned with that same terrifying hot white light I'd seen in the other dragons, only more so. It, too, had a ridge from head to tail, a jagged line of black ice. Instead of the spiked morningstar tails, the black dragon's tail was a long whip. It bellowed a triumphant challenge and both enemy dragons decided that vengeance for their fallen sibling would wait for another day. They fled towards the bridge.

The black dragon had saved us, but a shiver that had nothing to do with the cold still ran through me when I looked at it. The idea of something that *big* engaged in warfare staggered me.

A reddish slick of blood welled up from the spot where the green dragon had gone down. Barrels of it roiled and bubbled to the surface. The Goblins up in the sails wailed and moaned.

I looked back and saw the numb faces of the Dwarven carronade crew on the poop deck behind us. Some of them were still looking at the sea to see if the fallen dragon might come back up. Next to me, Avonstoke was looking too, his face drained and pale around the black mask, tears running down his face. Other Faerie were weeping openly. Two of the Goblins in the rigging above me were sobbing into each other's arms. I opened my mouth to say something about the dragon being the enemy and stopped.

I remembered what Avonstoke had said about the dragons. *When they die, all magic dies, and all of Faerie with it.* Was that true?

Avonstoke's head bowed, but his hand stayed on the tiller. I was sure I couldn't yet understand what kind of religious or cultural price these people were paying for this war, but it was clearly profound.

But someone still had to get the crew moving, or our cost was going to be higher yet.

I didn't see any of the officers. Possibly they'd gone overboard during the dragon attacks. A lot of people had. The *Rachaela* was still in danger of tipping over, but none of the Faerie seemed to know what to do next.

Swayle, the hard-faced commander of the Crow Whisper Brigade, climbed wearily up on the quarterdeck, followed by two of her marines and the Dwarven officer, Starling.

Swayle looked down at her bow as if suddenly remembering she had it. It was beautiful, layered strips of brown and gold, gilt all over with runes.

I knew from her face that she'd been one of the few archers to make a hit during the attack and that it was one of *her* arrows that had stuck in the green dragon's eye.

She made a noise of disgust, took one last look at the bow, and flung it into the ocean.

"You might need that again," Avonstoke said softly.

"I'll get another," Swayle said. "I'll not touch that one again. Not after what I did with it."

"Turn the ship the other way!" Mr. Starling snapped at me. "We're drifting too close to the bridge!"

"Absolutely not!" I said quickly. "We need to put the stay sail back in place or the ship will lay over the second we turn it."

"Nothing this barbaric contraption did would surprise me," he said with weariness, but he looked expectantly at Swayle. It seemed she was the next in the chain of command. "Captain Caine is in . . . surgery." His voice suggested that surgery was completely synonymous with horrific, painful and instant death. He looked around the deck, conspicuously empty of anyone else in an officer's uniform. His gaze, when he dragged it back to her, spoke volumes.

Swayle's face twisted and she said something foul-sounding that wasn't in English, but nonetheless needed no translation. She looked at Avonstoke, who made such a grand gesture of shrugging without letting go of the tiller that it might have been comical in other circumstances.

"You didn't fire," she said to him, "but you didn't run, either." She snorted. "Unlike most of the ship."

"No," Avonstoke said. "I didn't run." Seeing the two together showed that Avonstoke was a little shorter than the other marine and perhaps a little younger. I wondered how much younger then pulled my mind back to important things.

"We need the stay sail repaired," I said, "and the jib. That's just for starters. We're losing too much to windward."

Swayle shook her head, not understanding and clearly angry about it.

"If we don't fix them," I said, "we can't steep properly and we get too close to that." I pointed at the looming bridge and all the siege weapons pointed in our direction.

"I'm pretty sure that's bad," I said.

"On that," Swayle said, "we agree. Fine, we shall have your stay and whatever in blazes the other one was. But if you crash this contraption, I'll curse your name before I die."

"Fine," I said. "You!" I jabbed my finger at a gaggle of Goblins staring at us, goggle-eyed. "We need to drag that torn sail out of the water before it lays us over."

I turned back on Starling and said, "Do you have spare sails in store?"

Starling nodded. "Aye," he said, and bustled off.

By then we'd taken so much water on that I ordered a bunch of Dwarves onto the bilge pumps. Amazingly, they listened. The decking around the quarterdeck carronades needed repair and the massive damage to the forecastle had to be addressed. There was no replacement for the carronade lost there, but we would have to soldier on without it.

Slowly, very slowly, the *Rachaela* came back to life.

# CHAPTER 14

## Father Returns

I stood barefoot on the bowsprit, a long, narrow pole at the very front of the ship that hung out over the churning, sapphire sea. The ship swooped and sank, a motion amplified at the very front of the ship and it made me happier than I can ever remember being before in my life. The staysail rigging gave me plenty to hold onto and I couldn't bring myself to fear the sea, not even a little bit, for all the danger I knew it held. I'd been waiting to be here for too long to be afraid now.

All my life, really. I felt secure, despite the heaving and bucking of the ship and slippery footing. The *Rachaela* would not let me fall. The occasional plumes of foam drenched my bare feet and soaked my pants but I wasn't cold.

The sea was choppy and a fitful wind came out of the east, but the *Rachaela* rode easy with her sails trimmed and the sea anchor out for drag. The crew behind me worked small tasks on the deck and up in the rigging and I knew the purpose of all of them. Many I'd read about. Others, I just knew.

No ocean back home looked quite this blue, and certainly that creamy, gorgeous yellow sky wasn't there. How lucky I felt now! Not just at sea but at *this* magical sea. I felt more at ease out here than I ever had on land.

For a brief time, I'd had a miraculous command of a ship. But now that time was coming to an end.

Back aft and off to leeward, a small shell-like rowboat from *Seahome* fought the waves as Faerie seaman rowed toward us— Father and Mr. Sands returning, so they could lock me back up in Stormholt.

My stomach churned when I thought of what was coming next. Father was going to be furious with me. He might never look at me the same way once he found out I'd left Henry back in London. Anything could be happening to Henry right now and it was all my fault. Hadn't the trip been my idea? He might even be . . . dead. I felt cold and lost just thinking about it. Almost as monstrous as Henry's fate was the idea of explaining it to Father. How would he feel about me after I'd told him?

And would telling Father about Henry even help? Father hadn't been able to help Mother, if Avonstoke's story was true. Faith was right. Perhaps there wasn't any help for ourselves *except* ourselves. Which meant that *I* had to be prepared to do something about Henry. But what?

I looked further back to the quarterdeck where Faith and Avonstoke leaned against the rail, talking quietly. Faith's hair, almost white in this light, whipped around her face, but the moment the wind died, it fell right back into place again as tidy as you please. My hair was never that well behaved. Even now, it was a tangle of blonde waves and curls. But Faith, with her slender frame and regal bearing, could have almost been Faerie herself.

Faith was talking to Avonstoke, but I noticed, with a clandestine thrill, that Avonstoke wasn't actually paying any attention to her.

He was staring at me.

The slightest smile played over that wide mouth as he openly watched me sway on the bowsprit. His pale, golden eyes shone out of the mask tattoo, but even without irises or pupils, they conveyed a mix of emotions. Maybe expression had more to do with the lids or eyebrows or the rest of the face. I wasn't sure. I found the man infuriatingly confusing. Even now, I thought I saw wistfulness, philosophical acceptance, hope, doubt, fear, and a few more things I couldn't catch. With Avonstoke, it wasn't that I couldn't read his expression, but rather that I couldn't read them as quickly as they flew by. I didn't think I'd seen his face stay still for two seconds in a row yet.

The last was an insolent grin, because he'd caught me staring.

He waved.

I spun back towards the incoming rowboat, blushing furiously.

I stuck my hand in my coat pocket, where I still had Avonstoke's little silver and black pistol. It should probably frighten me, such a thing, but it didn't. The chess piece was in the other pocket, and I found myself checking one or the other constantly, touching them idly as if they were artifacts of power. Even my coat, Father's old black oilskin ulster made for the sea, had more meaning here to me than it had in London. And the hat I'd taken from Stormholt finished off the outfit of a true pirate scoundrel lass and no mistake.

I grinned in spite of myself.

Captain Caine came up to the forecastle, frowning at my antics on the bowsprit. He adjusted his cocked uniform hat twice, muttering darkly and revealing the long row of stitches on the temple the surgeon had left him. With his hat settled, he took out his pipe and a pouch of shag tobacco. He moved closer to me and pointed with the stem of the pipe at the giant Faerie ship sitting with unnatural stillness in the water.

"*Seahome*," he said, and spat. "Damned thing wouldn't float for thirty seconds, either, without their bloody magic."

Just as I'd suspected. I couldn't imagine that monstrous raft weathering a storm in the open sea. I pointed at the mismatched sails. "Do they control the wind, too?"

"Aye. No other way for that thing to sail. Not a real seaman among the lot of them. Faerie have been using magic at sea for so long they don't know how to manage without. Cheating, if you ask me. None of them would have gotten the ship back in line with the jib, the way you did. That's more seamanship than I'd expect out of a girl that's never been to sea."

I didn't have anything to say to that, so I didn't.

"Where'd you learn about ships, lass? Your Father?"

"Some of it," I said. "But mostly I read his books."

"Books? Tell the others that story, if you want, but not to me. You don't get sea legs from books. Most folks would be feeding the fishes their lunch over rail by now, not dancing on the bowsprit."

"It was books," I said, shrugging. "I always wanted Father to take me to sea, but he never did. Mother wouldn't let him." But that was the past, when all our family was together. Talking about things I did back then, it didn't even seem anything I did. I wasn't that same girl anymore.

Captain Caine leaned easily against one of the rails, moving with the motion of the ship and with one arm around the rigging in a slightly awkward manner. He lit his pipe. "Keep your secrets then, but I'll grant you this, you showed some real seamanship. Shame you're not a lad, it is. A *lad* like you would make a fine officer."

I glared at him. Bad enough I was trapped as a girl back in England, but did that have to happen in Faerie, too? There were women in the crew and Swayle, a woman Faerie, was an officer. Why couldn't a human woman be one too?

Caine didn't even notice my glare. He was too busy puffing angrily on his pipe and leveling a glare of his own at the Faerie ship. "Sailing is a dying art, girl. There's too few on this ship to my taste that can feel the difference between when to reef sail or when to run the top gallants. We've no ship's master or real navigator to speak of. Few of the English sailors Lord Kasric's provided have any modern seamanship and the Faerie have no seamanship whatsoever. Just bloody magic." He turned back to me. "You sure you've not sailed before?"

"No sir," I said. I couldn't say myself where my gut feelings on how to sail came from, now that I thought about it. Yes, I read plenty on it, but Caine was right. There was something else, a natural instinct, guiding my actions, too. That thought was a dark little tickle in the back of my mind that I pushed away.

The hatch to the lower decks opened with a heavy thump and one of the Faerie marines came up onto the deck. Her face was controlled, but her grip on the knife in her belt was tight enough to blanch her knuckles white.

Victoria Rose came up out of the hatch next, followed by another marine.

Caine had given orders to allow the fox-like Faerie some time up in the open air, which was standard treatment for prisoners, but caused some fearful grumbling among the Faerie crew. They all seemed to know Victoria Rose, at least by reputation, and the reputation wasn't good. Heavy shackles circled the Rose's wrists and ankles, and still she managed to walk gracefully. I couldn't help but look at the manacles and wonder about Henry. Was he in manacles like this even now? For that matter, I had the same questions about Mother and Joshua. Who knew what kind of trouble they'd walked into going into Faerie.

Father's rowboat drew up to the ship. One of the crewman threw down a line.

"Come, lass," Caine said. "Time to face the Lord of Thorns."

"Why do they call him that?" I asked. "He's not a lord back home."

"Don't know," Caine admitted. "Course that don't mean much. What I *don't* know about Rachek Kasric could fill the horizon. But I fought under his command in the Crimea and there's no man I trust more. The Faerie Outcasts call him Lord of Thorns. They practically worship him when they won't listen to no other man I know. He's the right one to defend against this pack of devil worshippers from the Seelie Court. I know that much." He tapped a blunt finger against his own head. "He knows how they *think*."

Caine led me to the rail next to Faith and Avonstoke, who grinned at me. Flanked as I was by the three of them, I suddenly wished for taller shoes. Or maybe stilts.

Father had to be hauled up carefully with block and tackle, as his arm was in a sling. He looked worn, haggard, stiff with pain. I took a good look with both my left and my right eye. I was more than a little relieved to see that he looked the same, and thoroughly human, regardless of which eye I used. He was dressed simply, without any uniform, only a dark brown, seamed, waterproofed leather coat and trousers, with a tan shirt. The white cloth of the sling for his arm looked newer and cleaner than the rest. An unadorned sword in a scarred scabbard hung at the waist. His face looked tired, but his blue eyes blazed with determination.

"They've agreed," Father said to Caine immediately before his feet even hit the deck. "They'll support us and we need their numbers. They agreed too easily, in fact. *She* wants something. We'll have to deal with that when it comes. One thing's for certain, they don't want to be stuck here. What news here?" He was too busy getting the lines off to even notice Faith and I standing behind Caine.

"The mizzenmast needs repair," Caine said, "as you can see, sir. At least a day to get us ship shape."

"The Outcasts will be sending engineers and carpenters over for that. What else?"

"No reports from our scouts, sir. Whatever else the Black Shuck did, he kept us from getting a good look at what he's hiding up on the bridge. Also, the messages from London are overdue."

"The Black Shuck may have found a way to stop the messages. That could make things tricky. We know his army hasn't crossed the bridge yet. Maybe we'd better check London, just in case. No one's used the door in the last twenty-four hours, so Sands and I will go back that way and alert the Hussars to what we need."

Mr. Sands himself clambered over the side. He was dressed far more fastidiously than Father in a dark gray suit and frock coat. His head was bare and the wild yellow hair was truly at its most windblown out here at sea. He, too, had a sword, a thin rapier from the look of the sheath. He noticed us immediately. The look of surprise on his face was almost comical.

"No sir," Caine said stiffly. "I'm afraid using the door back to London won't be possible."

"Someone's used it?" Father snapped. "I gave strict orders . . ."

Caine stood to one side and jerked his thumb at us.

Father froze. "Ah," he said, and ran his hand through his dark, ruffled hair. His face was suddenly difficult to read and very old.

I looked at Faith and took a deep breath. Best get all this out and over with and tell him about Henry first.

"We went . . ." I started.

"Did you find Mother?" Faith asked him. "You said you'd go after her. Did you even try?" So much for getting my confession out.

"I *did* seek her out," he said.

"Then what happened?" Faith said. I could tell it was all she could do not to scream.

"I found her," Father said, "and she nearly killed me." He looked down at his injured arm significantly.

"Did you at least talk to her?" Faith said.

He sighed. "I tried." He looked like he was about to say more, and then changed his mind. Faith opened her mouth again, but Father lifted his hand and there was enough of his old, masterful self to stall her next outburst.

"Benedict's still at Stormholt," I blurted, seizing my opportunity, "but the rest of us snuck out while the cats were being fed."

Father gave Sands a dark look, but the little magician was so surprised, staring at us, that he didn't even notice.

"Henry went with us to London," I went on, "but then the Faerie captured him. Or . . . killed him. We don't know which. London's overrun, too. There's Faerie trees and plants grown all over everything in London only no one can see them but me, and there's this massive tree looming over all the rest, like a mountain, Father. It's tearing London Bridge apart and that's just the beginning!"

"Henry killed?" Father said. He slumped heavily against the ship's rail, and Captain Caine had to reach out and steady him.

"Overrun?" Mr. Sands said. "The Faerie shouldn't have any real numbers in London yet. There aren't that many places to cross and we've been watching them all. Are you sure?"

"I saw it. They're everywhere. At least the trees are."

Mr. Sands blew out his cheeks. "Then the Faerie themselves *must* be."

Father's glacial-blue eyes surveyed the pair of us, then glanced questioningly at Mr. Sands. Finally, he mastered himself and regarded me again.

"I'll need to hear it all," he said. "Starting with how you got out of Stormholt. That would be your doing, Justice?"

I nodded, miserable. "Yes." My voice was terribly small with the sea and ship noises all around. The rest of the crew were still going about their business and more than likely couldn't hear most of what was being said, but their curious gazes lingered and there was no doubt we were the center of attention for the entire ship's crew.

Father's voice took on a different, softer tone, possibly to match my own, when he said, "I thought you trusted my judgment."

There wasn't any anger in him, but his words hit like a blow. I'd *wanted* to trust him when he put us in Stormholt, but I just couldn't stay on the sidelines while events tore our family apart. He had to understand that, didn't he?

"*We* did it," Faith said. "Together."

That was a lie. I'd pushed them into it and there was just no denying it. But I was grateful to Faith anyway. It felt good to have the connection between us back again, to feel like sisters, even in all the chaos and tragedy going on.

Father lifted his palms in a gesture of helplessness. "This is *exactly* the danger I wanted to keep you far away from. Why would you come here, of all places? How did you even find the door to bring you here?"

Everyone was watching us, including the Faerie marines, which was probably what gave Victoria Rose her opportunity.

The stifled grunts on my right didn't register until several seconds too late. When I turned—along with everyone else—it was to see the two marines guarding Victoria Rose crashing heavily to the deck.

She'd gotten her hands free somehow and the manacles dropped from her wrists with a clatter. Then the Faerie crouched and rocked onto her back in one fluid motion, yanking her left foot from the shackle.

A lot of blood came with it, but she was back on her feet in an instant.

Two more marines grabbed at her, missing outrageously as she jumped neatly up onto the rail. She balanced there for an instant, swinging her right foot around so that the loose weight of the manacle smashed into the nearest marine's face. The marine fell to the deck, spitting out a bloody mess of teeth.

I thought she meant to jump overboard and try and swim her way to safety, but escape didn't seem to be her intention at all. Victoria Rose looked over at us, flashed the kind of nasty grin that belonged in a dark and seedy alley somewhere, and started along the rail towards us, balancing as easy as you please.

The crew and marines shouted and crowded in her direction, but she evaded them with ease. The risk of striking the crowd on deck limited the use of any pistol or bow, and no one had their weapons ready anyhow. Other marines and sailors were trying to get to her, but everyone was getting in each other's way. Caine and some of the other officers shouted orders that no one could hear over the general outcry.

Avonstoke stepped in front of Faith and I, his face suddenly grim. He did something I couldn't see with his hands and there was soft whump as a curved and very deadly and dangerous looking sword appeared in his hands out of nowhere. Avonstoke looked suddenly very deadly and dangerous himself.

Victoria Rose stopped a few feet away from him and hissed like a stoat from her elevated, swaying perch on the rail. The red gloves she'd had on before were gone now, revealing knife-like talons. They glistened, dark and wet.

Avonstoke lunged and slashed at her feet with the curved sword, but she wasn't there.

Victoria Rose leapt from the rail, impossibly nimble, towards the center of the ship. She touched briefly on the vertical surface of the main mast, then landed on one of the yardarms and ran along it to pass by Avonstoke and us entirely and drop down onto the deck next to Father and Mr. Sands. A kick sent Mr. Sands back, but the real blow was a wicked slash from those glistening claws at Father's shoulder. It cut through the sling and uniform and laid the flesh open.

Father cried out, but managed to deliver her a backhanded blow across her face with his good hand that sent her to the deck. The damage was already done. He staggered with pain and clutched his bloody shoulder. Red seeped slowly through his fingers.

There had been a lot of weight behind Father's blow, but Victoria Rose was already up again. She grinned with triumph at him, despite the blood on her mouth.

Mr. Sands had his rapier out. He lunged at her. The rapier flashed in the sun and I saw it was silver, like Rose's own weapon.

The Rose danced backwards, then had to duck an arrow from one of the marines. Another jump onto one of the cannons avoided a British sailor's grab. She put a stiff kick into his face and the sailor went down.

I shuffled to one side to get a clear view. Somehow, Avonstoke's pistol had found its way into my hand. The glyphs glowed like red embers when I cocked it.

"Justice, you fool!" Faith hollered. "What are you doing?" I didn't bother answering her.

Everyone on the ship had some kind of weapon out now, a sword or pistol, but Victoria Rose was an elusive target weaving among the rigging and spars, making her way aft, climbing higher as she went. We had a lot of sail reefed, but there was still plenty of cover for her. A few arrows thunked into the mast behind her, and a thrown axe sailed past, devastating the mizzenmast rigging but leaving her untouched. I ran aft, trying to keep Victoria Rose in sight through the crowd on deck and the rigging. She'd have to come down somewhere! It wasn't that big of a ship.

Three Goblins from the sailing crew tried getting in her way, all of them clambering swiftly over the yardarm, bulky with reefed sail. Victoria Rose crouched and swept her foot out, as neat and pretty as ballet, and the closest Goblin screamed and fell twenty feet to crunch horribly on the deck amidships.

I got to the quarterdeck staircase just as Victoria Rose dropped down on the quarterdeck's port-side railing a mere three feet from me.

"Don't move!" I said, pointing the pistol.

Afterwards, it was the prevailing theory that she'd intended on destroying the tiller after she'd accomplished her attack on the Lord of Thorns. Another prevailing theory was that Victoria Rose couldn't swim, otherwise she'd have just dropped off the railing into the water.

Instead, she bared her teeth and swiped at me with those claws of hers.

I shot her.

I shot without hesitation, point blank. One pull of the trigger, and a sharp crack sounded. There was a second flash of heat from the markings on the gun, then a red splotch appeared, as if by magic, in Victoria Rose's neck. It wasn't very well-aimed. I'd been aiming lower, but I hadn't been ready for the kick a gun makes going off. Victoria Rose stared at me, stunned. A whistling bee went by my ears and an arrow appeared in the Faerie girl's chest an instant later.

Victoria Rose teetered on the rail, an expression of confusion on her face as she put a hand on the arrow. Not tugging, just touching it as if she were trying to make sure it was really there. Her face, empty of anything except that confusion, suddenly looked far younger.

I felt a shudder run through me as her eyes rolled up into the back of her head. The wound my gun had made in her neck was already bleeding all down her front, black on the scarlet cloth.

Then Victoria Rose toppled off the rail and down into the churning water.

*It's her this time,* I thought. *But that could have been me.* She'd been about my age and despite being on opposite sides I had the feeling we had had more in common than most. Maybe someday soon, it would be me.

The arrow had come from Swayle. She peered over the rail next to me, then nodded with satisfaction.

"Nice shot," she said. The intended compliment felt like a kick in my gut, and I just started at her.

Avonstoke was at my side instantly, staring in amazement first at me, then at the railing where Victoria Rose had gone over. He still had the curved sword.

"Did she touch you?" he said.

"What?" I was still looking at the railing, horrified now that I had time to think about it.

Avonstoke yanked me roughly. "Did she touch you?" He grabbed me by the hair suddenly, tilting my face so that he could look for any mark or sign.

"Get off me!" I shoved him away.

He was right back in my face. "What do you think you're doing?" he hissed. "An assassin reveals herself in our midst, and you run *towards* her? You might have been killed!" He was pleading now. His expression looked such a strange combination of anger and terror that it took me aback. Why should he care so much?

"I'm fine," I said, still a bit stunned by everything that had just happened. "That is . . ." I gestured helplessly at the place where Victoria Rose had gone over when I'd shot. When I'd killed her.

Avonstoke's face was very close to mine now and the strangest expression had suddenly crawled onto his. He looked like he wanted to say something, only didn't know how, which wasn't the Avonstoke *I* knew, by any stretch. He looked down at me and the swaying of the ship conspired to jostle us closer still. We were practically embracing now. His mouth opened and a sudden look of yearning came over him. For just an instant, I half expected him to kiss me right here in front of everyone.

Then his mouth twisted in a self-deprecating smile and he took a small step back.

"You're not hurt, then?" he said. "She didn't scratch you?"

I just shook my head. This was too much to take in. But I wasn't hurt. Victoria Rose hadn't touched me and I felt fine, physically. I stared down at the gun in my hand, belatedly remembering that most guns needed to be cocked first. Apparently, this wasn't one of those.

"I didn't expect you to use your gift so soon," Avonstoke murmured. His tone was clearly trying for casual, but it was strained. His expression was still frightened. Not for himself, but for me. He was trying to hide it with a wry smile, but I could still see it in his eyes, their strangeness notwithstanding.

He took a deep breath, visibly mastering himself. Then he seemed to remember suddenly that he was holding a sword. Not just any sword, either. This one was made of a dull black material, not iron, more like oxidized metal that smoldered with contained lightning, but black as a crow's wing. He made a motion with his hand like a stage magician and it disappeared. On any other day, or any other moment, it would have been astonishing. There was too much going on just then.

"First time you've ever shot at anybody, I expect?" He took the gun from my unresisting fingers.

"She tried to kill Father," I said blankly, then, "Assassin?" My god, he was right. Victoria Rose had been looking for Father, hadn't she? She'd admitted as much. Father's assassin, and I brought her right to him!

"Justice!" Faith shouted from the other side of the deck. She was standing by Father, her face tight.

I shoved Avonstoke out of the way and rushed across the deck.

Mr. Sands and two sailors were trying to hold Father's shoulders steady while Father spasmed helplessly on the deck. Father's eyes rolled, showing only the whites as his arms flopped limply. His thrashing feet knocked over a coil of rope, and foam flecked his lip.

"Father!" I cried.

"Hold him, I said!" Mr. Sands yelled. He looked at the shoulder wound, where a nauseating yellow foam had formed. Mr. Sands sniffed at it while the marines did their best to keep Father still.

I flung myself down next to them. "What's happening?"

"Yellow Veil," Mr. Sands said, his voice tight. "Poison."

"Can you cure it?" Captain Caine said.

Mr. Sands shook his head. "My magic doesn't work that way. Even if it did, Yellow Veil has long been used by blackhearts and assassins among the Faerie precisely because of its resistance to magical cure and its deadliness among the Faerie. Which may be our saving grace. We need to get him inside. Now."

They carried Father's jerking figure into the captain's cabin. I followed, my heart pounding and my stomach doing flip flops.

Mr. Sands put up a hand to the door, blocking me out.

"But I—" I started, but it was too late. Mr. Sands slammed the door in my face.

I stood dazed.

The wind was still coming from a northeasterly direction and the *Rachaela* still rode easily using the sea anchor in a calm sea, but somehow everything had changed.

Avonstoke and Faith were both staring at me.

"This is *our* fault," I said. "We brought her here."

"Oh god," Faith said. I could see the blood drain from her face as the realization hit her.

"You brought her as a *prisoner*," Avonstoke said. "We had her in chains and under guard after you told us how dangerous she was. This was not your fault." He grabbed me again, his face deadly serious. "This is *not* your fault."

"I..." I couldn't get any of the words right. "What are we going to do?"

Flashes of emotion crossed Avonstoke's face, but he finally mastered himself and seemed to realize that he still held onto my arm and suddenly let me go. "You carry on," he said. "You do what you can, when you can. Here, do you still have the ammunition I gave you?"

"Yes, but..."

"When the fight is over," he said, "and you're done shooting, always remember to reload. Don't wait until later. Do it as soon as the shooting's done. It might be too late if you wait." He took the gun and flipped open the cylinder and handed it back to me. His hands were warm when he gripped mine briefly to make me take it. "Do it now. Unloaded guns get people killed during war time."

After a moment of stunned incomprehension, I pulled out the bag of cartridges. The outside of each cartridge was brass, while the bullet itself gleamed silver in some places, with dull black iron in others, in an intricate pattern. Special ammunition made to kill Faerie.

The act of pulling out the cartridges and carefully fitting them into place wasn't easy with shaking hands, but by the time I'd gotten the sixth bullet in and closed the cylinder my hands weren't shaking quite as badly and I felt a little bit like I could breathe again.

I put the gun back in the holster and after staring at it for a long time and thinking about Victoria Rose's confused expression, I buckled the holster on. I couldn't get the gun to feel right at the side, so I settled with putting it in the front.

The waiting was agony. Captain Caine went in and didn't come out for a long time and still there was no news of Father.

An engineering team of Faeries from *Seahome* arrived, more of the Dwarves, who started a fury of sawing and hammering as they tore out part of the deck in order to fix the broken mizzenmast, which at any other time would have been interesting. I sat on the quarterdeck stairs and watched without really seeing anything.

Faith and Avonstoke sat with me for a while, and I began to wonder what Avonstoke's duties were. He didn't really seem a proper part of the marines, even if he wore the uniform. He just didn't go where the others did, never stood watch that I could see and clearly wasn't worried what Swayle, the commanding officer, might want of him. If anything, the other Faerie deferred to him. Whatever his duties were supposed to be, he wasn't doing them if all he did was provide us with his companionship.

When Caine finally came out, his face was grim. "They won't know anything about your father for some time. The magicians, are doing what they can, but of course they don't know anything."

"As to your brother, Henry," Caine went on, "he also lives. He's being imprisoned. Our methods of sending messages leave a bit to be desired, if you ask me, but Sands and the Outcast magician believe they can get a message through to Stormholt."

"Who are these Outcasts everyone's talking about?" I said.

Caine pointed at *Seahome*. "They're Faerie, but Faerie that challenged the Seelie Court's decision to invade England. Before you get all sappy-eyed about the Outcast cause, you should know that most of 'em *hate* humans. They'd rather have nothing to do with us. They want to tear down the bridge between our worlds once and for all, only there's the Seelie Court invasion force marching across that bridge, so for the moment, they're our allies.

"Anyway, our operative in England will stage some kind of breakout with the Ghost Boys there, or call in the Winged Hussars, if they have to. They're not usually used for city work, but Sands is determined. They should be able to do something about your brother. There's a lot of concern over your story, girl. No one here thought the Faerie had gotten across in any significant numbers, but your story makes a lie of that idea, doesn't it?"

"Yes," I said. "Yes it does."

At dusk, the yellow sky deepened to a pale grey, and the darker gold of the sun looked unreal as it slid into the shimmering blue-gold waters, but I could barely see it through my tears.

"What if Father dies?" I said.

"We'd lose a great man," Avonstoke said instantly. "The Lord of Thorns is a legend. Our greatest general."

"Father said the war was going badly." I hated myself for admitting it aloud, what it might mean. "Father is a great man, but he's no undefeated Faerie general. I think there might be some mistake."

"He can't be both, can he?" Faith said.

"That," Avonstoke said, "is a question for your father, isn't it?"

Faith scoffed. "There must be a religious taboo among the Faerie about answering questions. None of you ever will."

Avonstoke didn't say anything to that.

"Rachek Kasric," Faith said, with emphasis, "isn't this Faerie general you keep talking about. He's a merchant captain, that's all. He has a wife and five children. Normal English children. This famous Faerie general you think he is, that's just another story."

Avonstoke threw up his hands. "I only have stories, and none of them can I swear to. The Lord of Thorns is a bit like your Father

Christmas. No man can say what he has or hasn't done. Certainly not me."

"That's not an answer, either," Faith said. She pointed at the captain's cabin. "I don't know who that man is, leading this Faerie fleet of yours, but he's *not* our Father."

Avonstoke just lifted his hands again, as if he could believe anything and nothing about the Lord of Thorns with equal ease. "It's always been one of those things I thought I'd learn more about later, when I was older."

"Older?" Faith said. "Aren't you Faerie all ageless? How old are you now?" I found myself thrumming with a little thread of tension that ran along my spine as I waited for his answer.

Instead of answering Faith, he was looking at me with those huge eyes. "I'm only a year older than you are, my captain."

"Oh?" I could feel my eyebrows raise.

"Certainly," Avonstoke said, his hand pushing through his golden hair. He looked a bit ill at ease, something I had never seen on him before. "I'll need at least another eighty years or so before I'd be considered an adult among my people. Surely you'd noticed?"

"That," I said primly, "explains so much."

And it did. Knowing that the Court Faerie lived for hundreds of years, I'd assumed that he was some unfathomable number of years in age, just as Faith had. The sudden knowledge that he was only a year older than me . . . not that our ages should matter much for working together, but . . .

He gave me a wicked look with those golden eyes of his, and a grin that seemed to understand all my thoughts. The combination sent a hot shiver through me that wasn't at all blunted by the slight breeze coming off the water.

"None of that helps us with Father," Faith said.

"I've been thinking about what you said, Faith," I said. "About Father not being up to this task. The more I think about it, the truer that statement seems, at least." The follow-up thought to that might be that a man out of his depth in the Faerie was more consistent with what we knew about Father, but I didn't say that out loud.

What if Father really was this general and he died anyway? He couldn't, could he?

The white sun slid down into the sea and the repair crews gave up their work when the light failed and the ship grew quiet. Several of the crew strung hammocks on the deck while the rest disappeared below.

Bells rang for the changing of the watch and the officers and helmsman were replaced. Avonstoke didn't even seem to notice. For all the answers he had given us about certain things, he had withheld just as much, and I didn't know how far we could trust this man. With his glorious hair and elegant clothes, he was entirely *too* handsome in repose. He could be thinking anything, and we would never know. As for me, all I could think about was Father and Mother, Henry and Benedict and even Joshua.

The next shift moved silently about, talking to each other in whispers, the way people did at funerals.

# CHAPTER 15

## Henry: Mother's Offer

While I was worrying about the fate of both my brothers, gears were moving that would make all of us even more worried, if only we'd known.

Morning came to Henry in Newgate Prison, but it didn't bring much hope with it. Wan light trickled through the high window. Otherwise, nothing changed. The same two dog wardens sat, still and inert, in front of his cell.

Early in the day, Henry took a good look at the bars on his door and found deep impressions in the iron that matched his fingers precisely. He put his hands on the bars and took them off to make sure. They matched. He remembered swinging the heavy plank back in the London alley, too, without any real understanding how he could have done what he'd done. He didn't feel powerful now, and wasn't sure he ever expected to, despite what he'd remembered doing.

Henry decided to test it. He gave the bar a jerk and shockingly, the grate shifted in the heavy wooden door. The wolves suddenly snapped to attention with a growl that made Henry jump back. He backed away from the door and stayed in the far half of the cell for the rest of the day.

Mostly, he sat on the hard bench looking down at his hands. What had gotten into him? It was like the Faerie had leaked into every part of his world, including Henry himself. He thought a lot about that.

He also got very hungry.

He thought about his hands and the bars moving and looked longingly at the window above him. It was far out of reach, with the bench bolted into the corner so that even standing on it, he couldn't reach it.

"Oh, my son," a woman's voice said. "How could you have come to this?"

Henry jumped to his feet. "Mother?" Moving as if in a dream, Henry shuffled forward to the grate in the door. "Mother?" he said again. He gripped the iron grate, hardly believing what he saw.

It both *was* and wasn't the Mother he remembered. Martine Kasric wore a dark robe and scarlet cloak and sash like a bishop, only she had a heavy silver tree necklace where the crucifix should have been.

Her burnished copper hair was loose, longer than it should have been with odd and inexplicable streaks of gray in it. Her dark eyes glimmered with an occasional flash of green that made him think of Mr. Sands. Her calm, appraising look was even more unusual, and he realized how long it had been since he'd seen her with her eyes unclouded by either pain or medication.

"Mother?" he said again, suddenly not sure.

The grate creaked and shifted. He'd been pushing on it without realizing it. The wolves were still out there and growled a low warning. Henry lifted his hands and stepped back.

"I used to be," she said. "Maybe I could be again. That depends on you, Henry."

"Mummy," he whined bitterly, hating the little-boy voice coming out of him, but at a loss to stop it. "You left. Why did you leave?" A part of him was still reaching out for her in his mind, or wanted to. But another, deeper part inside remembered all the things he'd seen in Widdershins' mind, and knew that the Mother he'd known had never really existed. He just had to remember that he knew.

She hadn't been sick at all, at least not from brain fever.

She'd been slowly dosing herself, under Westerly's sinister care, with Faerie Absinthe. Faerie Absinthe was her key to power, too. Too much, and you went mad. Just enough, if you were very strong and very lucky, and you could learn to control the magic of it and gain a great deal of power. Mother had been both.

"Why do you hate us now?" Henry said. That whine was still there, but he didn't care.

"I was angry," she said. "After I found out how the man I'd married had been taken away from me. A stranger in my marriage bed tricked me into bearing Faerie children. I told myself that only Joshua was pure, and that the rest of you were dead to me. How could I trust you when I knew you'd all grow up to be just like *him*."

Henry had nothing to say to that, of course. He hadn't thought much about how awful those years must have been for her.

"Of course," Mother said, "if I could find a way to trust you, then I could love you again. You see? There is a way, Henry. Because of what you can do. I thought I was the only who had any defenses against Widdershins' little trick, but you . . . you turned it back on him. Now that I know you can do that . . ."

"He told you?" Henry said.

"Not in so many words."

"He doesn't know you're here," Henry said.

"He doesn't, but the Black Shuck does. The Black Shuck said that there could be a place for you in the new London government. We have a recent vacancy, you see, very high up."

"Me?" Henry said. "Help the Faerie take over London?"

"The Lord of Thorns doesn't have any use for his sons," Mother purred, "but we do. I could use your help, and the Black Shuck thinks that another of my sons could be very useful. Of course, we have Benedict, too. Joshua's approaching him right now. The Black Shuck has said there's only room for one of you. One of you will be given a title from the Seelie Court. Status, power, wealth, and my love to guide you to even bigger and better things."

"You can't ask me to do that!" Henry said. "Help you fight my sisters? I can't!"

"Only one of you gets these things," Mother went on as if Henry hadn't even spoken. "The other . . ." She tapped idly on the bars. "The other gets executed. There might be a trial before, but somehow, I doubt it. I picked you. Joshua wants Benedict, though. We argued about that."

"You're mad," Henry said.

"I'm not angry with you, darling. You can't help being Faerie. Anyway, a certain amount of time spent with Widdershins can alter even your viewpoint, just as he did mine. Joshua has already proven himself to the Black Shuck. He and I will be in a uniquely powerful position in the new government. Oh, Henry, we've done so much. Discovered ways to power that women never have in our world. Magic is real, my lamb, and the women of Faerie are by far the most powerful magicians. Think of all the implications, Henry. Can you imagine what that's like to a woman? I doubt it. Even with the fragments you pulled from Widdershins, I sincerely doubt it."

This was all too much. Henry pushed himself away from the bars and stumbled back to his bed and sat heavily down. His hands were shaking so badly he had to clench them into fists.

"Swear your fealty to the Seelie Court!" Mother called through the grate. "Renounce humanity, Henry, and enjoy the opportunities that wait for us. You, Joshua, me. Think about it! *We* are going to be the new ruling class. The Faerie bore easily and can't be bothered with anything as tedious as ruling subjects. They'll need people like us. Choose quickly, Henry. Benedict's probably jumping at the chance right now. If Joshua reaches the Black Shuck before I do, you'll be executed in a few days and there won't be anything I can do to stop it."

"I can't," Henry said. "Benedict won't, either. You'll see."

"Are you sure?"

"He won't!" Henry hollered, but in his gut he wished he could be more certain. He dropped his face in his hands and rocked back and forth, wishing more than anything that she would just go away.

"I can't, Mother," he moaned. "You know I can't!"

"Pity," Mother said. "My hands are tied, then. I *did* try, you know."

She left then, which was what he wanted. Wasn't it? He dropped his head back down and shook and wept great sobs that wrung him through and through.

# CHAPTER 16

## Benedict: Joshua's Offer

The call of a horn and the pounding of hooves . . . Cernunnos . . .
Herne, Wotan, The Henniquin . . .

Benedict pushed himself to a sitting position with a jerk, then a
drawn-out sigh. He ran his fingers through the curls of his soaking-
wet hair as if he might brush the Wild Hunt out of it. Cernunnos,
Herne, Wotan, the Henniquin . . . Benedict couldn't remember the
others, but he'd known them asleep. The indoor fire pit set in the
floor had settled to a dull red glow, which painted the otherwise
dark room around him with somber light.

The little apartment was a cozy sort of prison if you could forget
the monster roaming outside. Thick carpets, layers of curtains
with more curtains pinned to the ceiling. Low tables laden with

books in various languages, most of them tantalizingly unfamiliar. Benedict suspected it had been Sands' quarters. Trust a magician who worked with cats to think of putting his apartment up on the roof. He must have been half cat himself to climb up here. The importance of being this high up wasn't lost on Benedict, either.

He was to be a gift for the Wild Hunt. It seemed that even the Faerie feared them and clearly Mother and Joshua, who were now giving all the orders, thought they could appease the hunt by giving them what they wanted.

Benedict shuffled across the carpet to the very welcome brandy bottles on the table. Gifts from Étienne and Percy. One of the wine bottles was Armagnac. It took two glasses, a hefty dose of laudanum and the better part of thirty minutes before the sounds of hooves faded and he could think again.

Benedict crawled over to the door. (The ceiling was low and with all the carpets, the floor was soft.) Sure enough, there were a few more slips of paper slid under the door. Trust ghosts to get past even his new, unsettling guard. Sleep wasn't going to come back to him tonight, so he might as well see if there was a new report. He was still hoping to make Joshua regret dismissing him as a threat, but the best he could do now was make careful entries about the goings-on here, even if he had no way of getting them to Father or Sands.

Sure enough, the slips held Percy's careful lettering.

Benedict pulled over the Cervantes and carefully copied them into the margins. The first few were depressing. With no more Hussars to intercept them, more and more Faerie were making their way to Stormholt every day. Reports overheard by the Ghost Boys suggested that the main Faerie force was still en route across the Bridge of Sorrows, but Joshua was building a sizable advance garrison from the Faerie that found their own way across the Borderlands in ones and twos. A talking serpent this morning. A few Goblins. Still, the garrison grew every day. They must be nearing a hundred.

After that, the reports got better.

Étienne had taken it on himself to start a one-boy campaign to demoralize the Faerie troops for as long as they stayed at Stormholt and the last few notes always detailed these. Last week's entries had included: 'salt in the tea', 'tied twenty-seven pairs of Dwarf shoe laces together while sleeping' and 'dumped two liters of marmalade on one of them big cats'. Today's was probably Benedict's favorite, though: 'gathered at least sixty frogs, left in Joshua's office for morning'. It made Benedict smile. Being a ghost had its advantages.

Benedict took careful notes of the garrison additions and troop movements and then destroyed the written slips and put the Cervantes underneath a few of the other books. It wasn't much of a hiding place, but it was all he had.

∘✦∘✦∘✦∘

It was early the next morning when a ghastly scraping noise at the door woke him in a chill sweat. He stared, wide-eyed. They couldn't expect him to open it with that *thing* out there, could they?

The door shuddered again and broke open. It wasn't the monster Benedict feared, but a dozen of the rag-tag Goblins, hooting and dragging him out with their tough, horned hands.

The roof was cold. Usually, it stank of blood and cat urine. Now, the smells of sodden leather and wet Goblin fur overpowered the rest. The Goblins were in a muddled lot, bickering in what sounded like old Gaelic. The leader was a grizzled fellow with slits in his greenish copper helmet to let his batlike ears tilt and turn as he listened for trouble. Three other Goblins, one of them with buck-teeth, hustled Benedict over the roof top peaks slippery with rain. The largest of them was only waist-high, but even the smallest of them was stronger than Benedict was.

Just as the lead Goblin grabbed the cord handle for the trapdoor, the cat rose up from behind one of the gables. The thing was a monster, something out of the depths of Faerie. No real cat at all, Benedict was sure, but some foul thing in cat shape, like a Siamese-colored Siberian tiger. Benedict yelled a warning as it leapt.

It hooked the buck-toothed Goblin easily and pinned it to the roof. A few Goblins threw spears and hammers, but the blows didn't seem to do much other than make the cat mad. They ran like hell, Benedict very much included. The pinned Goblin cried out, but there was nothing that could be done to save him. Or her. Benedict never found out.

The huge cat, in no rush, dipped its mouth down and latched onto the Goblin's throat, searching for just the right grip. The terrible strangling noise was still happening while the leader threw open the trapdoor and everyone rushed through.

The Goblins pushed Benedict and he slipped and fell, screaming. He might have fallen all the way down the shaft and broken his neck, but one of the gibbering Goblins caught hold of his foot.

Benedict hung thrashing, upside down, while the Goblin clung to a twisting rope ladder, hooting and gnashing his teeth from the strain. The rest of the Goblin troop clambered over the two of them until they all swung like a bundle of grapes in a hurricane. If grapes screamed, that is. The last Goblin through pulled the trapdoor shut.

The Goblin leader shouted something and hauled Benedict upright so that he could grab the rungs of a twisting rope ladder put there to replace the iron one from before. Benedict managed to climb down to the bottom without falling. Most of the Goblins came down with him but three stayed on the ladder near the top. A wizened, gray-haired elder with a drooping white mustache crooned some kind of dirge for the lost.

The Goblins escorted Benedict down through the many floors of Stormholt, through armories and billiard rooms and libraries open to the sky and full of sodden, moldy books, to the main floor. They passed two other Goblin troops along the way and a burly giant with thorns growing out of his skull, who was feeding two large wolfhounds in a ruined dance hall.

They arrived at last to the room Joshua had annexed for his office. The door was partly ajar, and one of the elder Goblins made a soft *whuff-whuff* and pushed Benedict in.

Elegant, pristine. Other than the desk and two chairs, the room had no furniture or decorations. Nothing on the walls, leaving the room cold and open. No frogs.

Another of the Court Faerie appeared, holding a silver tray with a brandy bottle and two glasses. He set it on the desk and left, closing the door behind him.

"You look older," Benedict said to him.

Joshua nodded. "Years in Faerie will do that to you."

"Years?"

"It's been days for you," Joshua said, "years for me. Time in Faerie moves strangely, and there are some pockets where years pass in the time it takes us to finish a meal."

Benedict sat, trying to absorb that kind of information. It was patently impossible according to science, but he believed it all the same. There was no denying the gray in Joshua's hair, the bulkier build, the weathered face. Benedict couldn't make up his mind about Joshua's new age. The hair was gray, yes, but only at the tips. Joshua was bigger in the shoulders, heavier all around. But it was a dangerous bulk, powerful. The weathered face had more lines around the eyes. Twenty-five? Thirty?

"You've lost weight," Joshua said. "Probably the drink. I was just about to send for breakfast. Are you hungry?"

"No." Benedict lounged in the chair in front of the desk and helped himself to Joshua's brandy. It wasn't as good as the Armagnac he had upstairs, but it wasn't bad, either.

Benedict sighed. "What can I do for you, big brother? Or should I call you *Warden*? Where's Mother?"

"Mother isn't here." Joshua said. The long moment in which neither of them said anything stretched out to an uncomfortable silence.

"Is this where you start asking me questions?" Benedict finally said. "Gently at first. You won't need to use the hot poker until later."

"There's no need for that," Joshua said. "You don't know anything. How could you? You haven't left this house since Father put you here. Nevertheless, we should talk before Mother arrives."

Benedict spread his arms expansively. "I'm all yours, of course."

Joshua walked around the desk, tapping the edge of it thoughtfully as he went. "You're here because I want to offer you an officer's role in the invasion. One of our seven symbols has been killed. We need a new one. Accept, and we can save you from the Wild Hunt."

"Why would I want anything to do with . . ."

"You may want to let me finish. We have Henry, too. The Black Shuck will pardon whoever accepts first. The other will be executed. I can't imagine Henry refusing Mother. He doesn't have the stomach for it. She's probably heading to the Black Shuck right now with Henry's acceptance. But I know she'd rather have you."

"Mother's as crazy as a—"

Benedict's mouth exploded in pain and he fell to the floor. Joshua's backhand had been so snake-quick that Benedict hadn't even seen it coming.

His older brother was much faster than anyone his size had any right to be, and his face was an angry mask. The man was like a complete stranger.

Benedict lay a moment, gasping and dripping blood from his mouth onto the cold tile. His hand had a sliver of broken glass in it. It was hard to pull out with shaking fingers, but he did it.

"She's not crazy," Joshua said, and Benedict flinched. The cold anger in Joshua's voice sank icy daggers into Benedict's gut.

"All right," Benedict said. He spit a bloody tooth. He let it fall onto the carpet next to the glass. He climbed cautiously to his feet. It felt like more teeth might fall out of his mouth if he wasn't careful. The only glass left was Joshua's, so Benedict used that one to pour out more brandy. Joshua hulked over him the entire time. Benedict spilled some.

"She's not mad," Joshua said again.

"All right," Benedict said. He should be more worried about Joshua beating him to death, but with the Wild Hunt lurking out there, it didn't really seem to matter. Still, he had enough sense to wait until Joshua had gone back around the desk and sat down before he spoke again.

"All right, she's not mad. But she's evil."

Benedict expected another explosion, but this time Joshua only chuckled. "Evil? That's a word I haven't heard in a long time.

A church word. The Faerie don't use it. Mother's strong, is what she is. They tried to make her a victim, and she turned it around on them."

Benedict caught himself working his swollen jaw and made himself stop, but Joshua noticed the motion anyway.

"Oh hell," Joshua said. "I'm sorry about that. I've been around the Faerie too long. They only respond to status, tradition, or force. I don't have any of the first two behind me, so I lean heavily on force. But we don't need that between brothers, do we?"

"If you say so," Benedict said. "You're the one who's holding me prisoner."

"It doesn't have to be that way," Joshua said. "You could join us."

"Help the Faerie invade England?" Benedict. "No thanks. Besides, I thought Father was still mounting a defense."

"Him?" Joshua scoffed. "I don't think so. Besides, your father's dying."

"Our Father is?"

"No," Joshua said. "Your Father."

Benedict stared at him.

"The man Mother married," Joshua said, "*my* father, isn't the same as the man who's been calling himself our father for the past several years. *Your* father, and Faith and Justice and Henry's, is an imposter."

"That's ridiculous," Benedict said.

"Is it?" Joshua said calmly. "Well, I'll let Mother tell you the whole story. Let's just say that Mother has ample reason for trying to thwart the man calling himself Rachek Kasric. She's the one who made it possible for so many Faerie guerrilla units to come over in secret, while the main army is crossing the Bridge of Sorrows."

"The what?"

Joshua smiled thinly. "I keep forgetting. I've had years to absorb this information. It's the bridge over the ocean that separates England from Faerie. Created as an escape from England when religion made our world inhospitable to the Faerie. They took a forced march. A lot of them died, but they made it across the bridge and through the mist and into another place which they now call Faerie. It's a very hateful memory for them. They're very passionate about it. It's also how the Faerie army is traveling here. Father had planned a very dangerous defense of the bridge, but that's all shot to hell now.

"Now, thanks to Mother, the Faerie have managed to smuggle a great many forces into England before the rest of the army gets here. The Black Shuck has promised Mother a regency in England as reward."

The room went silent as Benedict tried to absorb everything he'd been told. Everyone else was fighting, it seemed, on one side or another, except Benedict. He continued to feel as useless as possible.

"I thought," Benedict said slowly, "that Mother's plan was to give me over to your hunt. That's what your jail keepers told me."

"It's not our hunt," Joshua said. "No one controls them. They could do anything. The Faerie fear Cernunnos as much as they fear anything. They're as much enemy as friend."

"Oh really?" Benedict said, a glimmer of hope rising within him.

"Don't bother getting excited," Joshua said. "They may not be *our* friend, but they're definitely an enemy to mankind. Cernunnos walked that Bridge of Sorrow into exile and now that he's back? He is, I assure you, no friend to England or the Lord of Thorns."

Benedict was watching Joshua closely. His poker face was excellent, but he must be nervous about something because he'd clearly said more than he'd intended to.

"It will be a new government here," Joshua went on, and now he sounded more comfortable. "With us in charge. There will be many new positions to fill, you see. Everyone will be looking to the few Lord of Thorns' heirs who are on our side. Imagine blood of Nelson, Napoleon and Wellington all rolled into one bloodline. That's you and Henry. Unique opportunity for both of you."

"So I'd be a general, big brother? Under your guidance, perhaps? How lovely."

Joshua said nothing, merely waited.

"You're wrong about Henry," Benedict went on. "He won't do it."

Joshua shrugged. "I hope you're wrong. It's not safe to tell Mother *no* these days. They're going to hang Henry soon if he doesn't accept. As in executed. Understand?"

"You *can't* be serious," Benedict said. "Henry's never had any bit of malice. He's only fourteen, for Christ's sake."

"Very serious. That's why we're having this talk. You need to agree to Mother's terms, accept her offer. The alternatives are too unpleasant. Don't take too long making up your mind, either."

Benedict couldn't help it. He burst out laughing. Somehow, Joshua and Mother couldn't hear the horn the way he did. They knew something about the Wild Hunt calling him, but they didn't know enough.

Because Benedict knew with bone-deep certainty that he didn't have the kind of time Joshua was talking about. Hearing about the Wild Hunt and seeing the edge of nervousness that it gave his brother—no, his half-brother!—to talk about it . . . Suddenly, going with the Wild Hunt seemed like a good idea. Hell, it might be the only way to contribute. He closed his eyes, and even deep in the belly of Stormholt, all he could hear was the sound of the coming storm that echoed with his laughter. Once he started laughing, he couldn't stop. He even thought Joshua would beat him again, but dear older brother just had him sent back to his prison.

Benedict was still laughing when they locked him away. Thunder rolled in the sky and the Goblins all looked nervously about.

# CHAPTER 17

## Prudence and Father's Story

The door to the captain's cabin opened, and those of us waiting all stood up. Caine and the other officers stopped conferring over the log book and looked down at us from the quarterdeck railing as Mr. Sands came out.

He had his coat off, his sleeves rolled up and a weary look on his face. He stumbled slightly with the motion of the ship before he caught himself. A silence fell on the crew, too, even way up in the topgallants, so the only noises around us were the wind and sea.

"He lives," Mr. Sands said. "But he is weak."

I felt the clench in my stomach release, just a little.

"For now," he said. "He'll have to stay bedridden for the next month or so, after that . . ."

"Then we're all dead men," Caine said from above us.

"He might still pull through," Mr. Sands said weakly. "Perhaps ..."

"It doesn't matter," Caine said. "The Outcasts are only here because he is. Can he lead us into battle?"

"No."

"Can he sail over and fence barbs with that she-bitch over on *Seahome*?"

"No, not for many weeks, and then, maybe not ..."

"Probably he can't manage a crossing, either, then. Can he?"

Mr. Sands sagged, defeated. "No. The door still works, but that's all."

"Then we're all dead men," Caine repeated bluntly. "Those of us from England, at least. Maybe we can make our way through the door by ones and twos, if we have that kind of time, but I think we all know how long we'll keep our freedom back there if the Seelie Court's forces aren't stopped out here.

"The rest of you lot," he sneered at the Faerie, "aren't going to follow an Englishman, are you? Not without your Faerie Lord to smooth the way." Most of the Faerie—the Dwarves, the Court Faerie marines, and the green folk with the webbed fingers and toes, like Mr. Lacon, that I'd learned were called Prowlers—all stared back, stony-faced. But the black, spidery Goblins up in the rigging chittered like angry squirrels. Avonstoke wouldn't meet my gaze, but at least had the decency to look embarrassed about it.

"You'll all slink into the dark alleyways of Faerie, won't you?" Caine said. "Try and hide. Won't help, if the Black Shuck has his way. He'll hunt you down to the last man!"

There was a murmur among the crew at that, but none of them spoke. Caine glared at all of them savagely, daring them to deny it. "Cowards, the lot of you!" He stomped down the quarterdeck stairs and stomped his way to the forecastle, pushing aside random crew members in his way.

There was a long moment of drawn-out silence before Mr. Sands turned to Faith and me. "He's asking to see you."

Faith and I went in. Surprisingly, Avonstoke followed and Mr. Sands didn't bat an eyelash. A dull glow filled the room from the yellow moonlight outside. The cabin was enormous by ship standards, with stern windows showing the way we had come and a small skylight above, but it still felt close and warm. Father was awake but looked dazed and horrid. His skin was yellowish and his breathing came in painful rasps. He struggled to sit up as we came in.

A plain, gray woman I didn't know was bending over his bed, helping him. I went over and carefully took his hand.

"It's all right," he whispered. "I probably look worse than I feel." He squeezed my hand weakly. Faith pointedly kept her distance.

"Hardly," the woman said. "You look like you've had a brush with death. Which you have. You're not out of it yet, not by a long shot." I took a second look at her. She resembled your average Londoner from the poor side of town, about thirty, with a kind, ordinary face and raggedly cut gray hair. She wore an equally gray dress, a long dirty shawl, and no shoes. In fact, once you looked for it, the overwhelming grayness of her was starkly unnatural. If you didn't count those eyes, which were an equally unnaturally bright blue.

"Who are you?" I said.

"You're doing better than expected," the woman said, still speaking to Father and ignoring my question. "You might be one of a handful to survive an encounter with Yellow Veil. That is, if you live the night out." Her tone and face were kindly, despite the heartlessness of her words.

"Who is this?" Faith said to Mr. Sands.

"She's another magician," Mr. Sands said, "from *Seahome*. Very skilled in poisons and their remedies."

"Not that anyone could do much for Yellow Veil," the woman said. "It's really his condition that made the difference."

"We've been right by the door all day," Faith said. "We didn't see her."

"I came in through the window, of course," she said, smiling at us in a pitying way. She cocked her head and looked at us with first one blue eye, and then the other. "I was coming anyway, as soon as I heard you two were here. I'm Prudence, but you already knew that. I'm so glad you got my letter."

I squinted and saw another shape superimposed on the woman shape. A bird. One I'd seen before, all in shades of gray. "You flew," I said, stunned by my own realization. "That's how you got in without us seeing you. You're a shape changer. You're the bird that delivered the letter, too."

She bowed, sweeping out the shawl and bobbing her head in a curtsy. "The same."

The motion filled the cabin with a gamey, outdoorsy kind of smell. She didn't seem right, the way she moved, as if her shape was a tenuous thing.

"Father told us you died," Faith said with a bitter look at Father.

"He had his reasons," Prudence said. "But of course I didn't die, or I wouldn't be here, would I? I wouldn't be very pleasant to talk to, either. And the smell . . . ugh. I *hate* talking with the dead."

I thought I'd been ready for adventure, but now it seemed that fate, with my ghost eye, had just given me the talent for seeing the danger coming. Someone had forgotten to give me some chance of defending against it.

"You," Father whispered to her. His voice was weak, but the anger was still palpable. "You helped them escape. How else could they get here?"

"They escaped on their own," Prudence said, picking a writhing bundle of cloth up from the table. "As you knew they would. All I did was give them some idea of where to go." She was looking at the bundle judiciously while it continued to writhe like a tangle of snakes. She nodded with satisfaction and laid it back on the table where it twitched constantly.

"They were supposed to be kept out of it. I told you . . ."

"You told me," Prudence said, "two decades ago, how critical it was that we get all seven sisters involved. The fate of all England and Faerie depended on the plan, you said." She drew a dagger and used it to cut the string on the bundle.

"What is *in* there?" I said.

"Did you say *more* sisters?" Faith said.

"Bloodflowers," Prudence said.

"Wait," I said as something she said a few seconds ago registered. "Decades?" Prudence didn't look old enough for that. It was hard to think with those things writhing there. Then the other part sank in and I realized what Faith had just said. "Wait, more sisters? How many more?"

"Certainly," Prudence said, looking back at us briefly. "Did you think we were the only ones?" She turned back to the table and flipped the cloth bundle.

Inside were a number of flowers. Orchids, I thought, blood and gold in color, as if each petal held the last of a vivid sunset. The yellow parts even glowed a little.

"I thought *we* were the only ones," I said. "I didn't know anything about you at all two weeks ago, let alone more of you."

Prudence glared at Father. "Haven't you told them *anything*?" She turned back to us. "There are seven of us, of course. As there were supposed to be. Hopefully this will make more sense when your powers start to manifest themselves."

Seven? Four more sisters after this stranger that I'd never even met, all related? Powers? Manifest? This was all too much.

"Only the three of us are full sisters," Prudence went on, "Temperance, Hope and Charity are also full sisters to each other, but only half-sisters to the three of us. Born to the Lady of Sorrows and Father. While Pyar was something else entirely. Sands, be a dear and hold his legs." She pulled out a long, wicked-looking knife.

"They don't need to see this," Mr. Sands said, looking at us.

"They do if they want to get anything intelligible out of him," Prudence said. "Look!" She pointed with the knife at Father. "He's already passed out again."

It was true. Father's eyes were closed.

"Just as well," Prudence said. "Certainly *he* doesn't want to see this." She stabbed the table suddenly, transfixing one of the still-moving flowers to the table. It thrashed wildly and the room was filled with its eerie rustling.

"It doesn't work right unless they're angry," Prudence said.

"I think I may throw up," Faith said.

Mr. Sands pulled the blanket back to reveal Father's naked feet. Mr. Sands then reversed his position so that he could hold Father's legs near the knees.

"This may sting," Prudence said, though Father's eyes were still closed. She pried the knife free and used it to drape the serpentine bloodflower over Father's nearest foot. Mr. Sands hurriedly covered flower and foot with the blanket. Prudence carefully wrapped the original package back up again.

"AaaaAAAAHHH!" Father bellowed, his eyes snapping open. "Bloody Hell, woman. Do you have to do that?"

"Of course I do," Prudence said. "I thought it might be easier while you were asleep."

"Well it bloody wasn't," Father snapped. "Damn! It feels like my . . . get it off!" He struggled weakly for a moment, but Mr. Sands kept his grip and Father fell back a few seconds later, panting heavily.

"I don't understand any of this," Faith said.

"I think," Mr. Sands said to Father, "that it is time you told them where you come from."

"This will help," Prudence said, and, to my horror, took her knife back up. But instead of disturbing the newly-wrapped bundle, she flicked the knife point with a practiced motion across her own wrist.

Faith gasped. We watched in horror as Prudence let the blood drip from the wound into a tin cup. Using her other hand, she added an equal amount of brandy, then pressed a white cloth to the wound. When she removed the cloth, her wrist was whole, though it had many old scars. She picked up the cup and put the horrible concoction to Father's lips. He grimaced, but he drank.

Father stared down for a moment after he finished, marshaling his strength. "Very well." There was a pause while Mr. Sands indicated that we should sit. Faith and I pulled over two slat-back chairs from the small table.

Avonstoke stayed at the door, looking dangerous and casual. The sea sloshed audibly through walls, and the walls creaked along with the ship's motion.

"It seems I can no longer shield you," Father said. "First, you should know that I was not born human. My real name is Lessard of the House of Thorns, and I was once a member of the Seelie Court until abdicating my position."

Faith caught my eye and gave me an I-told-you-so look. A sinking pit blossomed deep in my stomach as I listened to a confession that unmade the entire world I knew. I dropped my gaze to the maps on the table as a way to avoid hers. The map with all the railways marked was still on top.

"I rule Gloaming Hall in Faerie," the Lord of Thorns went on, "as the House of Thorns has always done. The original Rachek Kasric was born in Russia, I understand, then emigrated and later became a citizen of England. He went back to Russia as part of the British Navy during the Crimea, just as you were told. It was during the Siege of Sevastopol in the summer of 1855 that *I* first found him."

He sat up a little straighter in the bed. "Kasric's squad had been part of some midnight raiding party to shore. I don't know what their mission was, but Kasric got separated from his squad south of Sevastopol. Near the enclosures and trenches. Alone, with enemies all around, he would certainly have been discovered and killed.

"This is where I found him. I'd decided to come see the world that had once cast out the Faerie. It is a dangerous journey, a magician's quest among my people."

Father looked down at his hands.

"This was some time ago. Certainly, I would not do today what I did to Rachek Kasric when I found him back on that enemy beach."

"You were different back then," Mr. Sands said. "I think you have forgotten how different."

"Perhaps," Father said. "Now, I cannot blame Kasric for shooting me. He did what any soldier might have done, seeing an inhuman figure come walking out of the mist. Normal bullets are not deadly to us, but the pain is considerable and I was furious.

"In retribution, I disarmed him and flung him down. He was cowed by then and I crouched on the beach and regarded the mortal that had offended me and considered his sentence while the night howled with lightning and the sound of artillery.

"In the end, I offered Rachek Kasric a wager . . ."

"You what?" Faith said.

"You might want to let him finish," Prudence said tartly. "He only has a few minutes and it would be a pity if he passed out before he got to the end."

Faith glared back at her, but she kept her mouth shut. I couldn't blame her. I kept opening my mouth to ask questions, too, only I couldn't get it to work right. This was too much to take in all at once.

"I know," the Lord of Thorns said. "I was cruel. I offered him a chess game played for great stakes. If Kasric won, then I would transport him away from certain death, back to his ship. After that, I would see him free of the Crimean War not only unharmed, but also successful and wealthy far beyond measure. If I won, I would assume Kasric's shape and his life, while he would assume my own shape and life. But he would still have the chance to reclaim his life later on, and this, this was the hook that made Kasric agree. The worst part."

"You won," I said.

"Of course I won," he said, offended. "I was the greatest general who ever lived. I've had hundreds of years to study war in all its forms. After, I assumed Kasric's shape and went back to his ship in that guise. With my advantages, it was no great feat to distinguish myself in the following battle. I catapulted to the rank of captain in less than a month. I was a captain with an outstanding service record by the time the war ended and I went back to London to meet his wife and young son, Joshua. Now *my* wife and son. Martine had more children, my children.

"When I got an introduction to court, it was simple to curry the right favors. This appealed to your mother's family enormously. The Scarsdons were old blood fallen on bad times. More than anything, she wanted to see them rise again. I was the key to that rise, for a time."

"These are just more lies," Faith said, "It was later that you changed. Mother told me. She claimed you'd become an entirely different person in the past few years."

"Your mother perceived *a* change," Mr. Sands said. "But not until many years later. Shapeshifting has dangerous complications. When you assume the shape of a thing, you become it, in a very real sense. Stories abound of wizards, Faerie and otherwise, who take on the shape of wolves, birds, or fish and never return to their own shape, simply because they forgot how to be human. Your Father is forgetting what it was like to be Faerie."

Father spoke into the uncomfortable silence. "I'm becoming human. That's the change your mother sensed."

"It seems," Prudence said, "that she'd gotten used to the Faerie you."

"Yes," Father said. "The past few years have been something of a disappointment to Martine Kasric. She'd become used to my wild successes, you see. She saw the beginning of my meteoric rise in court, but that fell by the wayside once I diverted those resources in secret to the defense of England. You see, I knew the Faerie were coming and could no longer bear the idea of London under their capricious rule. Martine railed at me for our dwindling finances. I spent most of our resources and had nothing I could show her to account for it. The price of my secrecy.

"But my love, Faith?" he said, and there was something of the old fire in his eyes again. "Your mother is wrong about that. I loved her right from the start and that love has only grown, no matter how my other traits falter, because it was one thing that the Lord of Thorns and Rachek Kasric shared. How could I not love her? An Alexander the Great behind eyes that would make Cleopatra blush. What a queen she would have made me! The Seelie Court sent Mrs. Westerly to make Martine into their pawn, and Martine turned the tables on them all. Even when the Faerie came for her, she managed to come out on top. In my heart, she will always be my queen."

"Pity she doesn't feel the same about *you*," Prudence said dryly. "Not after years of lies, anyway. Of course, the lies might have gone over better if you still had all that wealth."

"But she left us!" Faith said. "How could she know what she knew and just leave us with the Faerie coming?"

"Westerly showed her proof of what she long suspected," Mr. Sands said. "That the Rachek Kasric in her bed wasn't the same man she married."

"She did *not* take it well," Father said. "She tried to kill me when I tracked her down a few days ago. I barely got away with my life."

I remembered Joshua's accusation that he and Mother were not family to the rest of us.

*That* must have been what he meant. Joshua had been born before Father came to England, and was fully human. The rest of us: Benedict, Faith, I, even plain Henry . . . we weren't even *human*.

Of course, it meant that Father really *was* our father, only I wasn't sure how I felt about that now.

I tried to imagine how Mother had felt when she realized how deep the lie of her life went. Then came Mrs. Westerly and her absinthe . . .

"So Mother decided to fight for the Faerie?" Faith said. "If she's against the Faerie so much, that doesn't make any sense."

"She hates the Faerie," Father said softly, "but she hates me more. If I fight on one side, she'll fight for the other."

"Perhaps," Prudence said. "Or perhaps Mother just likes to be on the winning side."

I wanted to shout at that.

It felt like an invasion of privacy for this stranger to say nasty things about my family.

"What happened to Rachek Kasric?" I said.

"He assumed my life. He went back to Gloaming Hall and managed my affairs and, I must admit, did not handle them too badly. He angered my wife a bit, over the years, but I cannot blame him for that.

"But he always longed to return to his family in England. Each year, on the anniversary of our agreement, we would meet and play again. If Kasric won, he would be able to return to his world. If he lost, he would return to another year of exile. He always lost. Year after year, Kasric lost and failed to earn his freedom."

"But that's coming to an end," Mr. Sands said to Father. "You've held onto this human for longer than any magician I know of, but you cannot hold out indefinitely. There's some irony and blessing to this," he said to us. "It's his humanity that's saved him today. Yellow Veil is deadly to Faerie but harmless to humans. That dosage would have killed him outright a few years ago."

"But if the resistance falls," Prudence said, "the Seelie Court will have us anyway. And England. We'll be just as dead."

I stared at her until she sighed and said, "The House of Thorns is known throughout all of Faerie as spawning a long line of brilliant tacticians. Since the Sethfyr war, no army with a Thorn leading it has ever lost a battle. It's *this* legacy that has brought all these different factions of Faerie together in England's defense. When they find that the Lord of Thorns they're expecting can't even stand to lead them into battle, this weak alliance will break. We'll have lost this war before it's even begun."

"I knew my time was coming to an end," Father said sadly. "As I've been taking on more and more human traits, the same has been happening to the real Rachek Kasric back in Faerie. He's more the Lord of Thorns right now than I am, with all that entails, and our yearly match is coming. In a very real sense, I will be facing the Lord of Thorns in the chess match this coming Christmas, not him, and I cannot hope to prevail. When I lose, the Faerie will have me back. I'll be executed for fighting against their invasion. The Seelie Court does not take betrayal lightly."

"Then why?" I said. "Why did you do it?"

Father reached out weakly, and I took his hand again.

"Someday," he said, "when you have children of your own, you will understand."

I was having a hard time seeing now with the blurriness in my eyes.

"But why didn't you tell us all this before?"

He looked surprised, and then ashamed. "I didn't tell you because I didn't want you to know who I really am. That I was . . . a monster."

"A monster?" I said.

"You said it yourself, that night in the woods. I didn't want to be a monster anymore. I thought . . . I thought that if I could put that behind me, then . . . then I could be a better father."

"I was just a child when I said that," I said, shaking my head. "I didn't know what I was talking about."

"Yes, you did. Even then, you understood things no one else did, saw things no one else saw in quite the same way. You were right to call me that, even if you didn't know it. I stole Rachek Kasric's entire life. Only a monster could do that. I needed, I still need, to make up for that somehow."

"You do carry on," Prudence said. "Don't you?" She stood up and patted Father's hand fondly. "You've changed far more than you realize." She turned to the others. "The Faerie never dote on their children the way you humans do. Something about the mortality . . . it must be different when it all happens so fast. Babies, children, women, then—poof!—old ladies and dead, all in less than the blink of a century. It's a wonder human parents even get attached to their children at all."

"Aren't you human?" Faith asked her. "You said you were born in London."

"Well," Prudence said with an expression of surprise, "I didn't think it showed." Prudence looked so much like a common Londoner that Faith and I shared a look of confusion. Faith shrugged in a way that said, *not all there, either,* as plainly as if she'd spoken.

"I was born in London," Prudence said. "But then the Lord of Thorns brought me to Faerie."

"We were told you *died,*" Faith said. "That's cruel. Did Mother know you were still alive?"

"I never thought to ask," Prudence said, astonished. "Does it matter?"

"Of course it matters," Father said. "One more thing I have to answer for. She had, from the start, visible magical talents. At the time, I thought her safer hidden in Faerie, but it was a cruel thing to do."

"But Joshua isn't yours at all, and that probably explains his unswerving devotion to her, too," Faith said. "Just the two of them against a strange and magical world. *Us. The Faerie.*" Her voice broke at the last.

"Forgive me, Lord," Avonstoke said. It was the first he'd spoken in a long time. "What was the original plan for when your powers failed you? Surely the Lord of Thorns prepared for that?"

"Of course there's a plan," Prudence said. "It's us." She made a waving gesture with her hand that included herself, Faith and me all together. "The Seven Daughters of the House of Thorns."

"No!" Father said. "I told you. We're not following through with that plan. I'm not exposing you to that kind of danger."

Prudence ignored him, turning to Faith and me. "Now that you've come into contact with the Faerie, your powers are asserting themselves, as we knew they would. But it's more than that. It comes down to magic and symbols. What you people would call superstition. It's not enough to rise up against the Faerie invasion. There needs to be a symbol of defiance. Seven daughters. All the most powerful magicians in Faerie have been women. It was Father's idea to name us after virtues. Nothing strikes fear into the Faerie heart like the whisper of human religion. A nice touch, don't you think?"

"Us three," I said, "Charity, Hope and Temperance you said. But the other name you used wasn't a virtue at all."

"Pyar is another word for love." Prudence patted my hand. "Do try and keep up. Of course, it's not a very accurate list of virtues, from the Christian sense, but we can't have a girl running around called Fortitude or Courage, can we? You only have to be close with symbols."

"What can *we* do?" Faith burst out. "We're not magic symbols."

"You sang open the lock back at Stormholt," I said, "and you fought the man in black when he had all the rest of us frozen."

"You can see ghosts," Faith said.

"That's my damaged eye," I wailed. "I can't *do* anything."

"Oh dear," Prudence said. "You just need training. We'll see to that."

"No!" Father said. "It's too dangerous. You two will both go back to Stormholt."

"Don't be stupid," Prudence said. "We've no chance at all without the plan."

"It might be more dangerous for them *not* to fight," Mr. Sands added. "They've already met Widdershins from the sound of it, and I wouldn't be surprised if this Soho Shark and the assassin . . ." he looked at me questioningly.

"Victoria Rose," I said, trying not to remember how confused she'd looked right after I'd shot her.

"I wouldn't be surprised if those two and Lady Westerly were all numbered among the Seven they've raised to fight for them," Mr. Sands said. "And the Black Shuck."

This was getting worse and worse, like a terrible dream you wanted to wake up from. Faeries I'd never even met out to kill me and my sister. *Sisters.* I had more than one now.

"Seven Sins to march against mankind," Prudence said. She talked as if it were of no more than academic interest. "To match the Lord of Thorns' Seven Virtues he's risen to protect them."

"The Black Shuck and the rest of the Seven Sins are coming for your daughters," Mr. Sands said to Father. "They've caught wind of your plan and you haven't even *started* training our seven yet. Hiding is their surest way to the slaughterhouse. The Seelie Court already has Martine, Joshua, and Henry, despite your efforts with Stormholt. Hiding isn't working, is it?"

Father had nothing to say to that. He closed his eyes, as if in pain and a silence fell on us all, broken only by the sounds of the ship and the rhythm of the water.

"There's another thing," Faith said, and her voice quavered a bit. There was something in her voice that made everyone, myself included, stop and listen to her.

She drew an envelope out of her pocket. It was canary yellow and folded several times, with the look of having been in her pocket for some time. She was sitting near the table and dropped it onto the surface as if the envelope was something distasteful.

"This . . . appeared in my pocket after we escaped," Faith said. She was looking down at the paper, not meeting anyone's eyes. "I'm pretty certain that Victoria Rose or the Soho Shark somehow put it there without me noticing. I don't know which one."

"Faith," Father said. "What is that?"

"It's a letter from Mother," Faith said. "Which confirms that she's working with the enemy, though we already guessed that a long time ago, I think." She sat frozen in place, staring at the letter.

"What," I said, "does it say?"

For answer, Faith, moving very suddenly, opened the envelope, drew out two slips of paper, and dropped them both on the table with a flick of her fingers, as if touching them caused her discomfort.

"The smaller one," she said, "is a letter from Mother. An invitation to write her."

I was the closest to her, and she reached out and slid the smaller piece of paper towards me. I picked it up. A simple piece of foolscap, very ordinary, that said: 'Write to your mother'. Mother's handwriting. No question.

"This other piece of paper," Faith said flatly, "is the interesting one." She unfolded the larger piece of paper, also canary yellow. It was rich and thick. When she smoothed it out, it seemed pristine and blank, as if it had never been folded. Ready for ink.

"Do you have a pen?" Faith asked of no one in particular.

Mr. Sands wordlessly went to the small desk and pulled out a fountain pen and ink bottle. He handed these over. Faith uncorked the ink bottle, dipped the pen in, and wrote out 'Dear Mother' on the paper.

"Now wait," Faith said, setting the pen down and putting the stopper back into the ink. "It takes a few minutes."

The ship creaked around us.

No one said anything.

"Lor!" I said. The ink was slowly fading away. Avonstoke whistled low. The paper wasn't just clean, but unnaturally clean. Even the indentations that Faith had made with the pen, not just the ink, had completely vanished.

"I assume," Faith said, "that whatever I might write there would find its way to Mother. Perhaps there is another piece of paper in her possession that she reads it from. Perhaps unicorns sneak into her room before breakfast to whisper the messages to her, I don't know. But I've carried that letter with me . . . waiting."

"What have you told her?" Father asked.

Faith met his gaze, her expression angry. "Nothing," she said. "But I've carried it all this time. I wanted to find out what you were hiding before I made any kind of decision."

"And now that you have?" he asked.

"Justice," Faith said, "will you pass me that lantern?"

Faith took the lantern from me and held the envelope and letter up in the light. She was still looking hard at Father. "You have a lot to answer for."

He nodded wearily. "I do."

"Mother has every right to hate you," Faith said. "You ruined her life. Stole her husband. Stole her *children*. I think I would hate you, too, with the same blind passion that she does, if you did that to me. How bad will it be when the Faerie come?"

Her question dropped in the room and it was a long moment before anyone answered it. Finally, Avonstoke stirred himself and spoke.

"I said before that I knew something of Faerie rule," he said. "I was part of the invasion force when the Seelie Court made war on the Prowler folk. I did not . . . participate. Our troops camped outside the water city of Levtramain. But many of the conquering heroes did not abstain, and the screams and laughter that drifted out of that city still haunt my dreams." He took a deep breath, mastering his memories. "Justice tells us they may have started in on London faster than we realize, making it safe for the Seelie Court. If the Court comes to England, it will be very bad." He spoke quietly, his face grave. It was a side of Avonstoke I'd never seen before, completely serious.

"London will likely survive as a city," he went on, "but its citizens will live as the dormouse lives, creeping around the manor looking for scraps while their masters make merry with their great metropolis. The Seelie Court members will take what they want, change it, and cast it aside a month later when their fancy lands on something else. I can't guess the details, but the welfare and survival of England's human inhabitants will be of very little concern to the Faerie. Whatever kind of place this Stormholt is, it will not keep the Faerie out for long unless the army is driven back. The Black Shuck is in a precarious position, hampered and limited by the influence of the Seelie Court and their army. But if he takes England, they'll make him a member of the Court and his power and influence will increase tenfold. Then nothing will stop him."

Faith took a deep breath. "That what I thought."

The lantern was made of brass, with thick, glass windows that opened up. She slid it open and held the bundle over the flame until it caught, then dropped the flaming mass and closed the little window back up. It burned very quickly, and left no ash or residue whatsoever.

Faith looked at Father again. "None of what you did is England's fault. Right now, the best hope England, and my family has, is with you."

Father held her gaze. He looked infinitely sad, but a spark of hope shone in his eyes. "Thank you," he said.

Faith shook her head. She hadn't done it for him.

"It seems we are all going into battle together," Avonstoke said.

"What?" I turned to him.

He gave me a wry, almost apologetic smile. "I'm with you to the end, of course. I promised the Lord of Thorns that I would protect his daughters, to repay the debt our house owes to yours . . ."

"You *what*?" I burst out.

Avonstoke flinched, but continued. "We must fight. The Black Shuck will hunt you down. With the invasion of England, nowhere will be safe. If you can attack, you must."

"Keeping them safe by sending them into battle?" Father said.

"I do not say this lightly," Avonstoke said, "since it means risking my own skin, too, which I value *rather* highly. But you cannot allow England to fall."

The maps on the table caught my eye again. Something about the railroads . . .

"You're not even trying to save England," I blurted out. "Not at first. You're going to let him right in." I pulled the map closer. "This can't actually work, can it?"

Mr. Sands chuckled. "You see?"

"The Seelie Army is making its way to England the only way a group of their size can," Father said. "Across the Bridge of Sorrows. Though technically the bridge runs through the Borderlands, it's more part of Faerie than anything else. It's where the Faerie are the strongest."

"Our force is one tenth their size," Mr. Sands added. "We've no chance of stopping them there."

"It's true," Father admitted. "The Outcast Resistance had stratagems to try and keep the Black Shuck from bringing his army across the Bridge of Sorrow, but they've all failed, as I expected they would. But once they reach London, the Black Shuck's plan is to bring chunks of the Faerie land with them, so that his powers, and the powers of his army will have no trouble with overwhelming England. England has never needed a large standing army at home. Can you imagine the Horse Guard dealing with even a single dragon?"

I shuffled several maps of the coast to the top. "You're going to let him take London and as much of England as he can hold, and trap him there with sea power while railroads made of black iron contain him. I wondered about all the black iron railway spikes, but now I see it. You've put enough black iron into the railways to slow down troop movements on land. That doesn't entirely work on the stronger Faerie, I guess, because we met the Soho Shark and Victoria Rose on the train."

"They looked uncomfortable," Faith said. "More than that. As if the train caused them pain, remember?"

I nodded and looked down at the map. "So it helps, but it's not a perfect defense. We need more. The coast, right? If we control the coastline, we'll have the advantage. Caine said they aren't very good sailors."

"See?" Mr. Sands said, more forcefully this time. "She's the one to replace you. She has the *eye*, marked like the sorcerers of old. She understands the tactics and what it takes to win a war at sea. *She's* the one we need in charge right now. Not you."

I jerked my gaze up, suddenly realizing the full import of what we were discussing.

"Our resistance needs a leader," Mr. Sands said. "One the Faerie can believe in. An admiral from the House of Thorns to replace your father when he is taken. If we are to survive, this has to be our next step. Will you do it?"

"No," Father said again, but his voice lacked conviction.

"You can't be that admiral anymore," Mr. Sands said relentlessly. "But *she* can."

"I don't want to hide in Stormholt," I said, "but I can't be the admiral you want. I'm just a . . ."

"We believe you can," Mr. Sands said. "The Faerie Outcasts will follow you."

"Caine won't," I said. "He doesn't think women should even be on a ship."

"British superstition," Mr. Sands said. "He'll come around. You won't be alone. You'll have help."

"But . . ." I was looking from Father to Mr. Sands to Avonstoke to Prudence, and they were all just watching *me*.

"You're bossy enough," Faith said wryly. "You're not going to stop telling everyone what to do anyway. You might as well make it official."

"And she won't be alone," Prudence said.

If Faith had felt left out of the attention before, it also meant she didn't feel the fear of what they were asking me to do, until now. Her eyes widened at the pensive way Prudence was looking at her.

"My tenure as magician ends when your father steps down," Sands said. "Our powers are linked. Just as yours will be. I mean for you to replace me, Faith."

"I'm not a magician!" Faith wailed, jumping up. "I'm not!"

"You have the magic in you, Faith," Mr. Sands said. "I've seen it. You've seen it."

She pointed at me. "She's been dreaming of this stuff for as long as I can remember, but I . . . I can't!"

"Our new Admiral will need a new magician," Prudence said. "Someone who doesn't follow her blindly. Someone who won't be afraid to speak up when she makes a mistake. That's you."

Mr. Sands stood and took Faith's hand in his. His face was filled with resolve, but I also saw the reverence he held for her. I was reminded of their encounter on the stairway back at Stormholt. Clearly, Mr. Sands was too. But it didn't dampen the resolve in his eyes.

Faith met his gaze. I could see fear of the unknown in them. God only knew what becoming a magician might entail. But she nodded and Mr. Sands let out a deep breath.

"It seems as if my hand is forced," Father said. That seemed to be the end of it. Father lay back and closed his eyes, and Avonstoke led Faith and me from the room.

"By this time tomorrow," Prudence said, "You'll be General and Magician."

"Admiral," I said. "It's admiral on the sea."

"Of course." She closed the door.

Avonstoke brushed his hand across my shoulder as I passed him, and I saw that curious yearning expression on his face again. He looked like he needed to say something to me. Badly.

We stood on the deck facing each other while the boat rocked around me.

He opened his mouth to speak and then I felt all the terrifying things that I'd just discovered come to a full realization inside of me. Without conscious thought, I spun and ran to the rail, bent over, and emptied the entire contents of my stomach into the passing waters of the sea.

# CHAPTER 18

## Justice Takes Command

"**F**ire!"

The shout sent a bloodcurdling fear through me. Fire was a terrifying thing on any ship.

Even worse, the fire was coming from the captain's cabin.

The sailors were hauling up buckets of water even before Mr. Starling battered down the door with one burly shoulder.

Sands turned from his contemplation of the smoldering and held up a hand.

"It's quite all right," he said. "There's no danger of the fire spreading. It's quite . . ."

But the sailors were already handing in buckets and Mr. Starling, clearly not hearing any of Sands' words, took the bucket handed him and flung it without thought. The water splashed Sands right in the face.

At least it got the door too. The wood gave an angry hiss.

"Quite . . . safe," Sands finished lamely. He lifted one dripping arm, shook out some of the water and put his hand on the door. "Charred from the London side. It's not even . . . ow!" He snatched his hand back.

Starling hastily threw another bucket of water and the door hissed again. At least he'd gotten more door than magician this time.

"Well," Sands said, wringing out his cravat, as we gathered around the table a few minutes later. "They must have found the Faerie door in London and burned it. There'll be no going back to London that way."

Faith, Sands, Avonstoke, and I were all there. Father too, if you counted him, which was getting harder and harder to do since he was passed out or in a haze of pain most of the time. The eerie rustling of the bloodflowers had joined the wind, waves and creaking as background noises. Constant, conspicuous only in their absence.

"So we can't use the door anymore," I said. "We need to get back to English waters. What was the original plan for taking the *Rachaela* back?"

"Him," Avonstoke said, nodding at Father. "Sands could lead us through, but he'll lose that power after the ceremony."

"We might be able to follow *Seahome* and their magician through the mists," Sands said. "But if we lose sight of them, we could be lost forever."

"The *Seahome* magician," Faith said. "You mean Prudence?"

"She's a different kind of magician," Sands said. "She can no more navigate the mists than I could. It takes a certain discipline of magic for that. His name is Drecovian. You'll meet him soon enough."

"We need to get back to English waters," I said again. "Barring the Faerie army isn't an option anymore, not one that large. We need to pull our forces defending the bridge and have them retreat to the rendezvous at Land's End."

"We do," Sands said, "but . . ."

"Can my ghost eye help us back?" I said. "I've seen through a lot of Faerie magic with it."

Sands considered. "It *is* possible, but it's incredibly risky. Better not to lose track of *Seahome*, I think. But there's no guarantee that either of those will work. It's a tricky business. Better, I think, to abandon the *Rachaela* and go back on *Seahome*. I think the Faerie on *Seahome* would allow that."

"Of course they would," I said. "But then we'd be under their control, and I get the impression we can't rely on them yet."

"That's true," Avonstoke said.

"I need my own ship," I said. "*This* ship. Something small enough to slip into London in the confusion and get out again in a hurry."

"You're mad," Faith said. She knew exactly what I had in mind, but Avonstoke and Sands looked at me questioningly.

"We're going back for Henry and Benedict," I said flatly.

"Ah," Avonstoke said, "the so-mad-nobody-could-ever-expect-it approach. I do admire that one."

"Something like that," I said. "You all keep talking about Faith and me coming into our powers, but it isn't just us. You should have seen Henry battling with the dead wolves. Something's happening to all of us, and I'm not throwing any member of my family away. My whole reason for accepting this is to help England, but especially my family. I'm *not* abandoning my brothers just because your plan doesn't include them."

I expected objections. Forget your brothers because they're already dead. Send someone else. Someone expendable, or competent, or both.

Instead, Sands only looked over at the bed where Father was just sitting up.

Sands said. "If you get yourselves caught, that would be the end of the resistance right there."

"Then *we* don't . . . get . . . caught," Faith said, and she glared at me, daring me to challenge the *we*. I nodded back, accepting the fact that she was coming with me.

"There's another deadline," Father said.

"We have less than a month," Sands elaborated, "before your father's next chess match with the real Rachek Kasric. He isn't strong enough now to work the crossing, but the magic around their pact will pull him to the World Tree. That's the center. He won't come back from that. It's a magical striving as much as a mental one, and Lessard's no match for Kasric anymore."

I had a momentary wave of confusion because it took me a second to remember that Lessard was Father's actual name. Doubt swam through me. If I didn't know that, how could I pretend to know anything?

"Then the Seelie Court will have their way with him," Sands said.

"No!" Faith said. "He can't go through all of this just to go back there!"

"We've run out of options," Sands said. "If he lives that long, he will be at the World Tree soon, no matter what we do. Then he will lose, and the Court will have him."

"Then we'd better get on with the ceremony," Father growled from his bunk. "It won't matter so much what happens to me after that."

◁◇▷◁◇▷◁◇▷

We brought Father out onto the deck in a makeshift chair made of spars and sailcloth with a wool blanket on his shoulders. He shivered in the cold, even though the sun was out and the deck warm with all the people gathered there. His feet were wrapped in a blanket which *moved*, and I could see small spots of blood and shuddered. He squinted up at the light as if it pained him.

We gathered on the quarterdeck with him, on display for the crowd on the main deck below.

"Are you ready for this, old friend?" Father said after they set him carefully down on the quarterdeck.

"We discussed this," Mr. Sands said. "It's going to happen soon anyway. Better for it to happen on our terms."

"It's one thing to talk about how brilliant it would be to saw off your arm," Father muttered. "Another to actually do it."

We were all waiting as the last of the group from *Seahome* boarded. They looked a frightening lot. Avonstoke had already pointed out the Dowager Lady Rue—the highest-ranking noble among them and the leader of the Faerie Outcasts. She was a tall woman with a face like an ice sculpture and her hair done up like two spiny sea urchins poking out to the right and left.

"She looks friendly," Faith murmured, echoing my own thoughts. "Are you sure she's on our side?"

"Only as long as our interests dovetail," Avonstoke said. "But she controls *Seahome*. They are an uneasy alliance of the Seelie and Unseelie Courts, and your Father and her kept them together.

She also brings several wizards, a dragon, and triple the number of forces your Father commands to the table."

The small group from the *Seahome* with the Lady Rue were mostly other Court Faerie, like Avonstoke and the Crow Whisper Brigade. But they weren't all Court Faerie. Avonstoke didn't know any of the others: a one-armed beggar, a small group of Dwarves, and a monster with a woman's face and a lion's body.

"Sir," Captain Caine growled, "there's still time to reconsider. It's no damned way to run a ship. You can't possibly expect the men to follow a slip of a girl into battle. She's not a general."

"The correct term ought to be *Admiral*," Avonstoke said sweetly, "us being at sea and all, hadn't it? Perhaps, *My Admiral Ladyship*?"

"Enough," Father said, "I've made my decision, Caine." He summoned enough strength to put some bite into the word, but it still fell flat. Partly because Father clearly couldn't see where Caine was on account of the sunlight which pained him.

"Aye," Caine said. He didn't say anything else with all the other officers gathered around, but I could see as he glared at me that this conversation was far from over.

"Let's get this over with, Sands," Father said.

Mr. Sands nodded and stepped to the rail. He reverently took out his violin case and opened it. When he had the violin in his hands, he gave the case to Prudence behind him.

He pulled us into position so that we faced the throng on the deck as well. Swayle and Mr. Starling both watched us carefully, as did the rest of the crew on the deck. I had no idea what most of their names were.

The Lady Rue had a sour look on her face.

Mr. Sands pitched his voice to carry to the entire assembly.

"Justice Kasric, Faith Kasric, your Father and I can no longer serve the House of Thorns as Lord and Magician. We are ready to pass on the burden. Are you ready to accept it?"

Faith and I looked at each other.

"We are," we said together.

"Too late to back out *now*," Faith murmured. Avonstoke, standing behind us, snickered.

"Justice," Father said. "Take out the chess piece I once gave to you."

I took out the wooden knight, somehow not surprised at all that he knew I had it. The wood throbbed in my hand like a living thing, warm to the touch. Father struggled to a sit up straighter.

"I'm sorry this fell to you girls," he said. "I'd lift this from you, if I could."

Mr. Sands had his violin out and played a slow melody, languorous and heartbreaking. His eyes were closed and he was whispering along with the music: "Acta Santorum, Acta Santorum, Acta Santorum." He whispered the name so fervently it might have been a lover, or a prayer, or both.

The notes soared, overpowering the slap of waves. The wind picked up, whipping through the rigging with a sound oddly in pitch with Mr. Sands' violin.

There was a shimmer of white off the port rail and a murmur went up from the crowd on deck. Three feet above the rail, standing on a ground none of us could see, was the beautiful white horse we'd seen Mr. Sands on before. Acta Santorum reared up once, and whickered softly. Then snorted and reared, angry and wild.

"Do you," Father called out, "swear fealty to the House of Thorns *and* the Outcast Resistance? Do you promise to serve them, and lead them well?"

Oh god, I couldn't speak. They meant us. It was time for us to speak and I couldn't get my mouth working right. The magically summoned horse was angry, rearing up and neighing, higher up than it was before.

"I do," Faith said, but it came out a whisper. "I do," she repeated more loudly, then nudged me.

"I do," I said. The chess piece was warm in my hand.

"Acta Santorum," Mr. Sands whispered, "forgive me."

He flung the violin bow out into the sea and took the violin itself in both hands. It gleamed in the sun, a delicate work of art. "Forgive me," he said again, looking up at the angelic horse, and smashed the violin across the railing.

The pieces burst into blue flame. I jumped and someone behind me shrieked.

Acta Santorum screamed like she was on fire.

The scream was a horrible thing, long and loud and full of pain. She reared up, then burst into a cloud of pearl-colored smoke. The smoke was rent by the wind, and then there was a flash of something else white, and then the cloud shredded and tore away.

Just like that, Acta Santorum was gone.

A smoldering heat burst in my stomach, burst and swelled until I felt the sudden flash of searing heat would tear through me and everything around me. My skin radiated heat and then it settled in my eyes like hot pokers, then focused on my left eye, which now felt a world on fire. Faith cried out next to me so I knew the same thing was happening to her.

Maybe worse, to judge by the scream. Another voice moaned with her, but it wasn't until the deck started tipping and someone caught me from behind that I realized the second voice crying out was mine.

Then a cool, soothing wind sluiced all the heat away. A part of me, even now, automatically tried to gauge the direction so I would know best how to weather the ship, but I couldn't even see in order to tell what direction I was facing. The whole business scattered in my mind like smoke, dissipating to nothingness.

I gradually came to, finding myself in Avonstoke's unsettling grip. His arms around me were warm and the heat of the one supporting the small of my back made me flush.

"Careful, my Lady," he murmured in my ear. "You almost began your new career as admiral by dashing your brains out on the deck."

"Get off me!" I said, swaying as I tried to stand up properly. "I'm fine!"

Father had collapsed. Prudence, who was directing several sailors to pick him up and carry him back into the cabin, saw my look and nodded reassuringly. "We expected this." Then her glance got more worried, and I followed her gaze to where Faith was lying.

"Faith!" I said.

Sands was with her, had pulled her head into his lap and was brushing the hair away from her face.

"She didn't have a token," he murmured. Then he looked up and snarled at Prudence. "I told you the transition would be harder for Faith than it would be for Justice! She didn't have a token to absorb the impact."

I looked down at the horse-shaped chess piece in my hand. It was hot to the touch, something I realized just now, though I'd been holding it all along. More than just hot. Smoke curled up from the black, glossy wood.

"I heard you," Prudence said, her mouth tight. "So did Lessard. We knew she'd have the worst of it, but thought it worth the risk."

Lessard. Right. Father's real name. That was going to take some getting used to.

"Will she be all right?" I said. "Why didn't you tell us . . ."

"Tell you there was danger?" Prudence said with a brittle laugh. "It's *all* danger from here on out. We're at war with the Seelie Court, girl!"

"Faith?" I said, crouching next to her and Mr. Sands on the deck. "Don't die, Faith! I couldn't bear it if you left again." I took her hand in mine.

"S'all right," Faith murmured. Her hand squeezed mine. Her grip was weak, but it was there. "Not going to let you have all the . . . fun."

"Thank the World Tree," Sands breathed.

"Good," Prudence said, her voice weary but relieved. She put her hand on my shoulder. "Don't worry. She'll be all fine now."

"Mr. Sands," I said, "Acta Santorum, your horse, what happened to her when you broke your violin?"

"My magic was bound up in the violin," he said. He looked over at a blackened spot on the deck that had once been his beautiful violin. The violin, the alabaster chess piece, both gone.

"Acta Santorum," Mr. Sands said softly in his lilting speech, "has left. The magic that bound her to me is gone. It's with you and Faith now."

"Does Faith have Acta Santorum now?" I asked.

"No," Mr. Sands said. His eyes filled with a pain so profound that I had to look away. "She has the power, but has yet to shape it. She'll have to learn how to do that, but there's no telling what form it will take."

"Let's get her inside," I said. Standing up, a sudden wooziness took me. Avonstoke had been lurking behind me and steadied me with a hand to my elbow. I glared at him. Instead of backing away, he captured my hand with a slightly bemused expression. Then he knelt and brought his warm lips to my knuckles. Inside the mask of his dark tattoo, his pale eyes went suddenly serious.

"Let me be the first," he murmured, "to welcome our new leader, my Lady of Thorns."

There was a murmur of appreciation from the crowd, who seemed delighted. There were still a few grim faces, however, among the Faerie. The English part of the crew looked even more dubious than before. Caine looked like death himself, glaring at me.

Dear god, what had I gotten myself into?

◦◈◦◈◦◈◦

"He has progressed even further," Sands said. "Be warned. He is not entirely lucid."

They'd had to move Father on account of the light from the stern windows, which was starting to be unbearable to him. The new quarters were half the size of the captain's cabin. There was barely enough room for the five of us to stand.

Sands did not lie. The last twenty-four hours had not been kind to Father. His eyes looked clouded and sunken, his face was noticeably thinner, wet and pale. I could see the cup that Prudence made her medicine with, and the knife. Both looked well-used and Prudence looked almost as pale as Father. The blanket at Father's feet twitched and moved and I knew that more than one bloodflower was at work there.

The table next to him held the chessboard. I noticed with a start that both knights were now on the board and hastily fished in my pocket.

"It's still there," Sands said behind me.

He was right, I found the reassuring carved piece right where I kept it.

"You've entered the fray," Father said to me, pointing at one of the black knights menacing the white queen.

I looked at the board again. Most of the pieces were still on the board, but white had occupied the center and forced the black line of defense back. The black queen was captured and white looked certain to take a handy victory.

"What a comfort," Faith said, "for all of England to be wrapped up neatly on one little board. Ships and countries and people all manifest here, with no blood or pain, just black and white. It's very tidy, looking at it this way."

"It is, isn't it?" Father said.

"But war won't be tidy," Faith insisted, "will it, Father?"

"Hmm?" Father said, starting back to alertness. "No. War is filled with blood. Blood and sacrifice."

"It's not just the pawns that get sacrificed," Avonstoke said. "All the pieces are expendable in war."

"Except the king," Father said bitterly, "the mighty, powerless, feeble and oh-so-important king. Incapable of defending himself. Woe to any king who loves his defenders."

"The board isn't meant to be a perfect analogy," Sands said. "It's an abstraction of a complicated situation. You *know* this. You shouldn't look for a one-to-one analogy."

"The bishop would be the closest approximation for *you*," Father said brightly. He pointed at Faith.

"Me?" Faith said. She didn't bother hiding her astonishment.

"The Faerie have moved faster into England than we expected," Father said. "A number of my plans and tricks have failed, but perhaps the largest trick may not."

The sky was still a constant and disconcerting yellow as we readied to sail to London. Beautiful weather they had here in the Borderlands. I was sad to be leaving it.

"We need to get to London," I said to Captain Caine.

"That's not my intention," Caine said.

"Father left her in charge," Faith said. "Your orders come from the House of Thorns. Father passed leadership of the house to Justice. Haven't you been paying any attention at all?"

"If you think," Caine said, "that I'm taking orders from a little wisp of a girl, you are sadly mistaken. This ship will participate in the harassment of troops as they cross into England, as planned."

"No," I said.

A sudden shifting of perceptions occurred. Faerie and men had been working two minutes ago, side by side with every outward sign of tolerance, but now that feeling evaporated. The Court Faerie marines, most of them cleaning weapons, were all as silent and frozen as a snow-laden cliff face before the rumbling start of an avalanche. Goblins paused up in the rigging. Dwarven carpenters and gunners stopped working.

Even the non-soldiers all seemed to have weapons of some sort at hand: fishing knives, the weighted end of a rope, a wrench, or length of spar. Avonstoke moved from his place at the railing to come stand behind Faith and I. He didn't speak, but he was a solid, comforting presence at our back.

One of the Goblins croaked in a cheese-grater voice, "We follow the 'ouse of Thorns, we do!"

"This is a British ship!" one of the human officers said. "Faerie rule is exactly what we're fighting *against*."

"We make for the end of the bridge," Caine said with finality. "Mr. Starling, make ready to haul anchor and set sail."

Mr. Starling wasn't even looking at him. He was looking back and forth from Caine to me and rubbing his beard thoughtfully with his heavy, stubby fingers.

None of the Faerie sailors had moved. Not so much as a muscle. They might have been statues on deck, lining the quarterdeck and forecastle railings looking down at them on the deck, hanging motionless from the rigging. Only the ship moved with the sea, and the listless and desultory shifting of the human members of the crew. It was as if the entire ship held its breath.

"Marines," Caine said, "relieve Mr. Starling of his duties. Escort him to the hold. He can reconsider his loyalty in chains."

Swayle walked over toward Starling, but not quickly. Her glance slid over to me, very briefly, and then away. It happened so quickly I almost missed it. The other Faerie, too, were casting glances my way. Caine was captain here. On a British ship, no ad hoc promotion such as Father had given me would hold water, but here . . .

But the Faerie were all looking at *me*.

They were waiting. Waiting for me to do something. I looked again at Swayle and Starling.

As the officers on Father's ship, not counting Caine, they'd been anything but warm towards me. Even so, I had to hope that Faerie lineage trumped naval rank in this topsy-turvy fleet. Father had asked me to take the tiller of his defense fleet. It was time to do so, with both hands.

"Mr. Swayle," I said. "Belay that order." I nearly got caught up in the sticky terminology of calling a naval officer 'Mr.' when she wasn't a mister by half, but I forged on.

If the Faerie crew had been watching me covertly before, it was open as all get out now. I could feel the weight of their combined expectations. Avonstoke's presence was still a comfort at our back, but he'd shifted position subtly and I got the distinct impression that he was tensed to leap in front of us should things turn south.

"Swayle," I said, "you will relieve Captain Caine of his duties."

There it was. I'd committed myself now. I did my best to exude stern confidence. Everyone shifted in place, eyes wide. The collective gaze slid toward Swayle.

She didn't look happy, but she nodded. She turned from Starling to face Captain Caine. No, not *Captain*. That was over now. I'd ended that. Swayle put her hand on the Caine's arm.

"Get your hand off of me!" Caine snarled. "Put her in the brig!" He pointed at swept his arm to include Swayle, Starling, Faith, me, all of us. "All of them in the brig!"

Swayle's grip didn't budge. He yanked again, but he might as well have been fighting the main mast. "Let me go!" he said again, and this time his voice had lost the tone of command. He nearly squeaked.

Several of the human sailors stepped forward to object. I'd nearly forgotten about them. But two dozen of Swayle's Court Faerie marines nocked and drew their bows. The creak of bows being drawn was shockingly loud. At least one of them targeted Caine. The Faerie outnumbered humans three-to-one on deck. The English sailors gulped and their faces went white. One of them wet himself, openly. They stepped back.

"Let's go," Swayle said. She led Caine off to the brig. Everyone, Faerie and Englishman, watched. No one spoke.

"Mr. Starling," I said. "Signal *Seahome*. Order them to take up station behind us. Let them know we're going back to London. Then prepare to wear the ship."

There was the briefest of pauses as Starling absorbed all of this, but then he was all business.

"Aye, captain," he said. He spun without a beat and bellowed at the crew. "You heard the captain! Get moving, you sea dogs!" The clustered group of sailors broke at once in all directions and the ship was quickly bustling with activity.

"That," Avonstoke said, "was bravely done." There was a clear admiration in his voice.

"Not too shabby," Faith said. She was grinning from ear to ear.

I became suddenly aware of Avonstoke's close proximity. The danger was past, but he was still standing awfully close to me, his golden eyes looking down at me in total amazement. As if I was the wondrous person on board on a ship full of the Faerie.

"The danger," I said, "appears to be over."

"Quite right, my captain," Avonstoke murmured back. He looked flushed, his mouth parted slightly.

I don't know what came into me, but I reached up and tangled my hand into his golden hair, right where the braided warrior's queue met his scalp, which felt like warm silk, and pulled his face down to mine.

"My captain," I said, my lips very close to his now. "I like the sound of that."

He leaned even closer and I pulled his mouth to mine. He tasted like cardamom, or cinnamon, or something else I couldn't name. It was warm and made mine tingle and his breath was somehow manly and pleasant. I forgot, briefly, about Faith, Starling, Swayle, the ship, the crew, about everything.

"That," he said when I pushed him away a few moments later, "was . . ."

"Yes," I agreed. "It was."

Faith looked at me, astonished, then her face burst into a grin.

"Now then," I said. "Mr. Starling, is the sail crew ready!"

"Aye aye, sir, my lady . . . um . . ." Starling was clearly at a loss for title.

"Captain will do just fine," I said. "You may begin wearing the ship."

"Aye, Captain Justice," Starling said. The words gave me a tingle almost as intoxicating as the brief contact with Avonstoke had been.

I watched Starling keenly as he bellowed out orders.

"Stand by there, at the capstan! Loose the 'eadsails! 'ands aloft to loose the topsails!"

I allowed a soft smile. Starling had clearly learned more than he thought he had from Caine. With the anchor broken out, the *Rachaela* gathered sternway. With the wheel hard over and the forecastle hands drawing at the headsail sheets, she brought her head round. I saw now that I could rely on him. In a moment we were slipping forward through the water, rudder balanced against pressure from the wind in the sail, a living ship, alive and lovely.

Our voyage had begun. I savored the pleasure of being afloat as the hands raced to set the topgallant sails and then the courses. The ship was a bustling hub of commotion, as everyone, Faerie and otherwise, went about their business.

"Ship underway, Captain," Starling said.

Captain. The title of 'captain' meant more to me than Lady, admiral or general all rolled together. I took a moment to savor it. Avonstoke, who was still standing disconcertingly close, took that moment to grin brilliantly at me. Faith put her hand on my arm.

"I hope," she said, "that you know what you're doing."

"Me, too," I said.

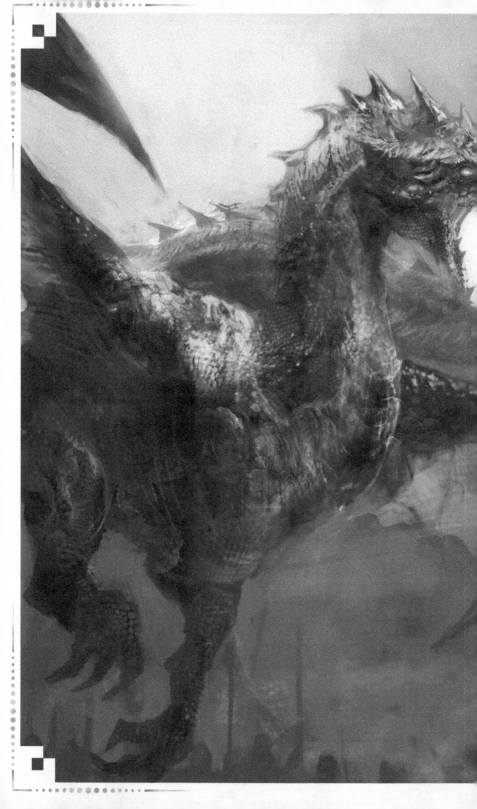

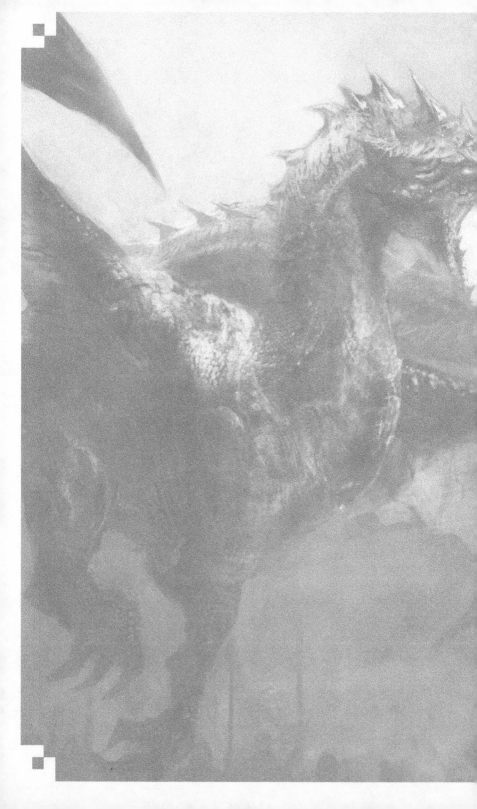

# Acknowledgments

Tremendous thanks to Sarah Zettel, Steven Piziks, Cindy Spencer Pape, David Erik Nelson, Diana Rivis, Mary Beth Johnson, Christine Pellar-Kosbar, Jonathan Jarrard, Erica Shippers, and Ted Reynolds of the Untitled Writer's Group who suffered innumerable versions of this story with grace and aplomb and many colored pens. Also to Janine Beaulieu, Heath Lowrance, Ron Warren, and Carole Ward for helping with a version *so* many versions back that they might not even recognize the final product anymore.

Also to my agent Lucienne Diver and editor Cassandra Farrin, who provided extraordinary levels of encouragement and understanding.

To my parents, Craig and Pam Klaver, and my mother Suzanne Klaver, who encouraged me in this endeavor for far longer than I care to admit.

Also to my wife, Kimberly, for the same, and for endless tolerance for a husband constantly sequestered.

And lastly, to my daughter Kathryn, who beats out both Horatio Hornblower and Lucy Pevensie as the inspiration for the most irrepressible facets of Justice's personality.

# About the Author

Christian Klaver has been writing for over thirty years, with a number of magazine publications, including *Escape Pod*, *Dark Wisdom Anthology*, and *Anti-Matter*. He's the author of The Empire of the House of Thorns series and the Classified Dossier—Sherlock Holmes and Count Dracula.

He has worked as a bookseller, bartender and a martial-arts instructor before settling into a career in internet security. He lives just outside the sprawling decay of Detroit, Michigan, with his wife Kimberly, his daughter Kathryn, and a group of animals he refers to as The Menagerie.

More from Christian Klaver

**JUSTICE AT SEA**
*The Empire of the House of Thorns*
*Book 2*

# CHAPTER 1

## Estuary Raid

The mist.

It pooled ankle-deep on the deck, moving in little eddies around our feet every time we moved. A slow, dank current of it flowed silently down the forecastle stairs in wispy trails, then down to the main deck where it pooled again before draining out the scuppers and down the hull to the ocean. But no matter how much fog drained out, there was always more. Made me itch to grab broom or mop and get it all off the deck, only I knew it wouldn't do any good. There was plenty more out here where that came from. All around us, in fact.

I was at the front rail near the bowsprit, the very front of the ship. A lantern threw yellow light that clung to the deck behind me, but didn't penetrate more than a dozen feet or so out and all I could make out was more fog pooled on quiet, black, still water. The ship's prow barely made a ripple as we cut soundless through the water. We'd been forced out into the Channel and now coming back towards the English shore had a forbidden feel. We weren't welcome here in England anymore. You could feel it.

The mist had a way of dampening sounds, so that I kept looking back to make sure that everyone else was still there. I could see the rest of the quarterdeck that Faith, Sands, and Avonstoke shared with me, but the rest of the ship was lost in the haze.

Quiet should have been good. We were prowling in enemy territory. I'd given the orders for silence myself, but now the heavy, unnatural feel of it was making my skin crawl. I thought the darkness was starting to show a little gray in it, at least, as if dawn might not be that far off.

"Justice," Faith hissed from behind me. "We're too far in!"

"Shh," I said, craning my neck to listen for signs of other ships, or possibly the English shore. England used to be home, before the Faerie took it and shrouded it in this bloody fog. Now it was enemy territory and there was no telling what changes the Faerie had wrought to it.

"Too far in!" she said again. I was supposed to be captain, but one of the problems with having your older sister on board is that she'd never taken orders from me and wasn't about to start now. Didn't matter if I was a captain, admiral, or a bag of rutabagas.

Faith looked unnatural in the eerie yellow light, with her white London dress and her long ash-white hair. No pants for her, despite being at sea. The Faerie might have conquered London, but they hadn't made much of a dent in Faith's sense of propriety or fashion. At least she'd forgone any hoops or a bustle.

She stepped closer, her dark eyes wild with panic. "You *know* the strain it takes for Sands to keep the shield up. He's going to collapse if we keep him at it."

I pushed my weather-beaten wide-brimmed black hat back on my head to peer up at her. She had to be prettier and older *and* taller. Life's not fair.

"What about *you?*" I snapped. "Do you feel anything? Anything at all?"

Faith's lips went tight. "No, same as the last time you asked. If I felt anything, don't you think I'd tell you? Everyone keeps calling me a magician, but that's all they can tell me. You don't learn magic as much as feel it, but I don't feel anything! I'm about as close to singing fish into a hat as raising a shield! You have to take us back!"

I shook my head. "You know we can't do that. They get one ship across the channel and it's all over." I turned my back on her. She made a smothered, frustrated noise behind me.

The worst part about Faith's warning was that she was probably right.

Sands looked an absolute and unmitigated shambles. The man's face, when I glanced back again, despite myself, was covered in sweat though he shivered in the cold damp. His black coat and tails were spattered with salt and he'd lost his hat. His cheeks showed two day's growth around the blonde mustache and goatee and his blonde hair stuck out in all directions. His eyes, a startling emerald green under normal conditions, now shone like a cat's eyes or undersea lanterns, washing the forecastle deck and our boots with lime, eldritch light. He stared out over the water, looking for dangers most of the ship couldn't even see.

The Faerie invasion force had put the mist up to keep us out, of course. The Outcast Fleet stayed on the edge of the mist, where the rest of humanity couldn't reach us, but venturing further in, like we were doing now, was like taking a rowboat out into a monsoon.

My ghost eye, which helped me see through Faerie magic, helped a little, letting me see through the first line of defense, the illusions. Or glamours, as the Faerie called them. Dark flocks of predatory birds, specters gliding on top of the ocean's surface. That sort of thing. It was enough to scare the crew into a wailing froth and I was just barely holding that fear in check, constantly reminding them that the glamours weren't really there. The only person not showing any fear was Avonstoke and I had him to thank for bolstering the crew. Without him, I'd have a mutiny on my hands for sure. I looked back to where he stood, supporting Sands.

Avonstoke was tall, slightly inhuman-looking, a Court Faerie like the stern and uncompromising Faerie marines. But Avonstoke wasn't stern, not by a long shot. Normally, I found him endearing, distracting, and exasperating in equal measures, but he'd become a sturdy support, my rock when things got dangerous, like now. His eyes, like the others of his kind, all pale gold, without any pupils. They were an echo of my ghost eye, a solid black marble in my left eye.

That ghost eye also allowed me to see the visions that really *were* out in the mist. Dark shapes cresting the water, ghost ships, an enormous bat-winged shape far overhead. But only Sands and I could see those, and neither of us mentioned it to the others.

"Ghosts," Sands muttered when another of the ships went by.

"Intangible?" I said, keeping my voice equally low. "So they can't hurt us?" Avonstoke and Faith were both close enough to hear, but I trusted them to keep their mouths shut.

Sands turned his glowing cats-eyes to me and shook his head. "*Probably* not." There was the hint, like always, of France and other places I didn't know in the lilt of his voice. "Ships, or other things, caught by a vortex and wrenched free of their place in time. If they are ghosts to us, or we are ghosts to them, I cannot say. Now they move through *when*, as well as through *where*. Let's hope they are not close enough in the fabric of time to reach us. Years spent in the mist would leave you quite mad. I should know."

I wanted to ask more, but now wasn't the time. He turned away, peering with those luminous eyes out into the fog.

What we were *really* worried about out here were the vortexes.

Dark twisters, like supernatural tornadoes that threatened either to tear us to pieces or pull us entirely out of the world we knew. One false step and we could be ghosts ourselves. Or we could just be dead.

Even as I watched, another black tornado lurched out of the mist, moving far too quickly for us to avoid, and battered itself against Sands' shield. The shield, which I could see through my ghost eye as a soft green shimmer around the ship, rippled under the impact. But it held. It was all eerily silent and unreal. I felt no sign of the impact under my feet, which was even more unnerving.

But Sands shook under the impact, as if he, himself, had been the one hit. Avonstoke's grip on him was the only thing that kept Sands from falling.

Faith wasn't wrong. The little blonde man couldn't take too much more of this.

I could see back to the rest of the ship this way, which was a far cry from a comfort. Every face I could see was tight with sullen fear, watching me, or Faith, but mostly watching Sands, our only magician.

Except Sands wasn't a full-fledged magician anymore, which was most of the problem. Since passing his mantle to Faith, his powers had been slowly fading. To make matters worse, Faith, his replacement according to Father's plan, didn't seem close to taking his place. I gnawed my lip.

The air was still, the rigging quiet, the splash of water soft, while we all struggled not to breathe too loudly. Everyone was listening hard enough to make their ears bleed. The ship itself made barely a creak under my feet. No scent of land came with the bare excuse for a breeze, even though I knew we had to be close. The chill off the water was like something off the grave.

A Prowler crew member ran up to report, knuckling his forehead. "Foretop lookout is seeing branches, sir."

"Branches?" I said, raising an eyebrow. The man blanched, his greenish skin going visibly paler, but nodded. "Yes, sir." I forgot, sometimes, the reverence the Faerie from Father's domain, most of our crew, regarded our family. If they only knew.

I opened my mouth to get a better explanation, but by then there was no need.

"There!" Faith said, pointing. "What's that?"

The mist parted to reveal a tree growing up out of the water, craggy and black and dripping with lichen and slim. The trunk was easily as wide around as the *Specter* was long, with branches angling up in all directions, long, jagged shapes that disappeared into the fog.

The tree was festooned with bodies.

There were dozen of them, all very dead, hanging from the branches on nooses. They'd been tall, when alive, and not at all human, with great horns on their heads, white or black hair, gray skin, and talons on their hands and feet that immediately reminded me of the Soho Shark. The talons swayed, very gently, though there wasn't any breeze to speak of. Drops of moisture dripped down into the water with a morose and solitary dripping sound.

## CamCat Books

VISIT US ONLINE FOR
MORE BOOKS TO LIVE IN:
CAMCATBOOKS.COM

FOLLOW US

CamCatBooks  @CamCatBooks  @CamCat_Books